HER
MOTHER'S
CRY

BOOKS BY ROBERTA GATELY

HER
MOTHER'S
CRY

ROBERTA GATELY

bookouture

Published by Bookouture in 2021

An imprint of Storyfire Ltd.
Carmelite House
50 Victoria Embankment
London EC4Y 0DZ

www.bookouture.com

ISBN: 978-1-80019-031-3
eBook ISBN: 978-1-80019-030-6

A good book is an unforgettable journey. I hope that readers will travel that mysterious and absorbing road with me. ♥

PROLOGUE

"Nine-one-one. This call is being recorded. What's your emergency?"

"A woman... oh, dear God, a woman..." The caller is breathless, her words too rushed, too garbled to be clear.

"Slow down," the dispatcher says calmly. "You're calling about a woman? Take a deep breath and tell me what happened."

"I don't know." The caller begins to cry, her sobs punctuating her words. "She jumped, from the roof, I think."

"Where are you?"

"Where are we?" the caller shouts to someone in the background, but her words are almost hidden in the crush of shouts and car horns. "The corner of Washington and Tremont, by the garage," the caller says after a pause. "She jumped. She jumped," she repeats, "or maybe she fell. I don't know for sure. I heard a scream and I looked up and... she was falling. Oh God..."

"Does she have a pulse? Can you check?"

The caller shouts to someone. "Is she alive?"

And then someone else has the phone. "Just send help. We're not sure. Please, just come."

The call is disconnected, and as the call taker moves to dispatch police, ambulance and fire, she realizes that the flurry of calls that her colleagues are logging all contain the same general information—a woman has jumped from a roof. Though the callers sound frantic, the message is clear—a woman has fallen from a height of eight stories and her life hangs in the balance.

1

He hadn't known that he'd enjoy watching these fools try to save a dead woman as much as he did. And the people watching, mesmerized by the spectacle, by seeing someone die before their very eyes, turning another dull, ordinary day into one they'll recount forever, depicting themselves almost as heroes for trying to save her. He can almost hear the whispers.

"She was dead for sure, but I breathed life into her, that beautiful young woman."

"I could feel her heart beneath my hands. I felt it come to life."

"She opened her eyes and looked right at me."

The crowd was growing. Concern and worry etched on their weary faces. He watched with a smile until he realized he needed to wipe the satisfied smile from his face and look as aggrieved as the rest of them. He couldn't afford to draw attention to himself. He had to blend in once again before he slipped quietly away.

The emergency medical technicians packed the woman's lifeless body into the ambulance, her lips blue, her deep brown eyes shut tight almost as if she was knowingly avoiding the hot glare of the sun. But of course, her eyes were closed not in sleep, but in death. So why were they doing CPR?

And then he heard it. The first murmurs.

"A terrible shame," one onlooker whispered.

"But maybe they can save her," another said.

Impossible, he thought as an elderly woman drew a string of rosary beads from her bag, her fingers sliding soundlessly along the beads, her lips moving in prayer.

As the first trickles of sweat gathered on his forehead, a tight knot of worry formed in his stomach. He swiped at the perspiration trickling down his face as he backed away and disappeared into the crowd.

2

SUNDAY, DAY 1

Jessie could feel it as soon as she woke. Today would be different. A bright sliver of sun seeped through her blinds, and as she sat and parted them to peer out, she knew it would be one of those perfect days, the kind you'll remember forever. It wasn't just the sun, though it was glorious to see that golden glow as she yanked her blinds fully open and pulled her window up, drinking in the fresh air—it was that the splendid days of spring had come to South Boston when she wasn't paying attention. Already, neighborhood women were out pushing baby carriages, their young children lagging behind, eager to stop and play.

She rose, headed for the shower and ran her fingers through her sleep-tangled mass of mahogany curls, her hazel eyes sparkling, her creamy skin shivering beneath the sudden burst of cold water. She pulled a towel from the shelf and dried off quickly. Life was just about perfect. She'd only recently learned that she had a mother, that she hadn't been abandoned as a baby as her father had always told her. His anger and lies didn't really matter now. *She had a mother. Maybe.* It was complicated, and she still needed time to absorb that information, that connection to someone who, kind as she was, still felt like a stranger.

But she was dating Sam Dallas, the homicide detective whom she worked alongside as a forensic nurse, bringing her ER expertise to homicide investigations. Four months ago, she'd been recruited by the already overworked medical examiner to help assess injuries and potential causes of death both at crime scenes and in the morgue, and then to liaise with families and detectives to help bring the case to closure. Although she was still new to her position, and still working in the ER, she'd learned to love the Forensics job. The ME had been right—bringing answers to families and finding justice for the victims was as gratifying as saving someone in the ER.

It was also fair to say that Sam Dallas was every woman's dream—tall, handsome, athletic build, kind, funny, smart and forgiving. And perhaps it was that last part that she needed most in her life. She had inherited her dad's quickness to anger and maddening impatience, unfortunate characteristics that she was working on.

But as blissful as her life was at the moment, she had no time to linger with her thoughts. Today, she was due in the ER to cover another nurse's shift. And, if she wanted to be on time, she had to hustle.

She brewed a pot of coffee, swiped a swath of color along her lips, pulled her curls into a neat ponytail, found clean scrubs, inhaled her coffee and hurried out, stopping to knock on her downstairs neighbor's door.

"Morning, Jessie," Rufus said as he pulled open his door. "Do you have time for a cup of tea?"

She puffed out her lower lip. "I'm sorry, I can't today, Rufus. I just wanted you to know I'm going to work a little early today if you're looking for me."

"On a beautiful day, you have to work?" he asked, more a statement of concern than a question. "Well, you go in and take care of yourself. You hear me?"

A smile burst onto her lips and she leaned in to plant a kiss on his lined cheek. "You too," she said softly. "Make a grocery list. I'll take you tomorrow."

.   .   .

Jessie parked in the hospital garage and made her way to the ER where she looked for Susan Peters, the nurse she was replacing. "Hey, Jessie," Susan called when she saw her. "Thank you for coming in. I have to get to this family party. I owe you one."

"No problem," she replied. "Anything going on here that I should know about?"

"We have a jumper on the way in. ETA of three minutes. She apparently fell about eight stories from that garage not far from here. Hard to believe she's still alive. Tim Merrick's on his way down."

A swell of relief surged through Jessie's veins. Tim Merrick was Boston City Hospital's Chief of Trauma Surgery. He could be a colossal pain, but he was a damn good surgeon and Jessie was relieved to know that he'd be directing the trauma team today. If anyone could save somebody who'd suffered near-fatal injuries, it was likely Tim Merrick. She took the beeper from Susan and headed to her locker.

"Thanks again," Susan called as she grabbed her things and headed out. The wail of a siren was all the notice Jessie needed to pull on a pair of surgical gloves and head to the ambulance bay where the medics were just pulling in. Tim Merrick appeared behind her.

"Hey, Jessie," he said. "I'm glad you're on today. Is this our jumper? When Susan paged me, she said the woman was in pretty bad shape."

Jessie turned. "That's what I heard, too. Sounds as though her condition is grave, but let's see what we can do. Now that you're back from leave we'll have a chance again."

A medic was pumping air into the woman's lungs when Tim pulled open the ambulance door and helped to bring the stretcher out. "Trauma One," Jessie said, guiding them along the hallway to the trauma room where another nurse, two residents and a medical aide were waiting.

"Unknown female reportedly jumped," the medic began as the trio backed into the room. Hands reached out to gently transfer the patient to the ER gurney. "She's pretty bad. Looks like she has an open skull fracture in the back of her head, and a lot of facial trauma—that's what the blood's from. Bilateral arm fractures, maybe her back too. We have a collar on her neck to protect her cervical spine. Right pupil is fixed and dilated, left eye too swollen to assess. No blood pressure, no pulse, but she has a disorganized heart rhythm on the monitor. We initiated CPR, intubated her and started an IV. We have no other information, no medical history, no name, nothing. She was apparently alone at the scene and had no ID, so all we know is that she appears to be a thirtyish-year-old woman who apparently jumped from that garage roof."

"Haven't there been a few other jumpers from garages in the last year?" one of the surgical residents asked.

The medic nodded. "She's the second one from a garage in the last year. There were complaints about those open garage rooftops, and I thought they were gonna close the roof access, but apparently they haven't, and there's still no cameras, so it's a natural spot for somebody who's decided to jump. Pretty damn depressing on this first beautiful spring day."

The medical assistant took over chest compressions as the respiratory tech arrived to take over ventilations with the football-shaped ambu bag—which forced oxygen into the lungs—while Jessie helped to cut away the woman's clothes—too-tight jeans, a long-sleeved blue shirt and underwear—before placing the EKG leads onto her chest and covering her with a sheet, the crisp whiteness stark against the faint bronze of her skin. The monitor revealed a sporadic cardiac rhythm, likely not a true rhythm, but artifact from electrical interference and the irregular spikes of a dying heart. Still, the team would try to save her.

"Help me to roll her," Tim directed one of the residents. Jessie leaned in to assist. The body was as floppy and loose as a rag doll. The sheet beneath the woman's head was splattered and wet, the back of her skull fractured and wide open, allowing tissue but curiously little blood to seep out. Tim grimaced. "Will you take that c-collar off?" he asked, and the resident gently pulled it away, revealing only a thin gold chain which held a small cross. Aside from the facial scrapes, swelling and bruising, which she may have suffered in the fall, there were no other wounds: no bruising, no evidence of assault. Tim examined her neck, felt for a carotid pulse, shook his head and exhaled noisily. "Any blood pressure?" he asked.

The resident shook his head and, "Nothing," he said. "As you just noted, no pulses either now, despite the intravenous fluid bolus and a round of Epinephrine."

The team watched as the erratic waves on the cardiac monitor turned into one long, straight, flat line, the beeps fading to a drone. She was officially dead, though with that terrible head injury, she'd likely died on impact, Jessie thought. She felt an unexpected wave of sadness for this poor woman who'd been so desperately unhappy on this seemingly perfect day when Jessie had been thinking how wonderful life was. She turned the monitor off, unhooked the IV, and closed the woman's right eye, still wide open with fright as though she'd been watching them as they gave up on her and declared her dead.

"Time of death," Tim said, snapping off his gloves and glancing quickly at the wall clock, "is twelve thirty-two p.m."

"Noted." Jessie turned and entered the time in the woman's chart.

The team dispersed, all back to their assignments, leaving Jessie and Tim behind. "Hey," Tim said, "thanks, Jessie. Always a pleasure to work with you."

"Likewise," she said as he turned to go.

He slipped out quietly, leaving Jessie alone with the unknown woman.

3

She heaved a long sigh. The body had to be readied for the morgue and for Dr. Dawson, the Chief Medical Examiner, so he could have a look and decide if an autopsy was required or not. Though in the case of a suicide or maybe an accidental death, she was sure he'd opt for the autopsy.

She pulled open a drawer and removed a prepackaged shroud kit. She hated this aspect of her job—wrapping and tagging the dead—but she felt strongly that she'd never assign a chore that she didn't want to someone else and so, this task was hers. She collected the woman's clothes first, fishing in the pockets for anything that might help to identify her. But they were empty, save for a tube of lipstick, a wrinkled gum wrapper and some change.

She took another look at the woman, the long shiny waves of her dark hair, the ends tipped in blue, fanning out around her face, too bruised and broken to be recognizable. Her chipped red nail polish, the last hints to who she was. *But who was she? And what happened today?*

Jessie couldn't imagine feeling as sad and despondent as this poor woman must have felt just hours ago, before she jumped to her death. No matter how hard it had been for Jessie, and God knew, there had been hard times, she'd still always known that things would be okay. But this poor woman hadn't had that same luxury of thought.

She plucked the shroud and tags from the bag and nudged the body over a bit to slide the plastic underneath. And Jessie remembered Sam's instructions to really observe the scene and then the body from every possible angle. She hadn't been at the scene, but she could step back for just a minute and take a good, long look at poor Jane Doe. Her wavy black hair almost concealed the terrible open wounds on the back of her head, bits of tissue still stuck in the strands. Her arms appeared to be broken as well. Jessie lifted them gently to tuck them by her side and her gaze was drawn to the woman's wrists. There were red indentations around her wrists, as though from hair ties or bracelets. Jessie looked closer. There were full-thickness abrasions on her knuckles and along her slender fingers, as though she'd fought to hold onto something to break her fall. Several of her fingernails had been torn off as well. Had she changed her mind too late? Had she tried to grab onto the edge of the building to save herself?

It was then Jessie noticed the bits of debris under the woman's remaining nails—skin and visible blood—hard to imagine it was her own unless she'd scratched at herself while she fell. Jessie looked closer. The woman's fingertips were blue, something more likely found on a body that had been deceased for a while but a curious sign in a woman who'd just died. Her skin was cool and gray, her back floppy and pliant and likely broken, the skin on her left hip mottled and spongy, her leg bent at an impossible angle. Her right leg seemed intact, sturdy and straight: no unusual angles, no open wounds, no obvious fractures. Considering the facial and posterior skull trauma on the left, maybe she'd landed on that side.

Jessie paused. She'd only taken care of one other jumper—a young man who'd jumped from a height of twenty feet in a failed suicide attempt. He'd survived, though his back and both legs were badly broken, his pelvis almost crushed. And she'd assumed that was how jumpers would present—with devastating fractures to the lower extremities and covered with blood from open wounds. But aside from her facial wounds, this woman had no evidence of other bleeding; her lacerations and injuries were almost too clean, too pristine in such a traumatic death.

Strange, she thought as she padded the woman's wrists before securing them together with string and wrapping a yellow tag on her great toe with the little information available. "Unknown female; no further information."

She began to pull the plastic edges of the shroud together and leaned in for a final look. Something just didn't feel right. She stepped away from the stretcher just as the door swung open.

"Hey," Detective Ralph Thompson said, standing back a little from the trauma room.

A friendly smile draped her lips. She and Ralph, a detective with a résumé that read like a Rhodes Scholar, had started with Homicide within weeks of each other, and he and Jessie had developed a friendship born of being rookies together. Ralph had a long, impressive background as an army officer, policeman and now a law student. He followed rules and protocols to the letter never, at least as far as Jessie knew, deviating from that hard-line policy. She'd do just about anything for him, and she knew he'd do the same for her. They were the newest of Detective Sergeant Sam Dallas's squad, which included several seasoned detectives. Jessie was their forensic nurse, the liaison between the Homicide unit and the medical examiner's office.

Ralph tugged a notebook from the pocket of his perfectly pressed suit. That was the other thing about Ralph. His appearance was flawless, his hair trimmed just so, his clothes impeccable; not even a smidgen of lint dared to linger there. With his coal-black eyes and ebony skin, he looked more model than detective. He was just too perfect. Until she got to know him and realized that was his first line of defense against people who might question a black man with his résumé and experience. His persnickety adherence to rules was his second, and his unquestioned expertise was a third line.

"Hey, Jessie, sorry to bother you," he said. "I'm here about Jane Doe. She still here?"

Jessie pulled the door open and nodded toward the stretcher. "Hey, Ralph, I'm glad you're here. I was just finishing up with her, getting ready to send her to the morgue."

"Okay if I have a quick look?" he asked, his voice soft and respectful.

"Take your time. I'll stay with you," she said, to reassure his unspoken anxieties. "Do you know what happened? Did she really jump?" She was about to mention the broken fingernails, the debris under some of them, and the dusky, blue skin—cyanosis—but she wanted to give him a chance to view the victim.

He shrugged. "Hard to say. One of the witnesses said he thought that maybe someone else was up there, but he was looking up, said he was squinting at the sun, which probably blocked his full view. He'd turned away not thinking much of it until he heard a scream. And that was when he saw her falling backward, her body just dropping like a sack of potatoes. He's pretty shaken up. We're checking to see if anyone else saw someone up there, but so far that doesn't seem likely. The remaining witnesses only saw her right before she landed with a loud thud. I'm just here to have a look and get some preliminary information. Time of death?" he asked.

Jessie checked her notes. "She was pronounced at twelve thirty-two p.m.," she said.

"Any ID on her?"

"Nothing," Jessie said. "She has a cross dangling from a chain around her neck but no wallet, no papers, no other jewelry. Just this," she said, holding up the lipstick, gum wrapper and loose coins she'd found in the woman's jeans.

"What's your impression?" he asked.

Jessie moved to one side of the stretcher, pulling the shroud away from the body. "She has a few injuries that made me wonder. She has significant facial trauma, enough that she'll be hard to identify, and she has abrasions on her hands—broken fingernails as though she was struggling. She doesn't have any obvious lower-extremity fractures. I'm no expert, but I think that's unusual in jumpers. She has plenty of other injuries but there's no active bleeding. She's already cyanotic, her skin mottled, and that doesn't happen immediately. It takes time. I don't see any stab wounds or gunshot wounds, no signs of strangulation that would explain that. And the facial trauma wouldn't have killed her." She sighed loudly. "When I add everything up, I think she was probably dead when she fell. But that final determination will be up to the ME."

Ralph nodded. "Nice observations, Jessie. And why didn't she have any ID? Did she just not carry one, or did someone remove her IDs? Maybe she was robbed." He leaned in for a closer look. "Her hair is so dark, and her skin has the slightest tinge of brown." He looked up at Jessie and caught her eye. "Hispanic?"

"Maybe," Jessie replied. "To tell you the truth, I hadn't even thought of that, but now that you mention it, probably."

"Hmm, makes me wonder if she's an illegal. Sorry, undocumented. And maybe that's why she had no ID." He sighed and stepped back. "Well, you never know, that cross, gum wrapper and lipstick might be a start. I'll take her belongings. Can you remove that chain for me? Forensics might be able to find something we can use."

Jessie gently ran her gloved hands around the woman's neck, her fingers searching for the clasp. The thin chain slipped away, and Jessie dropped it into a small envelope before passing it to Ralph with the rest of her belongings. "Just tragic that she died this way. Poor thing. Can't imagine what she went through, *if* she jumped."

"Tragic as it is, we've had a few of these jumpers the last year or so. Two of them were in the last six months—young female college students, one from the roof of her dorm, the other from the window of a sixth-floor classroom. Both had IDs, but no suicide notes, no hint, according to family and friends, that either was suicidal. I don't know if this one is related, but she's the third young woman. Very sad," he said, shaking his head.

"So, what's your gut telling you, Ralph? Do you think this woman jumped?"

"I don't know. Maybe she fell. Sometimes when people jump, they change their minds too late. If she really did scream, maybe that's why."

Jessie nodded. "That might explain the abrasions on her hands, and debris under her nails. But the cyanosis and mottling?" Jessie shook her head. "It doesn't make sense."

"We'll have to wait for the ME's report," Ralph said.

"Do you know the circumstances of the other girls' deaths? Did Homicide look into them?"

"I don't know the details, and if the ME rules a death a suicide, we don't interfere unless there's overwhelming evidence that points to something else."

She turned to the counter to collect the EMTs' reports so that Dr. Dawson, the medical examiner, would have them. "Will you be calling Sam?" she asked over her shoulder. Sam was away for the weekend to see his mother, and Jessie had felt a tinge of annoyance that he hadn't asked her to accompany him, to meet his family, become a part of his life. She'd had to remind herself that they were still new, and that the best things took time.

Ralph nodded. "Well, you know he's not around, so I'll fill him in tomorrow. To tell you the truth, I'm surprised to see you here. I would've thought you'd be with him."

Jessie smiled. She could almost see the sparkle in Sam's gray eyes, hear the tenderness in his voice. Ralph was the only person in the Homicide unit who knew that she and Sam were a couple. They'd decided it was best to keep it quiet, to navigate this new relationship without outside interference. But since Sam spent most of his work time with Ralph, who would surely notice the increased calls and texts between them, they'd decided to let him in on their secret. He'd been pleasantly surprised and supportive, even insisting they make plans for dinner with him and his wife.

She crossed her arms and shrugged. "I kind of thought so too, but maybe it's too soon."

Ralph snorted. "You know how he feels about you, Jessie. He's probably telling his mother about you right now."

Aware that his eyes were still on her, she smiled. "Bless you for that. Maybe he'll ask me next time."

Fastidious as ever, Ralph flicked an imaginary piece of lint from his suit jacket and folded his hand over the belongings bag. "Sam—"

"So," she said, anxious to end this line of conversation and any discussion of her relationship with Sam, "if we're all set, I'll just finish up and call the ME's office to pick her up."

Ralph nodded and moved for the door, before turning back. "Want to come for dinner tonight?"

She smiled and then laughed. "Thanks, Ralph, for trying to keep me occupied and out of trouble, but I'm working till eleven thirty."

He pulled her into a quick hug. "Okay. And keep us posted on the autopsy?"

"I'll definitely let you know what he says. I'd like to be there myself to share my own findings." She turned back to the body. "That cyanosis might just change the time, and manner, of death."

He smiled. "See ya later, Jessie," he said as she turned back to the body, the door closing softly as he left.

Jessie finished wrapping the corpse, leaving the breathing tube and intravenous catheters in place for Roger so that he could differentiate original wounds from any injuries that a vigorous resuscitation at the scene and in the ER might have caused. When that was done, she called for transport to take her to the morgue. No need to ask for a pickup by the ME's staff. Transport could take her through the tunnels that ran under Albany Street and into the morgue.

She held the door open for the transporter and turned to the loudspeaker. "Housekeeping to Trauma One," she said just as Carmen, the housekeeper, swept in.

"Thanks, Carmen," she said, glancing one last time at the room.

4

"Jessie Novak, line one," the clerk called over the loudspeaker.

Jessie had hoped today would be quiet—the first really warm day of spring with so much promise in the air, but she hadn't even been at work an hour and already things were going south: a multiple trauma had just arrived, and another was en route. "Hello," she answered tersely.

"Umm, hello," a timid male voice said. "I was told I had to speak with the charge nurse. Is that you?"

"Yes. How can I help you?"

"Well, I'm calling about that woman who jumped. I was wondering how she is."

"And who are you?" Jessie asked, hopeful that maybe the caller knew the woman and could rescue her from the abyss of being a nameless corpse. "A friend? A relative?"

"I... no. I was there. I just wanted to know if she made it, if she's alive."

"I can't tell you anything," Jessie said, her hopes for an ID dashed. "I can't even confirm if she's here."

"But, please. I just... I was there."

Jessie wondered if he was the witness who'd claimed that someone else was there on the roof and she felt a momentary bit of sympathy for his having had to see such a tragic death. Still,

HIPAA was clear even with an unknown. She couldn't tell him anything. "You should speak with the police. If you give me your name, I'll ask them to call you."

She could feel his hesitation through the silence. "Hello?" she said after a pause. "I can pass on your name. That's all I can do."

She could hear the caller take a deep breath, and then she heard the click as he hung up. She shook her head. There'd probably be more calls like that. She reminded herself to let the clerks know to direct any curiosity calls to the police. She checked the trauma rooms to see that the staff were managing—and they were. With Tim Merrick in charge, things would go smoothly.

"Carol," she called to one of the nurses. "If you need anything, page me."

Tim turned at the sound of her voice and smiled. "Will you call the operating room? Tell them we'll be up in twenty minutes. Just gonna get a CT scan."

Jessie nodded and headed for the hallway phone. She'd just notified the OR when she was paged to the front desk. She gritted her teeth and strode to the registration area. She spied a female police officer, a tiny boy in her arms, a thread of tears tracking silently along his cheeks. The clerk nodded to the officer. "Can I help you?" Jessie asked.

"I hope so," the woman said, patting the boy's back. "We found this poor kid wandering alone on Tremont Street. No ID, no name stenciled into his clothes, no one that we can find looking for him. There were only a few apartments in the area where he was found, and most of those were student apartments and dorms. No one knew him. And he hasn't spoken one word. I'm not sure he even understands us, though he looks to be about three, and probably should be speaking. I was thinking maybe he doesn't understand English, or maybe he's autistic. Either way, we can't help him, so we're passing him to you. Someone will be in later to get some photos and see what they can come up with, and I think they'll ask the media to help."

The little boy, his deep brown eyes big as saucers, turned away from Jessie before burying his head in the officer's shoulder. "I'll have to bring him to Pediatrics," Jessie said as she moved in and patted his back. "Are you hungry, sweetie?" The boy lifted his head to glance at Jessie but his eyes, still red with tears, blinked and he looked away once again.

The policewoman huffed out a sigh and held the boy out to Jessie. "Sorry, love," she whispered to him, "but I've got to get back to work." When he was secure in Jessie's arms, she pulled out a card. "Call if you need help. The Department of Children and Families, DCF, are sending someone in but I think it'll be a while before they show."

Jessie's own memories of DCF flickered through her mind, the anger rising from her gut like bile, leaving a bitter taste in her mouth. She remembered wandering the streets alone as a little girl, not much older than this tiny boy. Her father had been working extra hours, her mother had long since abandoned them and most days, there was simply no one to watch her. It wasn't anyone's fault. It was just the way it was. But she could still hear and almost see the elderly woman who'd shouted at her when Jessie was busy yanking flowers from a tiny garden. She'd only wanted something pretty for herself, and it had seemed harmless enough until the old lady had shouted that she'd call the police or better yet, DCF. And even Jessie knew that DCF would be a death knell. They'd take her away from her dad and place her in some crummy foster home, the stuff of Charles Dickens. Jessie could still feel the humiliation that had erupted in red splotches on her face. She'd dropped the flowers and raced home, and never again wandered along that street. Instead, she lingered in backyards and doorways, trying to keep out of sight of nosy neighbors who had too much time on their hands. And it was just about that time that the lie about her mother having died was born, a lie that had served her well until her mother had turned up, only recently, with a whole different story.

The policewoman, likely aware that Jessie was preoccupied, cleared her throat and ran a hand along the boy's cheek. "You'll be okay," she said, turning to go.

The child whimpered and Jessie hugged him close. They both watched as the policewoman headed for the exit. Once she'd disappeared from view, the boy eyed Jessie warily as she set him on his feet and knelt to have a good look at her new charge. Once he was standing, she could see that he was almost three feet tall, his jeans were clean but faded and worn, and the zipper on his red sweatshirt was broken revealing a threadbare t-shirt underneath. She ran her fingers through his dark curls, hoping to get a smile. But he kept his lips in a tight, serious line, his eyes sizing her up before he dropped his gaze to the floor and stuck his thumb into his mouth.

A silent sigh slipped through Jessie's lips and she wondered if this boy understood what DCF meant. "What's your name?" she asked softly. He looked up at the sound of her voice, his eyes focused on hers, but his stare was empty.

She tried another tactic. "My name is Jessie," she said. "What's yours?" He didn't answer but he didn't look away. One small victory. She pointed to herself and repeated her name before pointing to him. "You?" she asked, but he only blinked. *Maybe he doesn't understand English*, the policewoman had said. Jessie knew only a handful of phrases in French and Spanish, and most of them had to do with pain or allergies. "*Je m'appelle* Jessie," she said in the weakest of French accents, but he simply stood and continued to stare. "*Mi nombre es* Jessie," she said with a barely passable Spanish accent, and he tentatively offered a half-smile, his thumb dropping from his mouth. "*Su nombre?*" she asked, hoping he would tell her his name.

"Julio," he whispered and repeated it, his eyes focused on Jessie's.

She racked her brain to come up with the words she needed but finally just spoke in English. "Mother, where is your mother?" she asked, enunciating each syllable. His little shoulders shook in reply and a fresh trickle of tears ran silently along his cheeks.

She traced the line of his tears with her fingers, trying to dry his eyes. He sniffled and drew the sleeve of his sweatshirt along his nose and face, and she couldn't help but laugh at the universal way of all children to wipe a nose or a tear. He grew serious again, and Jessie's heart all but melted. "Come on, Julio," she said as she stood and took his hand. "Let's get you something to eat."

He tugged at her hand and pulled away, raising his arms to be lifted. "It's a good thing you're light, Julio," she said as she bent and gathered him into her arms. "Hey, Cheryl," she said as she passed the front desk. "I'm just going to take my friend to the cafeteria. We'll be right back, but I have my beeper if you need me. Okay?"

Cheryl nodded. "You're a natural with kids, Jessie," she said.

She bounced him on her hip and giggled. "Who knew, huh?" It did feel natural, holding a tiny body so close. She could feel his heart beating against her own, and she smiled. "Julio, we are off to get you some chicken nuggets and fries. I'm guessing those foods transcend language."

In the cafeteria, she balanced him on her hip as she glanced at the choices. He leaned forward, planting the palm of his hand onto the smudged glass that stood between him and the chicken and fries. "I'll have those," she called to the server, "and two of those big cookies." Julio nestled into her shoulder but kept his eyes on the food as it was placed into a bag and passed to Jessie. She grabbed a small juice and a carton of chocolate milk and swiped her ID at the register to pay.

The ER was quiet again when she returned, the trauma rooms emptied—one patient to the OR, the other to x-ray. She settled Julio in the staff lounge and watched as he devoured the nuggets and fries, barely taking time to breathe between bites. When he was finished, he wrapped the remaining cookie in a napkin and slipped it into his pocket and smiled. And with that tiny movement, as though he was planning for the possibility of leaner days ahead, Jessie fell in love with the small boy across from her.

But DCF would be looking for him shortly, and though she'd love nothing more than to sit with him until they came, this was a busy ER, she was in charge and the Pediatric ER was better equipped to meet his needs. She took his hand and this time he walked alongside her as they turned into the hallway that led to

Pediatrics. As soon as the door leading to the children's waiting area swung open, Julio came to a full stop, his eyes wide and dancing with joy. A giant fish tank bubbled in the corner, the over-sized fish swimming leisurely. Next to the tank, a wooden toy box overflowing with trucks and dolls stood untouched, while a Disney movie played on the widescreen television mounted on the wall. It was a child's dream room, designed to keep a sick child occupied with happy things, and though Julio wasn't sick, he needed these diversions as much as any child who wound up here. She paged the charge nurse and reluctantly gave a quick report on Julio's situation. The pediatric nurse was no stranger to stories like his, and she nodded quietly while Jessie spoke.

"So, will you page me when DCF shows up? I just want to be sure they take care of him and find his mom." She hoped that she could find out where he was going, maybe arrange to see him again. She knew that was a long shot, knew better than to get involved, but she couldn't help herself. She felt certain that nobody would understand him or his situation as well as she did. She knelt beside him on the floor. "Julio," she said softly, "I'm going now. *Adiós.*" She'd expected him to cry, maybe claw at her, but he was so engrossed in the truck he was playing with, he barely acknowledged her as she stood and turned to leave. She felt a tug at her heart. He was still a baby, as resilient as she'd once been, but none of them could know what lay ahead for this sweet boy who'd stolen her heart in a way no man ever had. She put out her hand and ruffled his hair before she walked away.

And only then did he look up and lock his eyes on hers in a silent acknowledgment.

5

"Jessie Novak, line two," the overhead speaker blared. She glanced at her watch. It was only six o'clock, and though the trauma rooms were quiet just then, it had been one of those days with a million little hassles. A nursing home's first floor had flooded after a pipe broke, and they'd sent in fifteen frail, elderly residents, wheelchair- or bed-bound, filling the acute side and part of the hallway to wait for the cleanup. They had only just left, and she muttered to herself, "What is it now?" She picked up the nearest phone. "You paged me?" she asked softly, not wanting to dump her grumpiness onto the caller.

"Sorry to bother you," Cheryl whispered, "but there's a man here asking for the nurse in charge."

"Did he say who he is or what he wants?"

"He won't say. He wants to speak to the nurse in charge."

"Does he look like a reporter?"

"No, I don't think so. Too young."

"Okay. If he won't say why he's here, tell him to have a seat. He'll just have to wait."

Cheryl chuckled. "You got it," she said, and she disconnected the call.

Jessie replaced the phone and made her way to Pediatrics to

see if anyone had come for Julio. She hadn't intended to let so much time pass before she checked on him, and she crossed her fingers that he was still there, or even better, that his family had come forward and collected him. She rounded the corner, swiped her ID against the reader and heard the anguished cries of a baby being poked and another child resisting treatment. This was exactly why she couldn't work in Pediatrics—the tormented wails of the poor kids who didn't understand what was happening to them. She stepped into the hallway, her eyes scanning the area for the young boy, but there was no sign of him, not by the fish tank, or the toy box, or even in front of the large-screen television. She felt a tiny prick of unease in her chest as she turned for the nurses' station hoping to find out where he'd gone.

"Hey, sorry to bother you," she said in greeting to the secretary, whose name she was embarrassed to admit she couldn't remember. "Is the little boy the police brought in still here?" she asked, wrinkling her eyes to read the woman's name tag—Pearl.

She nodded and Jessie's eyes followed her gaze to the floor, where Julio sat at the woman's feet playing with cars. "He seems happiest almost hidden away, so we just let him be," she said.

"No word yet from the police or DCF?"

"Nothing. And Cathy left messages."

"May I, Pearl?" Jessie asked as she bent to her knees.

Jessie squatted down, the movement startling Julio who scooted back further under the desk. "Julio," she whispered, and he turned his gaze to hers, his eyes wide with fright until a glimmer of recognition flashed in them, a sudden smile lighting up his face. He took Jessie's hand and allowed her to guide him out. "Has he said anything?" Jessie asked Pearl.

"No, he sat with Marta for a while, but she went home at four."

Jessie sighed. The poor kid. He'd been hiding under the desk for hours, and she wondered if that was what he had to do at home —hide from someone. She wanted to convince this little boy that he was safe. She lifted him into her arms and stood, hoisting him onto her hip. She tilted his chin up and offered him a wide smile. "*Bueno?*" She hoped that he understood that in her imperfect Spanish she was asking if he was okay.

Julio erupted into laughter, that joyful language of children, a sound that Jessie had always loved, a sound that had always made her wonder why a mother would leave a baby just as her own had, and probably Julio's as well. She'd had to wait twenty-five years to find out what had sent her mother away. She offered a quick prayer that Julio would have an answer tonight. Surely, someone was missing him.

She sighed and turned to Pearl. "I'm just going to grab a few toys and bring him to our staff lounge. One of the nurses ordered pizza, and he must be hungry by now. Call me if anyone shows up for him, or if you need me."

Pearl nodded and turned to her work as Jessie bounced Julio on her hip. He smiled shyly and though he didn't speak, he reached his hand out to touch her face before closing his eyes and burrowing his head into the curve of her shoulder. In the minutes it took to get back to the staff lounge and the pizza that had arrived, he was already sound asleep. Marveling at how he'd so easily snuggled into her, Jessie slid into a seat, holding him close. She knew she should bring him back to Pedi where a crib and blankets sat waiting, but she wasn't quite ready to let him go. She hadn't realized that a bond with a tiny child could be created so quickly; that his little body's warmth could seep into her own and from there directly into her heart. She gazed at his sleeping face, the skin as soft as down, the lips curled into a gentle smile, and eyelashes so long they almost swept his cheeks, and she felt a sudden inexplicable ache, a deep longing in her chest.

"Jessie, line one," the overhead speaker announced, breaking into her almost-trance.

She picked up the phone and whispered, "It's Jessie."

"Sorry to bother you, but that guy is still asking for you."

She groaned. She'd forgotten all about him. "I'll be right out," she said, shifting Julio's weight as she hung up the phone. She grabbed a small blanket from the linen cart, covering Julio as she made her way to the front desk. "Cheryl, will you hold him for a minute?"

Cheryl nodded and held out her arms to Julio. "He's over there," she said, tilting her head toward a young man who was standing against the tiled wall of the reception area.

Jessie smoothed the front of her scrubs and studied the man who'd been waiting to speak with her. He was tall, well over six feet, with thick sandy-colored hair and piercing dark eyes. He might have been handsome except for an asymmetrical smile that pulled his mouth to the left revealing a row of crooked, yellowing teeth, the latter likely due to the acrid scent of old smoke that seeped from his skin. She almost held her breath against the smell when she realized that he was studying her, too. She offered a tentative smile and her hand. "I'm the nurse in charge," she said. "What can I do for you?"

His smile faded and he cleared his throat. "I'm here about that woman who fell today. I wondered if she survived." He tangled and untangled his fingers nervously as he spoke.

"What did you say your name was?" she asked.

"Actually, I didn't," he answered, his voice soft in direct contrast to his sturdy athletic build. "I was there when it happened. I just wondered how she is."

Jessie shook her head. "Sorry, I can't even tell you if she's here. HIPAA."

His eyes crinkled in confusion.

"HIPAA, the federal privacy act. I can't confirm, or even deny, anything. Sorry. I know it must have been hard to witness that, but you should call the police. They may want to speak with you anyway, and they can probably offer you information that I can't."

"She's alive then?" he asked, his eyes crinkling at the prospect.

"Again," Jessie said, "I just can't say, but if you give me your name, I'll let the police know and ask them to call you."

He nodded, a fine sheen of sweat breaking out on his forehead, his eyes darting uneasily to the front entrance as a wail of sirens pierced the night air. "I think you're right, and thank you. I will call them."

But Jessie suspected he wouldn't call. There was something in the way he said it, as if to appease her. Like so many others, he probably didn't want to be involved in whatever had happened; he just wanted to know how it had ended. She shrugged. It didn't matter anyway. "It must have been terrible for you to witness that woman's fall. I can't imagine going through that, or how you must feel. Please know that we have services to help people get through traumatic events. You can see someone here in social work if you need to talk it through."

He almost seemed to consider the offer before he shook his head. "Well, anyway, sorry to have bothered you," he said, smiling again, the fluorescent overhead lights bouncing off the dull yellow of his teeth. He stuck out his hand. "I heard that lady call you Jessie, so thanks, Jessie. Have a good evening."

"You, too," she said, folding her arms across her chest and watching as he slipped through the sliding glass doors and disappeared into the night. She turned to see Cheryl rocking Julio, his head nestled in her arms, a half-smile on his lips. He looked so comfortable, she hated to disturb him, but she wanted to get him into a crib.

"I'll take him," she said, sliding her hands under him and wrapping her arms around him. "I'm just going to get him settled in Pedi. I'll be right back."

"If no one comes for him, you should see if you can take him home with you, Jessie," Cheryl said.

"I'd like to, but... I don't think they'd allow it."

Cheryl shrugged. "I don't know, but it's worth a try."

In Pedi, Jessie dragged a crib to the nurses' station and set Julio gently inside, arranging the blanket over him. "Sweet dreams," she whispered as she planted a quick kiss on his cheek. "Hey," she called softly, "I'll be back to check on him. Okay?"

Pearl nodded. "Still no word?" she asked.

Jessie shook her head. "Maybe that's a good sign, though, especially since DCF hasn't shown up. Makes me think they've found the mother and they're bringing her in to get him. Or maybe it's all wishful thinking."

6

As soon as she stepped back into the emergency room, the overhead page sounded. It was Cheryl again, calling her to the front desk. Thank God the ER wasn't busy, Jessie thought as she made her way out front where Cheryl caught her eye and directed her gaze to a slim black woman in a tailored suit, a string of pearls peeking through the jacket. Her back was ruler-straight as she rifled through her briefcase. She pulled out a sheaf of papers before glancing quickly at her wristwatch. Instinctively, Jessie looked at her own. Seven p.m. already.

"Hello," Jessie said. "I'm the nurse in charge."

"Ahh," the woman said. "DCF. Sorry to be so late. I was on call, but I was at a family wedding. Didn't get the page until an hour ago. Where's our boy?" The woman slipped the papers she'd held back into her briefcase before clicking it shut.

Jessie hesitated. The woman didn't seem interested in Julio so much as the official business of picking him up. "I don't understand. Has anyone at DCF been looking for his family, or trying to identify him? Anything?" Jessie felt her voice rising and she took a deep breath to settle herself down.

"No, we'll get to that tomorrow morning, first thing. I'm guessing you know how it is," she said, her eyes scanning the corridor and the waiting room. "Things are busy, and you just don't get to do everything that you need to do. I'd like to get going soon," she said, her fingers rolling over her glossy pearls. "Can you just show me where he is?"

Jessie felt the bloom of red blotches heating her cheeks. "He's been here for hours. Are you saying no one's lifted a finger to find out who he is?"

The woman stiffened. "I'm saying it's Sunday and we're short-staffed."

"We can just keep him here then," Jessie said. "He's asleep in Pedi anyway."

"Does he have any injuries?" the woman asked, pulling a pen from her bag ready to document any trauma he'd suffered.

Jessie swallowed the heavy ache of disappointment in her throat. "His only injury is that someone abandoned him, and DCF didn't bother to track anyone down."

"Anger won't change anything," she said, gripping the pen. "I'm here to take him with me."

"Where will he go? Is there a home available? Someone to take care of him? He's afraid, you know, and he's just a baby, really." She felt the first stirrings of a kind of panic burst into her chest.

"I do know, but there's nothing available tonight, no emergency placement. He'll have to go to a group home for the night. We'll work on placement tomorrow."

The red blotches on Jessie's cheeks spread to her ears and neck. "Can I take him for the night? He's comfortable with me."

The woman seemed to brighten a little at the prospect; it would certainly let her off the hook. "Are you a certified foster parent?" she asked, her tone friendlier than it had been.

"No, would I need to be? That seems crazy just to try to help out a little boy, doesn't it?"

"Those are the rules, and it's to protect the children. It's in his best interest."

Jessie wasn't ready to throw in the towel. "I'm a nurse here. I work with the police, too. You can call—check me out."

"It won't change anything. I have to take him," she said, her voice softening. "I do know how you feel, but we will take care of him. I promise."

The knot in her stomach tightening, Jessie motioned for the woman to follow as she pushed open the door to the Pediatrics waiting room. "Have a seat," she said. "I'll just check and have someone bring Julio out." She didn't think she could bear to hand him over herself.

The woman nodded and sank uncomfortably into the child-sized chair, her knees bent up tight against her chest. Jessie stifled a laugh and went in search of the Pedi charge nurse and Julio, who was wide awake and sitting on the floor, his eyes tracking her as she came into his line of sight. "Yessie," he shouted as he ran to her, his stubby little legs propelling him along, his delight at seeing her percolating into the air around him. Tears pricked at the backs of her eyes, but she forced a smile. She didn't want him to know that he was about to leave. She bent to pick him up as Pearl called out to her.

"He's been calling your name since he woke. Any news on a family?"

"No. They haven't even looked. The DCF social worker is here to take him to a group home."

Pearl grimaced. "Oh, no."

A hard lump caught in Jessie's throat as Julio rested his head on her shoulder and gently patted her back in that way of young children who are offering comfort, though he surely didn't understand why she needed it. She kissed his cheek and he giggled and looked into her eyes, a lone tear breaking free. Jessie whisked it away and took a deep breath, but it was too late. Julio sensed that something was wrong, and he tried to wriggle from her arms. "No, sweetie," she whispered. "It's okay," she added, though she knew it wasn't.

"Jessie," Pearl said, nodding to the doorway where the social worker stood watching.

"We really have to get going," she said, moving toward Jessie and the boy.

Julio sensed that something bad was about to happen and he

began to wail and stiffen against Jessie's arms. She wanted to cry and scream as well, but that would only make things worse. She sank to her knees and stood him in front of her, her arms still encircling him. "Julio," she whispered, racking her brain for the words she needed to say, but they eluded her. "It's okay," she finally whispered, again.

He sniffled and swiped his sleeve along his eyes. "Okay?" he asked, his innocence and helplessness so pure Jessie felt her heart break. She turned back toward the social worker.

"Please," she said. "You see how it is. Just one night?"

The social worker, to her credit, nodded sadly. "Sorry," she said, reaching down and taking Julio's hand into her own. Jessie could see his little hand trying to slip out of the woman's grip and when he couldn't, he let out a howl and reached back for Jessie.

"Let me walk him out with you, at least," she said.

The social worker flicked her eyes in response. *She just wants to get out of here*, Jessie thought as she lifted Julio once again and turned for the exit. He clung tightly to her, his fear seeping through his skin, his tiny hands trembling. Silently, Jessie cursed the system that would do this to a child. She pushed out through the doors into the deep chill and dusky sky of late evening.

"Here," the social worker said, pointing to a car parked by the entrance. She pulled open the door and reached for Julio, who turned his back to her and clung tightly to Jessie.

"No," he shouted, the terror in his voice ricocheting off the building and into Jessie's veins. She ran her hand along his back in a soothing motion.

"It's okay, Julio," she murmured softly.

"We have to go," the social worker said impatiently. She reached for Julio again and he wrenched away from her and let out a long howl.

Jessie twisted away from her. "I'll put him in the car seat," she said, sliding in back and placing Julio securely in the seat. He almost smiled then, his eyes wide. He seemed to think that Jessie would be coming with him. She stifled the sob that tore at the back of her throat and she kissed him gently on the cheek. "You are loved, sweet Julio. Wherever you are, remember that."

She backed out of the car and stood there blinking away the tears that pricked at her eyes. He reached for her. "Yessie?" he called.

The social worker slammed the car door shut. Jessie leaned toward the window and blew a kiss to Julio, who strained against the car seat, his mouth open in stunned protest. Jessie pressed her hand against the window, hoping he understood that she was heartbroken too.

"Can I call tomorrow to find out where he is, or what happened?" she asked, her voice cracking. "I want to be sure he's safe."

"I can assure you that he'll be safe, but I can't share any information about him. Sorry, but those are the rules." The social worker walked to the driver's side, her heels clicking on the pavement. She opened her door, gave the slightest of nods and pulled away from the ER, Julio's cries fading, though Jessie could still hear them loud and clear in her mind.

She was pretty sure she'd be hearing them for a long time.

7

MONDAY, DAY 2

Jessie slept fitfully. Stark images of Julio, alone and afraid, swirled through her mind. She rolled up her pillow and pulled the covers over her head, but it was no use. The city's early morning sounds seeped through her windows: the clatter of garbage cans being pulled to the curb, the groan of car engines coming to life, the occasional horn of an impatient driver. She finally rose, brewed a cup of strong coffee, pulled on her spandex running tights, a light sweatshirt and running shoes, and headed out, barely stretching her cold muscles before she stepped onto K Street, the houses buttoned up tight, shades still drawn, people just shaking off the night. It hadn't been so long ago that her evening runs had allowed her peeks into her neighbors' lives—shades up, lights full on, families gathering in front of the glow of television screens. She could almost feel the warmth of those scenes seeping out to her, spreading through her veins. She longed for that—a house and family of her own. And this morning, she wished that for Julio as well. She turned her attention back to her run and made her way to Day Boulevard and her familiar route along the beach and Castle Island. Lost in the sweet bliss of a good run, she wasn't sure how long she'd been out before she realized that already the roads were filling up.

She inhaled deeply, the salty air clearing her head and her thoughts of poor little Julio. She had to remember there were some things she'd never be able to change, and one little boy's circumstances—as awful as they were—was one of those things. But she might just check with DCF and find out if she could become an emergency foster parent for kids who were suddenly left all alone. It couldn't hurt to at least try, and though it was too late to rescue Julio, there might be another child who wound up alone and frightened in the ER, and she might as well be ready to fight back.

A sudden car horn nudged Jessie from her musings, her eyes and thoughts back on her route and the morning traffic. She knew she had to be vigilant when she ran on this busy road. She crossed Day Boulevard and Columbia Road and headed back up K Street, her footfalls light as air and almost soundless as she slowed to a walk and turned into the corner store, fishing in her pocket for money.

"Morning, Patrick, I'll have the usual," she called, her eyes searching the *Herald*'s front page for any story about the jumper. But the front page screamed out the usual politics and crime, though she sometimes thought the line between them was indistinguishable. She picked up the paper and scanned the pages, and there on page four was a short story about a woman who'd jumped from the roof of a garage near Northeastern University just as two others had in the last year. There was no definite mention of her death, although by alluding to the others they hinted at that. Neither did they mention that she was still unidentified, just a note that a bystander suspected she was a student anxious about finals. "Where do they come up with these people and their theories?" she mumbled to herself. The story ended with the usual plea from police for any witnesses to come forward.

"Here ya go, love. A muffin, blueberry today, and black coffee. Don't know how you can drink it that way." Patrick wrinkled his mouth. "Anything else?" he asked.

Jessie spun around. "The paper," she said, holding it up, "and a cup of tea and another muffin."

Patrick raised a brow and smiled. "Got company, have ya?" His brogue was thick as molasses today.

Jessie laughed. "No secrets in Southie, huh? But no." She shook her head to emphasize the point. "It's for Rufus."

"Ahh, lovely man, that one. Give him my best, will ya?"

Jessie nodded and slid her money over the counter. "I will. Thanks, Patrick." She rolled the paper under her arm, gripped her bag and drinks tray and hurried along the street, noting that the sky was grayer than yesterday, the air a bit colder, and the buds on trees and flowers seemed to have shriveled in the last twenty-four hours. Still, though the brakes might have been tapped on spring's arrival, it was here and that gave her hope. For everything.

She'd barely knocked on Rufus's door when he'd pulled it open as if he'd been waiting for her. "Morning, Jessie, what do you have there?"

"Breakfast, and I remembered the tea this time."

"You're a good girl, Jessie. Don't know what I'd do without you." He took the bag from her hand and led her along the hallway to the kitchen, where he pulled out a chair and motioned for her to sit.

She sat with a sigh and drank a long sip of her coffee, the steam tickling her lips as she swallowed.

Rufus took two small plates from a cabinet and passed one to Jessie as he sat across from her. "I was just making up my shopping list," he said. "It'll be nice to have a ride. I do need a few things." He peered into the bag of muffins. "Which one do you fancy for yourself?" he asked.

Jessie was about to say either was fine when she remembered that his cabinets often held the sparsest food supply: cans of soup, baked beans, cereal, stale bread and not much else. He just didn't eat as well as he should in the years since his wife had died.

"Actually," she said, "I'm not hungry. They're both for you. And we're still going grocery shopping, but a little later today. I hope that's okay. I just have to stop by the morgue this morning." She didn't actually *have* to stop by the morgue, but she wanted to see how Roger Dawson, the medical examiner, would approach the jumper's case. Would he just call it a suicide, or would he look for

more evidence to prove that? Her experience with jumpers was
minimal at best, and if she wanted to prove her worth as a forensic
nurse, she had to understand every aspect of cases like this one—
the how and why and even when of this woman's death. She had to
be there. No question.

"No problem, Jessie," Rufus said, dusting a sprinkling of
crumbs from the front of his shirt. "I'll be around all day. No big
plans for me. You go on and do what you need to. I'll be right
here." He washed down the last of a muffin with a gulp of tea and
smiled.

Jessie pushed back from the table. "I'll get going then. The
sooner I get there, the sooner I'll be back." She leaned down and
planted a kiss on his cheek. "See you in a while," she said as she
headed out.

Upstairs, she took a quick shower, and checked the weather,
groaning when she heard the forecast—a high of fifty-nine degrees
and cloudy, overcast skies. She slipped on a pair of well-worn
jeans, a soft sweater and her sturdiest boots. Yesterday had seemed
the prelude to those lazy days of gauzy skirts, sleeveless tops, and
glittery sandals, but she'd just have to be patient for a little longer
and hope that waiting would make the arrival of warmer days all
that much sweeter.

Jessie grabbed a light jacket, another surrender to cooler
weather, and headed out, maneuvering through early morning traffic, and parked before jogging across the street to the morgue. Once
inside, the sharp odors of formaldehyde and old blood prickled at
the back of her throat. She coughed the tickle away and wondered
if she'd ever adjust to the bitter scents here. She took the stairs to
the second floor and the autopsy suite in search of Dr. Dawson and
Jane Doe.

"Hey there," Tony Jones, the postmortem technician, called as
she pulled open the door. "Are you here to invite me for coffee?"
He winked.

"Sorry," Jessie said. "Another time. Is Roger in?"

"He is," Tony replied, nodding his head to the closed door.

"We're just getting ready to look at Jane Doe. Is she the reason for your visit?"

"She is. I was on when she came in and there were some conflicting stories about her fall. I'm interested in seeing how Roger decides to call it—suicide or something else."

Tony bobbed his head. "We're finished with the x-rays, about to start the autopsy. Go on and get changed. I'll tell him you're here. We'll wait for you."

Jessie hurried to the locker room, quickly changed into scrubs and grabbed her PPE, pulling it on as she raced back to the autopsy suite, a large, cavernous room that seemed designed to accommodate more than the three metal gurneys it held. "This was built for mass casualty events with multiple deaths," Tony had once said. "But we haven't had anything on that scale since the Coconut Grove fires in 1942. And that was long before my time." Adjusting her mask and goggles just so, she pulled open the door and stepped inside.

"Morning, Jessie," Roger said, snapping on a pair of gloves, a tuft of his thick gray hair peeking from under his surgical cap.

"Morning, Roger. I was on yesterday when she came in. I'm curious how you'll decide to proceed—or if you decide to proceed."

Roger pushed his eyeglasses up on his nose. "Come and have a look," he said, motioning Jessie to the x-ray view box on the wall, the skull film backlit and already marked up with a red Sharpie. Roger tapped his hand on the spot. "See here," he said. "This fracture of her left orbit?"

"I see it, and the soft tissue swelling that surrounds it. She had some bleeding at that site."

"Exactly," Roger answered. "And this," he said, pointing to a film of her left hip.

Jessie moved closer and examined the film. It took her a few minutes, but finally she turned to him. "The displaced fracture?" she asked, not entirely certain that was what he meant.

Roger pulled the x-ray films from the viewer and slid them into an oversized envelope. "Ahh, yes," he said, "and you know a hip

fracture results in significant blood loss, which appears as soft-
tissue swelling on x-ray? With the orbital fracture we saw that
expected swelling and tissue response, but there's none of that in
the hip." He folded his arms across his chest in a teacherly way, his
eyeglasses creeping down on his nose. "The same goes for her head
wound, that open skull fracture. There's tissue leaking out, but no
indication of active bleeding. Based on my quick initial assessment
I'd say that her orbital fracture and facial wounds occurred before
her death, and those other fractures, they happened after her
death. I think that her heart had already stopped pumping when
she fell from that roof, which makes this all very suspicious. But
we'll take a closer look and then we'll have a better idea of how she
really died."

"Has anyone ID'd her?" she asked, turning to Tony.

"Nothing on her yet. Sam Dallas and another detective are
coming in, I think. Maybe they'll have something." Tony posi-
tioned the body on the table, her head raised on a wooden block.

"Could she have overdosed, banged up her face and then fell?"
Jessie asked, but even as she said it, she knew it was unlikely.

"No," Roger said, reaching for the scalpel that Tony held out.
"Even if her heart stopped as she fell, she'd still have evidence of
active bleeding, and I don't see any of that. Instead, she has
evidence of lividity and mottling though rigor mortis hadn't yet set
in. I think she'd been dead for half an hour, maybe more, when she
fell."

Jessie smiled to herself. She'd noticed that in the ER. She was
good at this job. Suddenly she realized that Roger was still speaking, and she snapped to attention.

"We've taken blood, urine, spinal fluid and vitreous samples,
but unless we find something—heart disease, blood or liver disease,
toxic drug levels or poisons such as ricin, arsenic, cyanide—this
whole picture is strange."

He tapped his foot on the pedal located by the table to activate
the Dictaphone as he made the first cut in his Y incision from the
woman's shoulders to her lower abdomen. "Unknown Hispanic

female, age appears to be between twenty and thirty-five, height of sixty-six inches, weight one hundred twenty-one pounds, with an endotracheal tube in her airway, and one intravenous line in her left brachial vein, faded striae and loose skin on her lower abdomen consistent with a past pregnancy," he began as the door creaked open.

"Hey," a male voice called. "Just poked my head in to say hi."

"Ahh, hi, Al," Tony said. "Bad timing. It's good to see you, but we're busy and you're not in PPE."

"Yeah, sorry. Just wanted to say hi."

Jessie, her eyes trained on the body, could feel Roger's irritation at being disturbed, but he remained silent and she remained still.

"I'll catch up with you later," Tony said. "Maybe we can get a drink sometime."

"Sounds good," the man said as the door closed with a quick thud.

Roger shook his head. "How did he get in here?"

Tony shrugged. "I don't know, but he used to work here. People like him. No harm in saying hello, is there?"

"I guess not," Roger said grudgingly. "Let's get on with it. Initial x-rays revealed multiple extremity fractures including a depressed occipital skull fracture. She also had fractures of the c-spine at levels two to four, compression fractures of the thoracic and lumbar spines, a fracture of her left humerus and left hip, and multiple rib fractures, those likely due to vigorous resuscitation attempts. External exam also revealed petechial hemorrhages in both eyes."

"Suffocation?" Jessie asked, remembering that those tiny pinpoint hemorrhages were often indicative of asphyxia as a cause of death, usually due to strangulation or suffocation. She was going with suffocation, since Jane Doe hadn't had any of those telltale marks on her neck that indicated strangulation.

"We'll see," Roger said before launching back into his description of the corpse as he continued his examination. "Normal vascular system, no evidence of clots, heart and great vessels look good, liver looks good, no evidence of heavy metal toxicity or tissue damage and no obvious signs of drug use. No evidence of sexual assault or recent sexual activity either, but we'll take samples anyway for testing."

"What about the bruising on her wrists, the abrasions on her hands and the debris under her nails? Was that inflicted after she died? It seems strange, but..."

"No, just like her facial wounds, those were definitely inflicted before she fell, so before she died. Those wounds all show evidence of active bleeding and inflammation which you wouldn't see if they'd occurred after death."

"So, her wrist bruising was fresh? Not from a bracelet or something?"

He nodded. "Hard to say. Could be, or maybe restraint bruising from something wrapped around her wrists."

"So, she was assaulted before the fall?"

"Looks as though she was involved in some kind of altercation before her death. Maybe the debris under her nails will reveal someone else's DNA. And then there's her past pregnancy. She may have an older child or even a teenager who will report her missing. It could be a start in figuring this out."

Jessie's mind drifted to the young woman who lay before her. Twenty-four hours ago, she was alive and breathing and, in an instant, it was all over. The ER had taught her that life was tenuous and fragile, that everything could be lost in the blink of an eye, that violence and trauma and tragic death were a part of life. But this woman's death seemed somehow worse, maybe because she remained unidentified. Someone must be missing her.

Finally, the procedure over, Roger stepped back and peeled his gloves away revealing damp, crinkled skin on his hands. He sighed heavily. "I just don't see anything obvious. Maybe toxicology or even histology will come up with something for us. Right now, I'm stymied."

"Could she have been smothered?" Jessie asked. "With a pillow, or something like that?"

"She could have been, especially since she has debris under her nails. No indication of sexual assault, though maybe that was the intent but she fought back. Maybe that's how she received those facial injuries, but she has no bits of fiber in her mouth. And you'd have to hold a pillow pretty tightly to suffocate someone. That usually leaves bilateral bruising behind. I'm just not sure."

"Hey, Doc," Tony said, "doesn't this remind you of those two college girls who jumped this year?"

"Hmm, maybe, but the evidence on those girls was negligible. No signs of assault or a struggle. Nothing. Everything pointed to suicide, and suicide is the second leading cause of death among young people. Sometimes these are copycat deaths, coming in twos or threes. But..." He pulled his goggles away from his eyes. "This young woman does not appear to be a suicide, though someone may have wanted it to look that way." Roger made his way to the sink, where he tapped the foot pedal to activate the water before plunging his hands under the fresh stream. He scrubbed and rinsed and scrubbed again before turning back.

"We'll have to see what comes back on this woman's toxic screen, but my initial impression is asphyxia as the cause of death. These cases," he said, drying his hands, "are the ones that will stay with you, keep you up at night."

"I can let Sam and the team know," Jessie said, pulling off her goggles and face mask.

Roger jerked his head toward Tony. "They already called us asking for an expedited report on her, right?"

Tony nodded.

"I can give Sam a call, tell him I'll bring your preliminary report over, convey your suspicions." She peeled her own gloves off, the skin on her hands slick with sweat.

Roger smiled. "They were your suspicions as well, Jessie. Well done."

"Thanks, Roger," she said quietly.

"Give us fifteen minutes. Tony can retrieve the preliminary report on this Jane Doe and you can be on your way. Remind them that we still need toxicology and histology results before we can say for certain what killed this woman, and with luck, we'll come up with something."

Jessie nodded, and then remembered that Ralph had said she might have screamed when she fell. If it wasn't Jane Doe who'd screamed, and clearly it wasn't, then who was it?

8

When she exited the morgue, she had a text from Sam. *Call me,* he'd written. *Just got back.*

She smiled and texted. *Way ahead of you. On my way to your office. See you then.*

At police headquarters, she pulled her ID from her bag, held it up for the officer at the entrance and took the stairs two at a time, slowing only as she approached the row of cubicles that held the desks of the detectives in Homicide. "Got anything on Jane Doe for us?" Ralph asked when he saw her.

Jessie pulled the report from her bag and waved it in the air. "I do. You coming?" she asked as she made her way to Sam's office.

"I'll give you a few minutes," he said. He winked and jerked his head toward the open doorway, motioning for Jessie to go in.

Sam was sitting forward, his elbows resting on the desk, his hands massaging his forehead, too deep in thought to notice that Jessie had stepped into his office. "Morning, Sam," she said softly. "Are you okay?"

He looked up, his eyes crinkling with the sudden smile that lit up his face, his focus on her. And suddenly it was as though she was the center of his universe, the only one who mattered, and she felt that warm glow that coursed through her veins when she was with him.

"I am now," he answered, coming from behind his desk and pulling her into his arms.

She stood on her toes to plant a quick kiss on his lips before pushing him gently away. She glanced sideways toward the open door. "Better save that for later."

He reluctantly dropped his arms and retreated to his chair. "You're right. I just... I missed you this weekend."

"I missed you too, Sam."

"So," he said, leaning back, tenting his fingers before lacing them together. "Ralph told me about the jumper. Any word?"

As if on cue, Ralph poked his head in. "Ready for me?" he asked, slipping in and taking the chair next to Jessie.

She sank into a chair and passed one copy of the postmortem report to Sam, the other to Ralph, before slipping off her jacket and draping it over the chair back. After a few moments, they finished reading and looked up in tandem. "No obvious cause of death?" Ralph asked.

"Roger mentioned that she may have been suffocated, but aside from petechial hemorrhages in her eyes, there's not much else to support that—yet. But she did suffer significant facial injuries."

Sam sighed noisily. "Roger's certain that she was dead before she fell?"

"Yes," Jessie answered. "And so am I. In the ER, she didn't have any fresh bleeding from the fall, which meant that her heartbeat and her blood flow had already stopped."

"Oh, hell," Sam said, running his hand though his hair. "If she was dead when she fell, someone else was up there. Someone had to have thrown her off that roof."

"Ralph, was there anyone at the scene?" Jessie asked. "On the roof? I remember you said yesterday that one witness thought he saw a shadow, that maybe someone was up there with her? And someone screamed?"

"Yeah, that didn't really pan out. There was no evidence at all on the roof. Nothing to indicate that anyone had been up there, including her. The scream was likely a horrified bystander, though we can't be sure of that yet. And Jane Doe left nothing behind, no bag, no ID, nothing. The area was pristine. There were only three cars parked there. They were all still locked up tight. We checked with the owners—one of them had left his car there for two days, the other two had been there overnight, left there while they attended a frat party nearby. It was a Sunday morning, so the garage was quiet. Only a few other cars coming and going. I've asked the garage owner to pull the video for me, though there's no camera on the roof. I'll check neighborhood footage, see if they have anything. And that's where we are. For now, at least." Ralph nodded to himself as he flicked through the preliminary report.

"Any signs of robbery gone bad?"

Sam shook his head. "I suppose that's a possibility since we didn't find a wallet or phone on her. But until we find out who she is, we don't even have a motive."

"I had a call yesterday," Jessie said, "from a guy who said he was at the scene and wanted to know how the woman was doing. And later, another guy showed up asking the same thing. Might have been the same guy, I guess."

Sam leaned forward, his brows knitted, his gaze drifting from the report to Jessie. "Did you tell him anything?"

"I'm not even sure why you'd ask that," she answered testily. "Of course I didn't say anything. I told him I couldn't even say if she was a patient, and then I advised him to call the police. I even offered to take his name and have you get in touch, but he declined, said he'd be in touch with you. Has he?"

Ralph propped his elbow on the arm of his chair and turned to face her. "There've been a lot of calls to go through, but nothing that stands out. And I think we spoke to all the witnesses who were actually there. We've had a few calls from people who said they were there, and we've called most of them, but nobody had any new information. And there's still only that one guy who's convinced there was a shadow up on the roof. No one else saw that, but they hadn't looked up until they noticed her falling through the air. It all happened within seconds, and everyone remembers the scene a little differently. Maybe the video will give us more information, especially since she didn't leave a car up there. We're checking cars on the other levels to see if she might have parked on another level and walked up. But if she was dead when she fell, someone else brought her up there and likely left as soon as he, or she, dropped her from the roof."

A chill ran through Jessie and she tugged her coat over her shoulders before slouching low in her chair. "Tony Jones, Roger's assistant, told me about the two female college students who'd jumped this year in Boston, and it got me to wondering if someone wanted this death to look like a suicide. I'd like to check to see how many confirmed suicides there've been in the state recently." She turned to Sam. "There's just something so odd about this. Any chance this is related?"

"Not likely," Sam said, folding his hands on the desk. "The other two in Boston had no signs of assault and both were college students—young, identities known and ruled as likely suicides."

"Did any of them leave notes behind?"

"No," Ralph said. "One of the other guys checked on that."

Jessie nodded. "I checked while I was waiting for Roger's report and it seems that women don't usually jump, it's men who jump. Roger said sometimes there are copycat suicides but maybe someone wanted *this* death to look like a suicide. It just got me to thinking."

Sam leaned forward. "It means you're a detective if things get you to thinking, Jessie, but let's get back to Jane Doe for now."

"Okay. Some fingernails were broken off as well, and from what I heard, those missing fingernails weren't at the scene, but there was some debris under her remaining nails—blood and tissue. Roger took scrapings, so maybe Forensics can get some DNA."

"That's almost too much to hope for," Ralph said as he pushed himself up from his chair with a sigh. "Think I'll head over to that garage, see if I can pick up that footage and have a look. I'll see you later, Jessie, and Sam, text me if you think of anything else we need."

"I thought things would move more quickly," Jessie said. "I feel as though we're missing something that's right in front of us."

"Maybe," Sam said, "but unidentified victims are always tough, and we have to move with what we've got, so let's see what we have on video, see if Forensics has come up with anything, and plan for a meeting tomorrow morning. I need to have a closer look at the witness statements, too. Roger's report says he should have histology, the tissue examination, by then. If we have a cause of death and the video tapes caught something, we might get lucky." He turned to Jessie. "Can you make a meeting tomorrow?"

"As long as I can make it to the ER by three, I'll be here."

Ralph raised his hand to his forehead as if in salute. "See you then," he said as he strode through the door.

"I have a question, a request, really," she asked Sam, crossing her arms, anxious about what she wanted to ask.

Sam leaned forward, his fingers drumming on his desk. "Go ahead."

"There was a little boy yesterday, about three years old, I'd guess, who was found wandering alone and brought to the ER. He didn't have injuries or anything. He looked well fed, but no one ever reported him missing and DCF took custody of him last night. I was just wondering if you could get some information on him, find out where he is, or if his family showed up. I'm worried about him. The social worker who picked him up said they couldn't share anything with me. But maybe they would with you."

He shook his head. "Sorry, not likely that DCF will tell me anything unless there was a murder involved."

Jessie frowned.

"I'm not being smart. If you're worried, I can reach out to a friend on the Crimes Against Children Unit, see if they have anything. I can check too with the National Center for Missing and Exploited Children, see if he's listed there. Do you have the child's name?"

"Just a first name, and I'm not even sure of that. He said his name was Julio. That was it. He understood Spanish but he didn't speak much. Just his name. Nothing else."

"Do you know where they picked him up?"

"I'm not sure. Maybe Tremont Street? I guess I don't have much to go on, do I?"

"No, but there aren't too many abandoned or lost three-year-olds. I'll ask around."

"Thanks, Sam. I can't stop thinking about him. I guess it hit a little close to home. Child abandonment is personal to me. Guess I need to get past that."

"Speaking of which, have you spoken with Angela Novak? I mean, your mom?"

"No, a text here and there," she said with a shrug. "No calls yet. I don't think I'm ready." Her mother had disappeared for twenty-five long years and Jessie didn't feel any urgent rush to get to know her now. Or maybe ever.

"Want to get your mind off things? Lunch, maybe?" he asked hopefully.

"I can't," Jessie said. "I'm working evenings in the ER, and I promised Rufus that I'd take him shopping."

Sam nodded. "It seems we hardly see each other. Between your schedule and mine..." He shrugged. "I'd just like to see more of you."

Jessie slipped behind his desk and brushed her lips against his. "Me too, Sam, me too," she whispered, wondering again why—if he missed her so much—he hadn't invited her to meet his mother.

9

"Fluffy's sick," Rufus said when Jessie picked him up for their trip to the grocery store. Fluffy was his aging calico cat, the last living reminder of his adored wife, Mary, who'd died ten years earlier. Mary had adopted Fluffy as a kitten, named her and lavished her with the love and attention she might have squandered on a child had they been blessed with any. Instead, Fluffy was her beloved fur baby, and Rufus had carried on caring for the cat with love just as Mary would have wished.

"Do you want to take her to the vet?" Jessie asked. "See if she needs any meds?"

Rufus shook his head sadly. "Not yet. I can't see myself doing that right now. It'd just upset her. She's a fussy old girl, and it doesn't take much to get her riled up. I want to try a different food first, some cat vitamins maybe, and see if that helps."

"Alright. It's your call, but let me know if you change your mind."

At the market, Rufus bought more for the cat than he did for himself. "Whoa," Jessie said, eyeing his cart. "You need food, too. Let's pick up some more for you." Reluctantly, he allowed Jessie to add some frozen meals, some chicken, vegetables, bread and eggs to his cart.

At the register, as Jessie bagged his groceries, he counted out his bills slowly before fishing in his pockets for change. "I don't have enough," he said softly to the cashier, who huffed out an irritated sigh and placed her hands on her hips. Rufus seemed to shrivel a little. "I'll just put a few things back."

Jessie resisted the almost overwhelming urge to knock the woman over and instead, stepped in front of Rufus and passed her credit card to the woman. "Use this," she said, the anger in her voice unmistakable even to this stranger.

"Aww, Jessie," Rufus said as they headed to the car, "you didn't have to do that. I don't like borrowing money."

"Rufus, you didn't borrow any. We're friends, and how many times have I eaten in your kitchen? About time I paid up, wouldn't you say?"

He dipped his chin to his chest and smiled shyly. "I'll pay you back, Jessie."

Jessie ignored that comment. There was no way she'd take his money. "Now, let's get home and get Fluffy settled. I have to be at work by three."

Jessie spent more time than she should have checking on Fluffy, who was as lethargic as Rufus had described. "Call me if you need me," she said as she headed out.

By the time she'd parked at the hospital and raced through the tunnels to the ER, she was already ten minutes late. She took report from Donna, the nurse manager, quickly made her rounds and hurried to her locker, running right into the EMTs who'd brought Jane Doe in yesterday.

"Hey, Jessie, we heard you pronounced the jumper right after we left," Danny said.

"We did," she replied. "Got a minute? I have a few questions about her."

"As a detective, or a nurse?" he asked.

"Both." She pushed the lounge door wide open, motioning the two EMTs inside. "Have some coffee," she beckoned, "and relax for a minute." Danny helped himself to coffee, Steve declined the caffeine but sank into a chair by the table, plucking a stale donut from the box. Jessie smiled. EMTs and medics were like ER nurses —you never knew when the next emergency call would come, so you never passed up a chance to eat, especially if it was free. Jessie poured a cup of coffee and sat down across from them.

"What's up?" Steve asked.

"So, you know that we pronounced that woman pretty quickly after she arrived here. We just confirmed that she was already dead when she came in. But I wondered why you guys..." She paused and thought about how to say what she was going to say without sounding insulting. These were smart guys who had more years on the street than she did in the ER. She had to remember and respect that as she asked her questions.

"Don't take this the wrong way, but I wondered why you guys started CPR, intubated her, started a line. The ME said she was already dead when she fell. There was no bleeding from the wounds she suffered in the fall, which meant that her heart had already stopped, and she was cyanotic and pulseless except for that chaotic dying rhythm which was probably artifact. I know you guys, hands down, are the best at what you do, so I wondered if there was something at the scene that was different from what we saw here."

Danny bobbed his head vigorously and glanced at Steve, who offered a knowing smile. "When we arrived on the scene," Danny said, "there was a guy there who said he was a doctor, and he was doing CPR. He's the one who insisted that we continue CPR, get her intubated and get a line in. Neither of us found a pulse, but you saw the monitor rhythm—that crazy pattern. He insisted it was V-fib, a terminal rhythm. What could we do?" He shrugged. "He was a physician and he insisted that she had electrical activity and we couldn't stop CPR. I have to say, it was difficult to ventilate her once we got her endotracheal tube in. There was a lot of resistance in her lungs, and the O_2 saturation device didn't work at all because it couldn't pick up a pulse. Yeah, it was pretty strange."

"By then a crowd had gathered," Steve added, "and people were watching us closely. Neither of us felt or heard a pulse or heartbeat, but we both figured maybe he was right, maybe she was in an electromechanical dissociation cardiac rhythm. We put her in the truck, got a line in, intubated her and came here." He crossed his arms and sat back. "You guys confirmed what we saw, but you know things are different on the street. Everyone second-guesses you."

"I know," Jessie said. "Did you speak to the police?"

"No. We'd arrived on the scene pretty quickly. We'd been around the corner and we were there for literally only a few minutes, though I know it sounds longer. The police were pulling up as we pulled out. And no one called us, but they probably read our report, which really just says that we couldn't find a pulse but continued CPR and brought her here. There wasn't much else to say."

"Did you get the doctor's name?" Jessie asked.

Steve shook his head. "No, there was no time. Never even thought to do that."

"Do you remember what he looked like?"

"Not really. I'm not even sure I could identify him again," Steve said. Danny nodded in agreement. "We were focused on poor Jane Doe and trying to see if she had a pulse. I don't know if that helps you any."

"It does," Jessie said. "It probably doesn't mean anything, but I'm going to share this with the detectives, and they'll probably want to speak with you now that we know for sure that she was already dead. Thank you."

"Anytime, Jessie," Steve said, wiping a trace of jelly from the corner of his mouth. "Especially if you have donuts."

And as she watched them pass through the ambulance bay doors, she recalled the men—one by phone, the other in person—who had inquired about Jane Doe yesterday. Maybe one of them was the doctor who'd insisted on CPR. But as quickly as it crossed her mind, she dismissed the thought. A doctor who'd announced his credentials at the scene would surely have repeated them to her in an effort to get the information he was seeking.

She began to walk back into the hallway when she stopped suddenly. There were cameras all over the city. Maybe their mystery doctor would show up on one of them. And maybe, just maybe he could add to the little they knew about Jane Doe. She sighed, relieved that tomorrow, she'd attend the meeting with Sam and the others, and in a few days, she'd be back on rotation with the ME and Homicide. Perfect timing.

She stepped into the office and picked up the phone.

10

He held the wrinkled newspaper so close he could smell the ink. He knew she was dead, though the story only hinted at that, and already she was being described as a student who jumped. She'd been labeled a jumper! Just as he'd hoped.

It had all worked better than he could have imagined. Everything he'd learned from that egotistical doctor had served him well. Add to that, the special thrill of watching those fools try to revive a corpse that had prolonged his power, his pleasure. He was like a puppeteer pulling their strings, dictating their actions. It was almost more exciting than seeing her fear, but he knew that he would have to see that again. There was nothing like it—that terror when a girl knew for certain that he controlled every last minute of her life, and he was going to kill her no matter her pathetic pleas.

A familiar pleasant tingle ran along his back. He hadn't realized at first how magical this kind of power was. It was intoxicating, better than whiskey or wine or drugs, better than sex, better than killing small animals, better than anything he'd ever experienced. There was absolutely nothing else like it.

He tore the small newspaper article out, folded it carefully and stuck it into his back pocket along with the fingernails. He'd have to follow this story closely, see what else those idiots could come up with. But he was confident they'd never connect him to it. They weren't smart enough to catch him, but this cat-and-mouse game might be as much fun as the actual killing. He chuckled to himself.

No, it would never be as much fun as the killing.

11

Despite her determination to get to police headquarters early and speak to Sam, Jessie woke late, her eyes inching open slowly until she caught sight of her small bedside clock. Nine thirty! She threw off her covers, raced through her shower, pulled on jeans and a light shirt, packed scrubs into her bag for her evening shift and made it through the usual miserable mid-morning traffic to headquarters shortly after ten a.m.

Feeling pretty pleased with herself, but desperate for coffee and food, she checked her watch and with minutes to spare, she stopped in at the first-floor cafeteria where the scrambled eggs and bacon in the warmer caught her eye. She'd long known that food didn't just fill her stomach, it filled the void that her mother had left when she'd abandoned her. It was a miracle, or maybe her youth and an addiction to running, that she'd maintained her slim figure. "I'll have that, to go," she said, pointing to the breakfast. "And a large black coffee." With caffeine and food in hand, she took the steps only one at a time, careful to balance her food and drink and protect her much-needed sustenance. She passed through the detectives' area to the conference room to see that a bit of a crowd had already gathered.

"Morning, Jessie," a handful of detectives said as she slid into a chair, resting her plate on her lap and her coffee by her feet.

"Sorry," she said, tilting her head toward Sam. "Traffic."

"Traffic in the cafeteria?" he asked, to a smattering of laughter.

She smirked and bit off a chunk of bacon.

"Anyway," Sam said, "to bring everyone up to date, Dr. Dawson is here to explain his findings, and Ralph will update us on the videos." He turned to Roger Dawson, who sat quietly at the front of the room. "Dr. Dawson," he said. "You have the floor."

Roger stood and caught Jessie's eye. "Care to join me? I think you can add the ER perspective."

Jessie shoveled in the last of the eggs, gulped down a swig of coffee and rose to make her way to Roger's side.

Roger gave a brief physical description of the victim and began to go through her wounds, explaining that she was clearly dead when she fell from the garage roof. "Histology is negative, preliminary toxicology is negative—there is absolutely nothing to explain her death. Jessie suggested suffocation, and that is likely what we are seeing."

"Full toxicology will take at least another week, right?" Sam asked.

Roger nodded.

"And you're looking for heavy metals, poisons, all of that?"

Roger nodded again. "I'm here because this is one of those cases that will stay with me until it is solved. Without a definitive cause of death, and on the heels of our other recent assumed suicides—the jumpers—I'm determined to follow this to an acceptable conclusion. This young woman deserves that." He folded his arms and sighed deeply. "And there is one detail on our latest Jane Doe. Whoever her killer was, he or she likely restrained the victim's wrists. She has circular marks on both wrists, but she fought back, scratched at her attacker and they left some debris under her nails. Forensics is testing for DNA, and we can only hope they come up with something that will allow us to make a match." He turned to Jessie. "Anything you'd like to add from the ER perspective, Jessie?"

She looked out at the crowd. This would be the first time she'd be speaking in front of the group of detectives on a case. She took a long swallow of her coffee and began. "When she came in yesterday, just as Roger said, she appeared to be dead with no hope of resuscitation. The cardiac rhythm wasn't really a rhythm at all—it was the artifact we caused by moving her around. Dr. Merrick pretty quickly pronounced her dead. I was curious why CPR was started at the scene and last night, I spoke to the EMTs who'd brought her in. They said they had started the resuscitation because a physician at the scene was doing CPR when they arrived and he insisted that she had a pulse, that she was alive, and they had to get her intubated and on her way to the ER. They didn't feel pulses but they assumed that since he was a doctor, maybe there was some subtle sign of life that they were missing, so they moved her hurriedly and brought her to the ER. They didn't even get a chance to speak to the police." She paused, her eyes scanning the room. "I don't know if anyone has spoken to them. They don't know who the physician was and probably couldn't identify him again since everything was so chaotic. The interesting thing is I got inquiries on the dead woman from two men—one on the phone and the other in person. It may have been the same person, but both asked how she was and if she'd survived. Obviously, I didn't tell them anything. I told them to call the police. But I wonder if one of them might be the doctor on the scene. Even if it wasn't, maybe those two or someone else at the scene saw that guy and could describe him. I just can't see a doctor saying that an obviously dead woman was alive. It may have just been the turmoil and drama of the moment, but it's worth a look. I'm hoping the street videos caught him and we can identify him."

She dipped her chin and hurried back to her seat. "Oh, I almost forgot," she said, bouncing back up just as she was about to sit. "The red marks on both of her wrists were thin, maybe from those hair elastics that women sometimes wear so they can pull their hair up, or one of those cotton tie bracelets, but she didn't have either of those with her, so maybe she was restrained with something else. Anyway, it's another observation, something to think about."

Sam nodded thoughtfully and stood once again, pointing to the whiteboard which held the pertinent facts of the case of Jane Doe. "Jessie left me a message yesterday about the incident with the physician on the scene and asked us to check videos from that area." He directed his gaze to Jessie, the affection there evident in the silvery shimmer that danced in his gray eyes. She sank into her seat, hoping that no one else noticed. Sam turned his attention back to the group. "Ralph did the footwork on that yesterday, so I'll let him speak."

Ralph stood slowly, smoothing his suit jacket before clicking on the overhead projector. All eyes tracked to the screen. "These are the videos I was able to collect," he began as a grainy scene came into view. "This is from the closest camera, which was about thirty yards away from the scene. Here," he said, using the laser to point to the area of interest, "the camera really focuses on the street and the view takes in only the first four levels of the garage. This next scene is a little grim..." he said as he paused the footage, "but it's important to see." He turned to the screen as the video played again and suddenly the screen filled with the image of the woman, her hair streaming out, her head thrown back, as she fell through the air and landed with a thud.

Jessie gasped, her hand flying to her mouth. It was one thing to know the story of the woman's death and the facts that they had, but it was something else again to actually see the horror of it played out right in front of you. Aside from a few deep intakes of breath, the reflective silence in the room was intense. No wonder people at the scene were so upset. It was awful to see on video. Jessie's only question now was why hadn't more people called the hospital trying to find out what had happened to her?

Ralph read the emotion in the room and paused the video again for almost a full minute. "It's a pretty graphic video," he said as he got back to business and pressed the play button again. "A small crowd gathered around the body, a few lifting their cell phones, likely calling nine-one-one. We had a total of four calls almost simultaneously. There were a few cars stopping to watch, more people gathering, although not a big crowd since this occurred late Sunday morning. It's a college area, so most of those living in the neighborhood are students. You can see the grainy image of a man moving in close to the body and starting CPR."

Instinctively, Jessie leaned forward as though she were watching in real time and might get a better view.

Ralph cleared his throat and took a pull from the bottle of water on the table.

"Unfortunately, we can only see the back of him. The camera is too far away to really get a good look at his face, though we can see the blue t-shirt and blue jeans. He could be anybody, but he's doing CPR, which seems reasonable from this vantage point. *If she was alive.* You see the ambulance pull up and the medics jump out. That man speaks to them briefly and the medics take over the CPR and quickly get her into the ambulance. The man in question never turns toward the camera, just shoves his hands into his pockets and moves out of view. I'll be honest, I don't see anything in his behavior that sends up red flags or seems unusual, and I suspect that if we put out a call for the doctor at the scene to help us with information, he would answer. I also don't think there's anything he actually can help us with, but of course I will leave that to Sam's discretion. Any questions on the video?"

Jessie's hand shot up. "If you replay that last scene, you'll see that the man doing CPR is only doing chest compressions, no rescue breathing. He hasn't checked her for a pulse either. It's almost as though he already knew she was dead."

There was a hush in the room as Ralph replayed the CPR scene. "Good catch," someone said.

"Maybe he's our guy," said another.

"Moving on," Ralph said, "the next videos show the interior of the garage. There are no cameras on the roof, so we just have images of the actual parking areas, which were very quiet, only an occasional person exiting the elevator, walking to a car and pulling away. As you can see, each level of the garage held only a few cars, probably because it was a Sunday."

Jessie stretched and rubbed at the knot on the back of her neck. Coffee would have cured the tension there, but without a second cup, she was forced to try to massage it away. As the tension eased a bit, she focused on the video, though there wasn't much happening—no bodies, no women screaming for help, no argument, nothing.

Ralph stopped the video again. "There really isn't much to see. There was not an attendant in the payment booth—drivers going in and out used their credit cards to gain access and to exit the garage. Four cars exited between nine a.m. and noontime. We've checked them all out and they're all legit. Another team is checking the license plates of the parked cars in the garage, but our focus really is on the roof. There were only three cars parked there and they've all checked out, as we've already discussed. So, as you can see, there is no one walking around, no activity at all. The next video..." he said as he busied himself at the computer, "will show us the street view of the entrances—both pedestrian and drive-in."

Jessie's hand shot up. "Any neighboring rooftop cameras?"

Ralph shook his head. "There were four—all angled toward the street, nothing pointing at the garage roof." He turned back toward the screen. "These are pointing to the garage entrance, and again, not much to see. Two cars enter, each with a lone driver, and we've spoken with them. All of their stories and alibis were confirmed. And here," he clicked to the next video, "is the side street pedestrian entrance." The view was grainy, out of focus and frozen. "This door leads to the stairwell entrance. You can reach your car by taking the stairs. Unfortunately, that camera was broken. Nobody had checked it in a while, so all we have is this still image of the entrance. No activity, nothing up to date. I've also checked the street cameras but there's nothing down that little side street, which is really like an alley, so we're pretty much at zero where videos are concerned."

He folded his arms and looked out on the crowd. "Any ideas?"

"The DNA is where we'll start," Sam said. "And fingerprints."

"We can actually do that now," a Forensics technician said. "We have the DNA on Jane Doe logged in and we're running the DNA on the tissue that Dr. Dawson retrieved from under her fingernails. No matches yet in the database, but we're still working on that."

Jessie sat forward, eager to catch every word. She raised her hand and stood. "What about calling the media in? Get a description of her out there. Someone must know who she is, and maybe a description or artist's sketch will push someone to speak up."

"Good idea," Ralph said and flashed a quick smile toward Jessie. "I think there's a fair chance that she may be undocumented, and fear is holding people back. But this woman deserves to have a name. Her name. And knowing who she is will help us figure out how and why she died."

A murmur of approval rippled through the group. "We have face shots from the autopsy, but too grim to release," Sam said. "We can have our forensic artist see what he can sketch, and ask our media relations group to get a press release out asking for help with identification. Ralph, do you mind handling a press briefing?"

Ralph straightened his tie and smiled. He was born for this moment. "I'm ready whenever we can put this together."

Sam stood. "Okay, let's get moving on this." He passed out assignments—witness interviews, follow-up video checks and missing persons searches—to the detectives, and the room emptied within minutes.

Dr. Dawson said his goodbyes as well. "I'll let Jessie know as soon as I get final lab reports back. See you later this week," he said to her as he strode to the door, his hand held high in a wave. Only Ralph and Sam, the two that Jessie thought of as her team, remained.

"Sam," Jessie said softly. "Any news on Julio? The lost boy?"

12

A muscle twitched in Sam's jaw and he shook his head. "Sorry, Jess. I did put some calls out but no word yet."

Jessie's shoulders drooped in disappointment. "Is there any way to find out where those group homes are? Where they place kids overnight? The social worker said that's where he'd go. I'm just worried about him."

Sam squeezed her shoulder, his eyes crinkling with concern. "He's probably not there anymore, and we can't go around the system. Those places are not unlike the domestic violence houses where women and children go for safety. Their whole aim is to protect the kids. I'll try again, I promise, and hopefully we can learn something." He locked his eyes onto hers. "Don't let this little lost boy consume your attention. Wherever he is, he's being taken care of."

Jessie could only offer a half-smile. She loved Sam, but he didn't know what he was talking about. She saw abused kids all the time in the ER, brought in from crappy foster or group homes. He investigated homicides, not child abuse or abandonment, and he had no personal experience with that. She did. "Just keep me posted, will you?" she asked, not wanting to start an argument.

"I'm sure that little boy is fine," Ralph added. "He's probably been reunited with his family by now. Just hang onto that thought."

She glanced at her watch, her tried-and-true tactic to getting away from conversations she preferred to avoid. "I'm going to get moving. I'll let you know what else Roger finds."

"I'll walk you out," Sam said, reaching for her backpack.

"See ya, Jessie," Ralph called as they headed for the hallway.

Sam slowed as they reached the stairs. "Hey." He pulled her into a quick and furtive embrace. "I've missed you. Can I pick you up after work? Maybe a drink at Foley's? Or I can pick up wine and come to your place. What do you say?" he asked, tucking a stray hair behind her ear.

Jessie smiled. "Maybe," she said. "No promises. I'm trying to cut down on drinking and staying up late. So..."

"Just say yes."

"Call me later," she answered. "I'll see how the night goes."

He brushed his lips against hers. "I'm an optimist. I'll pick up some wine and call you." He passed the backpack to Jessie, who raised a brow and turned for the exit. She knew she had to get her mind off Julio and back onto the business at hand—Jane Doe. The garage was near headquarters. She'd just make a quick stop, see for herself where Jane Doe had been thrown to her death. Sometimes a fresh pair of eyes could pick up what experienced Forensics techs had missed. She pulled onto Tremont Street and turned left onto Melnea Cass Boulevard, heading toward the garage and away from the hospital. She took a left onto Columbus Avenue and slowed. The garage was directly in front of her, a looming eight-story building, ominous to Jessie's eyes.

She swung into the side alley for a look and just as Ralph had said, there was one camera perched above the pedestrian entrance. She pulled around and into the parking lot entrance, drawing a ticket before navigating the circular upward route. She reached the seventh level and turned her wheels sharply, intending to drive onto the rooftop, but the last ramp was closed off, blocked by orange cones and yellow crime tape. She maneuvered her old

Toyota into a tight space, locked the car, ducked beneath the yellow tape and headed upward to the eighth level.

Once she reached the top level, she blinked away the sudden glare of the sun, and had a good look around. The rooftop area was large with spaces for probably seventy-five cars. She knew that the area had already been swept for any evidence, but she also knew that even the most practiced eye could miss something and so she walked slowly, starting at the corner by the stairway, examining the ground as she proceeded before peering over the ledge and down to the street. The ledge was high, over four feet at least and at five foot three, Jessie had to stand on her toes just to get a good look over the edge. When she saw the area where the woman had fallen, she offered up a silent prayer.

The street was cleared of any debris left behind by the bystanders or EMTs. The only evidence of the woman's death was a tiny makeshift memorial set up on the sidewalk. She could make out a few flickering candles, several cellophane-wrapped super-market flower bouquets and what looked like—at least from where she stood—a small teddy bear. Jessie wondered who'd taken the time to remember this woman. Were they witnesses to her fall, or maybe loved ones? Whoever they were, they would likely be on video. Those street cameras had been working. They'd caught the woman's fall. They had to have caught the mourners. She'd text Sam when she was done here.

Her eyes moved back to the floor of the garage roof and she stooped low to scrutinize the debris there. There were bits of chipped cement, small stones, dirt, and a lone latex glove. She looked closer. The Forensics team's work, she knew from her own time with them, was impeccable. They processed crime scenes with experienced eyes and hands, leaving nothing behind. Could this have been left by a detective or another team member who'd come up later? She shook her head, answering her own question. It was unlikely; they were just too careful, and anyway, their police-issue gloves were purple. These were the soft blue gloves she used at the hospital and morgue. A common enough glove, but definitely not police issue. The only other outsiders on the scene were the EMTs, and she knew they hadn't been up here unless they'd come back for a look, but wouldn't they have mentioned it when she spoke to them?

Someone had been up here after the police had exited the area and in an unbelievably sloppy move, had left this glove behind. Killers, she'd learned, often came back to the scene of the crime or to their victim's funeral, to have another look at their work. Did this glove belong to the killer?

She reached into her pocket and pulled out her phone to take a picture of the glove. She typed out a quick text to Sam including the photo and asking that he send someone over. *ASAP*, she added at the end. She crouched low again, her eyes scanning the ground. If someone was careless enough to leave a glove behind, what else might be here? Focused intently on her search, she was startled by the eerie sound of screeching metal.

The door to the stairwell was opening. Someone was just behind her.

13

Despite the day's warmth, a sudden chill swept over Jessie. She turned quickly just as the door slammed shut. Whoever was there had surely been scared away by her presence. She sprinted for the door, pulled it open and heard the thunderous noise of footsteps bounding down the stairs, the echoes bouncing off the walls, filling the narrow space. Her heart pounding, she took the steps two at a time. She'd catch whoever this was. She had just reached the third floor when she heard the door that led to the street bang shut. She picked up her pace and reached the street level in less than a minute, but when she pulled the door open, the street outside was empty. Whoever it was had gotten away.

Breathing hard, a sheen of sweat running along her forehead, she closed her eyes and leaned her back against the door to catch her breath.

"What are you doing out here?"

Her eyes snapping open, she looked into Sam's silvery gaze. "How did you get here so quickly?" she asked. "Anyway, you just missed him. He might have run right by you."

"Who?" Sam asked, a line creasing his brow.

"I don't know. I stopped by here just to have a look for myself." She replayed her actions and her discovery of the glove. "I was crouched down looking for more evidence when I heard the door open and..." She turned and looked at the door, her mind flicking through what needed to be done. "We need Forensics to swab this door handle and the banister inside the stairwell again for fingerprints and DNA. I think whoever came here was looking for something. Probably the glove." She took a long breath. "Want to walk up or get the elevator?"

"Looks like you need the elevator," Sam said, taking her elbow and guiding her to the entrance and the elevator. "Why didn't you tell me you were stopping here? I would've come with you."

"I just decided after I left you guys. I was going right by it. I wanted to see it for myself. Get a feel for where she was. I thought it might help me to picture what happened."

He pressed eight on the panel and as the elevator began to rise, he pulled her into his arms.

"Hey," she said, pulling away and pointing to the ceiling. "Cameras. And I'm sure we'll be looking at these films at some point."

He hung his head in mock shame. "I can't catch a break," he said.

The elevator rose shakily, the door opening slowly to the rooftop. Once they stepped out, Sam took her in his arms once again. "I know for a fact that there are no cameras up here." He leaned down and kissed her deeply, his hands caressing the back of her neck.

Her skin tingled at his touch. She closed her eyes and kissed him back with an intensity that surprised her. She pushed him away playfully. "Work now, play later."

Sam shook his head. "I know, I know."

"I'm off tomorrow, and then I'll be back to work with Roger and you guys." She stood on her toes and planted a quick kiss on his cheek. "Did you call Forensics to pick up the glove?"

He shook his head. "No. I was halfway here when I got your text, so I haven't had time. Thought I'd have a quick look first. Show me what you found."

She led him to the area where the glove lay. "There," she said, leaning close.

Sam bent to his knees for a look.

"See," she said. "You guys at BPD wear purple, so I don't think it belongs to any of your team. EMTs, the ME and hospital staff wear blue, but the EMTs weren't up here. Neither was anyone from the ME's office. They picked her up from the street and took off pretty quickly. I think someone else, the killer probably, came back for a look to make sure he hadn't left anything behind and then dropped his glove. I think when he realized he'd dropped it, he came back to get it and knew enough about the cameras to take the stairs."

"He?"

She nodded. "Had to be from the pounding of the footsteps. Too heavy and too fast to be a woman. And I don't think a woman threw her over the edge. It's too high and besides, dead weight is heavier than it seems."

Sam stood and punched some numbers into his phone. "Ralph," he said. "Jessie came to the garage and found a glove on the rooftop." He nodded before continuing. "Yeah, just send Forensics. I'll wait for them."

Jessie mouthed that she wanted to speak with Ralph and Sam pressed the speaker button on his phone. "Jessie's still here. She wants to speak with you."

"Ralph, there's one of those memorials on the street—flowers, candles. Can we get the video? Get a look at the people who stopped by? Might be a clue to who she is, or maybe the killer stopped there."

"Great idea," Ralph answered. "I'll put in the request. Will you be in tomorrow?"

"I will. Might be a little late. I'm working till eleven tonight and then I think I have a date."

Ralph laughed softly. "I bet you do, and it's about time. Sam, see you in a while."

Sam put the phone back in his pocket. "Do you need to get to work?"

"I do. I'll see you later? My house or L Street Tavern. Okay?"

The silver flecks in Sam's eyes sparkled in the bright sun. "Anything you say, Jessie. I'll call you." He leaned down and brushed his lips against hers.

"Think I'll take the elevator," Jessie said. "I've had enough of those stairs."

Donna was waiting for Jessie when she arrived at the ER. "We've been waiting for you," she said.

"We? Who is we? Why?" Jessie asked, her brain on overdrive trying to remember if she'd forgotten to document a medication administration or had done something else against policy. *Why else would anyone be waiting to speak with me?* A flush of heat rose to her cheeks.

"Come on," Donna said, smiling. "And stop worrying. You're not in any trouble."

"Then what...?" But they had just turned into Donna's office, still decorated with the previous manager's leather chair, mahogany desk and plush oriental rug. Standing just inside was Steve Alexander, the hospital CEO, and Dr. Dawson. She'd just seen him at the Homicide team meeting. *What was he doing here?*

"Good to see you," Alexander said. "I hear you've been doing great work with Dr. Dawson here, and the police. Have a seat," he said, motioning to the wooden chair in front of the desk.

"I don't have much time," she answered nervously. "I have to take report from Donna in a few minutes. I'd rather stand if that's okay."

"Dr. Dawson, would you like to tell her?"

Roger Dawson adjusted his glasses and smiled. "Jessie, you've done just a great job for us and the Homicide unit, and, well... the truth is, we hate sharing you with the ER. We'd like to have you on with us full-time. We've gotten permission from the Boston Police, and Steve here agrees. So, I'm offering you a full-time position with me as a forensic nurse investigator and liaison with the police and victims. What do you say?"

Jessie was speechless. She looked toward Donna, who was smiling. "Full-time with you and Homicide? Really?"

Roger nodded. "Really."

"I..." Her heart was pounding, and her mind had gone totally blank. Forensic nurse was her dream job, but the ER was, too. She turned toward Donna. "What do you think?"

"I think it's a perfect opportunity, and you know you can work extra here anytime. You'll always have a home here."

"So, what do you say?" Roger asked again. "You've already been a great help with our Jane Doe. We'd like you to continue working on that full-time. Jane Doe needs you, and we need you, Jessie."

"I just left police headquarters. They didn't say a word about this. Roger, you didn't say a word. Do they know? Do they want me full-time?" Her tendency toward self-doubt and insecurity began to creep in. *And what about Sam? Would she still be able to see him?*

"Sorry about that," Roger said. "Of course, they want you. And, though you haven't met them yet, I have Pathology residents. Two residents who have been rotating out to the Westfield office will be returning to my office shortly, and on July first, I'll be getting two new residents. I'm going to be very busy with the four of them. I will definitely need you to get out to scenes, and as for not telling you earlier, I was just waiting to hear from Steve. I left that meeting this morning at headquarters to come back and find him. When Donna told us that you'd be in at three, we thought we'd just wait for you and make the offer here."

"Are you on board with this?" Alexander asked.

She smiled widely. They wanted her on their team. She felt almost breathless with joy, but she wanted to be one hundred percent sure that this was what *she* wanted—for herself, not for Sam, and not for anyone else. "I don't know what to say. I mean, I'm a nurse. That's who I am. Of course, I'm very flattered and yes,

I'm very interested. A full-time forensic nurse? Wow. I don't know what to say."

"Say yes," Roger said.

"I'm pretty sure it's a yes, but I have to give this some thought. Is that okay?"

Steve Alexander and Roger nodded in unison. A smile crept onto Donna's lips.

"Take all the time you need," Roger said.

"Thanks, I'm off tomorrow but planning to head back to Homicide to see how things are going, so I'll see you then, Roger. But I'm scheduled to work tonight here in the ER, so I have to get going." She looked at each of the three in turn. "Thank you for the offer and the vote of confidence. It means more to me than I can say," Jessie said, trying to keep her voice from cracking.

"Come on," Donna said, throwing her arm over Jessie's shoulder and guiding her from the office.

"Did you know about this?" Jessie asked when they were out of earshot. The flush in her cheeks started to fade. The reality of this incredible offer was just starting to sink in. *A forensic nurse!*

Donna shook her head. "They arrived right before you and told me then. I'm not really surprised, though. You've done great investigative work. I'm so proud of you. Do you think you'll do it?"

"I think so. How could I turn this down? But I'm a nurse. That defines me. I don't want to leave it entirely."

"But you won't have to. You can work here whenever you want, and you know I'll still be calling, begging you to pick up shifts."

Jessie laughed. "It's good to know some things will never change."

14

And just like that, Jessie was back to work. She'd taken report from Donna, made her rounds and was brewing a pot of coffee when she was paged for a call on line one. "Jessie Novak," she said as she picked up the phone.

"Hey, Jess, it's Sam. Got a minute?"

She poured a cup of coffee and sank into a chair. "For you, always. Did you call about the offer? Did you know about it?"

"I did," he answered, and she could almost feel the warmth of his smile through the connection. "It almost killed me to keep it to myself. What did you say?"

"I was shocked. It's exciting that everyone thinks I can do this, but I'm anxious about how this will affect you and me, and I'm not ready to give up nursing. I love both jobs. Donna said I could fill in here, so..."

"Will I see you tonight? I can convince you then."

Jessie laughed. "I won't take much convincing. Besides, I thought you were going to call later."

"I was, but I heard from a friend in Children's Services about your lost boy."

Jessie sat up straight. "And?"

"No one has come forward. They released a physical description and..."

"Why not a photo?"

"To protect him. They don't want any pedophiles coming forward. This way, they can ask for specifics from callers to be sure they really know him. They included the location where he was found and asked the press for help. It was on the local news last evening and in this morning's paper, but they haven't received even one call."

"Do you think he was abandoned?" She hated even saying that word out loud. It hit too close to home.

"No way to know for sure. I just wanted you to know."

"Did they tell you where he is? If he's okay?"

"No, and I did ask. They said only that he's safe."

Jessie exhaled noisily. "Thanks for trying. I've got to get back to work."

"Hey, what about tonight? Drinks at your place?"

And though she was tired already, she couldn't help herself. They hadn't been out in almost a week, and the chance to spend some time alone with Sam was just too good to pass up. "I'll text you when I'm leaving here."

He sighed. "Can't wait," he whispered before Jessie hung up.

The night was still young and there was work to do. She finished her coffee and headed back out to check the trauma rooms which, blessedly, hadn't been used at all today. The evening shift housekeeper, Carmen, always quiet as though trying to blend into the background, was busy in Trauma One cleaning the counter. She jumped when Jessie opened the door. "Sorry," Jessie said. "I didn't mean to disturb you."

Carmen turned, clinging to her bottle of spray disinfectant. "You're not disturbing me. I was hoping to speak with you tonight. I need some help." Her Spanish accent was heavy, and she spoke slowly and pronounced her words carefully.

It was the first time Jessie had heard her say more than a quick hello. She closed the door softly and stepped into the room. "What is it?" she asked.

"Before I speak, can I trust you?" Carmen asked, setting the bottle on the counter and wiping her callused hands on a paper towel.

"Of course you can," Jessie replied.

Carmen took a deep breath. "Something bad has happened to my friends, but they can't go to the police. I've heard that you work with them, the police, so, I said I would speak with you and see if you could help."

"What happened? And why can't your friends go to the police?"

"Because they are in this country without papers. They came from Guatemala. They live and work in secret and are afraid of the police. Understand?" She adjusted the hair-net that kept her graying locks in place.

Jessie nodded. "I can listen, but I can't promise that I can help. Has someone committed a crime?"

"No, no. That's not it," Carmen answered, her brown eyes flashing as she reached into her pocket and pulled out a small section of newspaper. She smoothed the paper and held it out for Jessie to see. It was the story of Jane Doe, though this particular story made it seem that she'd jumped to her death. "I think we might know her."

Jessie glanced at the story. "You have to tell the police. This woman deserves that. Come forward. I'll go with you and your friends."

Carmen shook her head vigorously. "When people are undocumented, illegal, they are afraid to speak up. Everything carries the risk of being taken away."

"But..." Jessie began.

Carmen shook her head. "We think it might have been a man who knows some of the girls and they are afraid for themselves." She swiped her hand across her forehead, whisking away the beads of sweat that had surfaced there. "Please," she said, "we need your help, so it doesn't happen again. Will you meet with my friends? Let them tell you what has happened?"

An image of Jane Doe flashed through her mind. Was it even

possible that Carmen and her friends really knew her, had information? She'd need to tell Sam if Jane Doe was the woman Carmen was describing. "I guess so, as long as you agree that I may have to involve the police, especially if someone has been hurt, or you can identify that woman. Understand?"

Carmen's shoulders slumped. "I will have to ask them." She shoved her trembling hands into her pockets.

Jessie moved closer. "I'll give you my number. Please tell your friends not to be afraid. I want to help. You can text me and I can meet you. Okay?"

"Yes."

Jessie wrote out her number and passed it to Carmen. "Text me anytime. I promise I'll try to help. And I won't say a word to anyone without your permission."

The evening was uneventful; no major traumas, and quiet enough that when the pizza they ordered arrived, everyone was able to sit and eat. But Jessie couldn't get Carmen out of her mind. She gave report to the night nurse and went in search of Carmen, who was just collecting her things from her locker. "Don't forget to text me," she said softly. "I want to help."

Carmen nodded and headed for the exit, leaving Jessie alone in the corridor. There was nothing she could do unless Carmen's friends agreed to speak with her. She huffed out a sigh, changed out of her scrubs and texted Sam at eleven fifteen. *On my way home. See you there.*

She arrived home just as Sam pulled into a spot across the street. Clad in a gray long-sleeve t-shirt and jeans, he hurried to join her, a bottle of wine and a bouquet of red roses in his hand. He leaned down and kissed the back of her neck as she stepped into the house. She turned and placed her finger over her lips. "Shh," she whispered. "Rufus." She pointed to his door and they crept silently up the stairs to her apartment.

Once inside, Sam set the flowers and wine down and pulled her into his arms and kissed her so deeply, a rush of pleasure surged through her veins. "Hey," she said, pulling away, "let me put these beautiful flowers in a vase."

"I'll open the wine and get the glasses," Sam said as they both squeezed into the tiny kitchen.

Jessie finished arranging the flowers before moving back into the living room where she kicked off her shoes and joined Sam on the couch. He passed her a glass of wine and tapped his glass against hers. "To more nights together," he said, his eyes sparkling.

Jessie smiled and sipped her wine. Everything about Sam was perfect. It wasn't just that he was tall and handsome, though he was, or that the silver flecks in his eyes made her forget everything, it was that he was good and kind to everyone. He never lost his temper; he was honest and understanding, and she'd be a fool to let him get away again. Though they'd been dating for just over two months, they'd made love only a handful of times, always tentatively, as though he was protecting her from himself, and he'd never stayed the night.

"I want to give you all the time you need," he'd said more than once. "I want you to be sure about us, Jessie."

But Jessie was sure. It was Sam she wondered about. He placed his glass on the table and leaned into her, his lips finding hers. He kissed her slowly and so deeply, it took her breath away. He pulled his shirt off and Jessie ran her hands over the taut muscles of his arms and chest before slipping out of her own shirt. They slid to the floor, fumbling with zippers and hooks and elastic, and once they were both free of their clothes, they fell into a deep embrace. At Sam's touch, Jessie felt her body come alive, her skin tingling, her nerves on fire. And when they were ready, he lifted her into his arms and carried her into the bedroom where he laid her gently on the bed, lifting himself on top of her, and she moaned with desire.

"Oh, Jessie, I need you," he whispered, his breath hot on her skin, their bodies moving in perfect rhythm, the blissful sounds of their coming together lost in the not-too-distant blare of police sirens and the sounds of city life. At last, they simply lay there,

Sam above her, the weight and feel of him its own unexpected bliss. They lingered there, legs and arms tangled together, slick with sweat and satisfaction.

Sam rolled away before pulling her close. "I have to tell you something," he whispered.

A sudden fog clouded her joy. "What is it?" she asked so softly she wasn't sure he heard. Her mind raced with endless possibilities —none of them very good.

He sighed and ran his finger along the curve of her shoulder. "I love you, Jessie. I think I have from the moment we met."

Jessie's mouth dropped open. Had she heard him right? "You love me?" she asked, anxious that he might take his words back.

He pulled her into his arms, his embrace firm and sure, and then he kissed her. "I do. I love you, Jessie Novak."

"I..." She wanted to say she loved him too, but declaring her love for someone had never turned out well. She'd always chosen the wrong man, and though she wanted desperately to change that, the knot in her stomach held her back. She hadn't said those words in a long time. And when her mother had recently reappeared and uttered those same three little words, Jessie had instinctively pulled back, afraid to trust, to let herself be vulnerable. Her mother had disappeared for twenty-five years, but suddenly *loved* her. Love was complicated. Jessie knew that, but she also knew that this was different. This was Sam—reliable, honest and steady. Everything her mother was not. "But why now?" She hadn't realized she'd said it out loud.

His forehead wrinkled in confusion. "I... I... it seemed like a good time to say it. And..." He sighed and pulled his arms away. "There's someone who's going to be in the office this week, someone I was involved with in the past. I saw my mother this past weekend to let her know that she'd be around. Anyway, I'm going to be working with her on an old case. And you know how those things go. Someone from the past shows up, gossip starts. I want to be sure you know I love you, and I hope you love me too," he whispered, a pleading in his voice now.

And the unpleasant fluttering that had begun when he'd mentioned *someone* faded, leaving only the sweet sensation of butterflies, a sure sign that she needed to throw caution to the wind. She did love him. She knew she did. She folded herself into his arms. "I do love you, Sam Dallas. I thought you already knew that."

15

"Hey," a voice hovering over Jessie whispered as a slight nudge startled her awake. Sam was dressed and sitting on the side of the bed leaning over her. "Morning, Jessie. I hated to wake you—you look so beautiful—but I didn't want to just disappear. I'm heading home to shower and change, and then to work. I'll see you there later?"

She pulled him to her. "Come back to bed," she said softly.

"Oh, God, you have no idea how much I want to, but I have to go."

She kissed him then, her fingertips sliding along the back of his neck. "Can't I convince you?"

He leaned closer and kissed her forehead. "Not this morning, but I'll see you in a while." He stood and blew her another kiss as he slipped from the room.

"I love you," she shouted after him.

"I thought I was going to have to drag those words from you again," he said with a laugh.

And she realized how freeing it was to say it. Was there anything better in the world than loving someone who loved you back? She hugged his pillow, inhaling his scent, listening as the door closed behind him and his footsteps bounded down the stairs. Was it possible, she wondered, that footsteps could sound happy?

Because Sam's sure did. She lay in bed a little while longer, feeling the emptiness, the absolute quiet with Sam gone. Then she dragged herself up, showered, dressed and gathered her things. She'd just stop and say hello to Rufus, to see how he and his little cat were doing.

"Morning, Jessie," Rufus greeted her with a wide smile. "Saw Sam this morning," he said with a wink. "Glad you're keeping company with him. I always liked him."

Jessie chuckled. There were no secrets where Rufus was concerned. "He is a good guy, isn't he?" she said. "But I stopped by to see how you and Fluffy are doing. Is she better?"

He shook his head sadly. "She's still quiet, mostly sleeping."

"Well, that's okay. If you decide you want to bring her to the vet, let me know."

"I don't know about that. She hasn't ever been outside. I think she'd die of fright. But we'll see. I may take you up on the offer."

Jessie leaned in and kissed his cheek. "As I said, let me know. I'll be around later."

"Tell your friend Sam I approve," he called as she closed his door behind her.

At headquarters, Jessie bounded up the stairs, a definite spring in her step. Maybe feet could sound happy after all, she thought as she passed through the main area where members of Sam's team sat hunched over their desks while others hovered deep in conversation. Ralph looked up and winked. "Morning, Jessie," he said. *Oh, God*, she wondered. *Does everyone know?* She nodded and continued on into Sam's office.

He was hanging up his desk phone as she entered. "Morning, again," he said, smiling.

"Rufus says hello."

"Great old guy. I take it he approves? I saw him this morning when I was leaving."

"He approves. Looks like Ralph does as well. You didn't say anything?"

Sam's forehead wrinkled. "You're not serious? Of course, I didn't."

She came around the desk and planted a quick kiss on his cheek. "Sorry. It's just that he winked at me."

Sam laughed. "He winked at me, too. I think he just assumed. He's been pushing me to spend more time with you. I must have been smiling when I came in today."

And Jessie's heart could have melted right there. A tingle of pleasure settled in her bones. This was what really being loved felt like. And she hadn't known until last night how much she'd needed that.

"Hey," Ralph said, poking his head into the office. "You guys ready to see the videos? Hear the updates?"

Sam stood and Jessie moved back. "We'll be right there," he said before turning to Jessie. "Do you need coffee, donuts, food?"

She suddenly realized she hadn't eaten this morning. No coffee, no muffin, nothing. And the strange thing was that she wasn't hungry or in need of caffeine. Somehow, Sam was enough. For today, at least. She shook her head. "I'm all set."

Sam tilted his head as if in deep thought. "Well, will wonders never cease? I never thought I'd hear you turn down food."

"I'll probably be starving in an hour. Don't get too excited."

He raised a brow playfully. "We'd better get going, Jessie," he said as he led the way to the conference room, a small, tightly packed room with mismatched chairs around a pockmarked oval table. A city street map dotted with colored pins hung on one wall. The red pins designated active Homicide investigations: green were solved cases, and blue were cold. The map was provided by the Boston Regional Intelligence Center—BRIC. Information gathered by them pinpointed areas of crime, shootings and gang violence, as well as helping to identify major players and ex-offenders. It was the heart of their investigations, Jessie had learned. The opposite wall held a small window which offered a glimpse into the public housing project nearby. An overhead screen had been pulled down on the far wall to share the videos.

Ralph was standing by a laptop hooking it to the overhead screen. "This first is the video from the memorial that sprang up outside the garage. Everyone, please have a look. See if you recognize anyone or see anything that I might have missed."

Jessie and Sam separated as they entered the room and slipped into seats across from one another. The less people here knew of their relationship, the better.

"Here we go," Ralph said, flicking the lights off as the screen came to life, the sidewalk memorial in front of the garage coming into view. Jessie leaned forward, her eyes glued to the scene as Ralph hit fast forward through the hours after the woman's fall. "These," he said, pausing the video periodically, "are the first images of the memorial. You can see the first to arrive is an older woman with a cellophane-wrapped supermarket flower bouquet. She sets that down, pauses and then leaves. I checked with the earlier photos we have of the fall and the witnesses there, and this woman was among them. We've spoken to her extensively—she was one of several who called to report the fall. That evening," he said, scrolling through the images before pausing, "two more sprays are left, one by another older woman, another by a young girl." He pointed to the screen where a youngish man, who kept his back to the camera, bent and placed a single flower with the other bouquets. "We never see this man's face, and he does not appear in the earlier photos, so I know this isn't much to go on, but he left a single red rose, which makes us think that he may have known Jane Doe. He's a person of interest. Unfortunately, we have no identifying features aside from his height of about six feet and his hair color, brown. Again, not much to go on."

Jessie raised her hand. "Ralph, doesn't he resemble the physician who was at the scene? Same height and hair color, and keeps his back to the camera? I'm not sure if that was purposeful to keep his face hidden, but it just seems like a coincidence."

Ralph nodded. "I wondered about that, too. The earlier photos depict a similar man but in different clothes. He could have changed clothes, or it could be someone else entirely. I've actually asked our media team to put out a request for the doctor who was at the scene to come forward, so he can share what he saw." He pressed a button on his remote and advanced to the next scene of interest. "This is the next day, after word has spread about the woman who jumped. You can see this older woman place one of those glass-encased candles at the site. She lights the candle, bends her head as if in prayer, looks around and leaves. At first, I thought maybe she was one of the witnesses, but I checked, and she wasn't in any of the scene photos." He paused as if for effect. "I'm betting she knows who our Jane Doe is. Does anyone recognize her?"

Jessie squirmed in her seat. She was looking at Carmen.

16

"Okay," Ralph said before scrolling through the video once again. The memorial grew, more people arriving to place flowers and candles. One young woman left a small teddy bear at the site. Jessie sat forward. The woman resembled Jane Doe—long brown hair, deep mahogany eyes and light brown skin.

"What about her?" Jessie asked.

"Good catch, Jessie," he said. "She stayed there for about twenty minutes. I wondered if she knew her. The artist's sketch of Jane Doe went to the media this morning. I think it's already been featured on the news, so we're hoping that someone will come forward."

Jessie's phone vibrated in her pocket. She pulled it out and noted the sender. "I have to make a call," she said, standing. "Be right back."

Sam looked at her questioningly. "Everything okay?" he mouthed.

She smiled and made a quick exit. The text was from Carmen, and she'd promised not to share anything with the police just yet and that included Sam. For now.

Once outside the conference room, she read the text.

My friends will speak with you later today. 12PM?

She included an address in East Boston, an area where many newly arrived Latinos lived.

Yes, she replied. *See you then.*

Though a part of Boston, East Boston was separated from the city by Boston Harbor. Home to busy Logan Airport, it was accessible via a tunnel that ran under the harbor and every time Jessie had to drive through, she kept her eyes on the tile walls looking for leaks. If that wasn't overwhelming enough, the constant roar of planes taking off and landing just above the crowded narrow streets added to the general feeling of chaos. Though she could count on one hand the number of times she'd traveled there, her unease persisted. Still, she had to go. Carmen and her friends knew something, and they were willing—at least she hoped they were—to share what they knew.

Jessie slipped back into the conference room where Ralph was still standing by the overhead screen, pointing to a frozen view of a street by the garage. "No suspicious behavior," he said. "No one running, no one seeming to get away. We think that whoever threw her from the roof hid in plain sight and joined the group hovering around the victim."

"We've identified most of them except for the doctor and another man, an elderly man who was visible in the frame but kept back from the victim," Sam said. "Our priority has to be to identify Jane Doe."

"What about the glove I found on the roof?" Jessie asked. "Any DNA? Has it been checked yet with the scrapings that Roger got from under her fingernails?"

"We're in the process of running that DNA through the database. We have some fingerprints from the glove, as well. We're waiting on Forensics to complete their search. So, okay, that's it," Sam said and began to assign interviews and follow-up calls to the detectives in the room. "Jessie—" he began, but she interrupted him.

"Sorry," she said as she stood. "I wanted to be here to hear the update, but I'm actually off today and I have a backload of errands to run."

Sam's forehead wrinkled in confusion. "I..."

"Sorry," she said again. "I should have mentioned that as soon as I arrived." But she hadn't known then that Carmen and her friends would agree to speak today. She offered a half-shrug.

Sam collected his notebook and the flash drive that Ralph had used to download the videos and stood stiffly. "Okay then, everybody. Let's get on this. Call me with any updates." He started for the exit and Jessie blocked his way.

"Can I speak with you?" she asked.

"Sure," he said, walking beside her back to his office, where he closed the door and turned back to her, his beautiful silver eyes suddenly a flat gray. "Am I missing something? Was it the call? Is everything okay?"

"I'm pretty sure I told you I was off today."

He sighed. "Maybe you did. I just forgot. I'm sorry. Tonight?" he asked, pulling her close.

"Can I let you know? I'm not being cagey. I just have a lot to catch up on."

He kissed her forehead. "Okay, just let me know."

She smiled and made her way into the corridor past Ralph and the others who were gathered around a coffee pot. "See you later," she called and headed for the stairs and the parking lot. It was eleven a.m. In her car, she pulled up the GPS on her phone and typed in the address in East Boston where she was headed.

The app provided a traffic update on the route, and she sighed noisily. What should have been a twenty-minute trip was now estimated at an hour. A three-car accident in the tunnel was to blame. She checked for an alternate route, but that would take her out of her way and last at least an hour. She opted for the tunnel route, checked her bag to be sure she had a notebook and pens, and pulled into traffic hoping the long, slow drive would give her time to think about what to say, how to convince Carmen and her friends to come forward and identify the victim.

The trip took fifty minutes, fifteen of that spent in the tunnel, where Jessie anxiously eyed the tile seams of the walls as she inched her way through. Once she pulled out into the glare of the sun, she took the first exit for East Boston. Her GPS was as confused as she was, leading her the wrong way down one-way streets and noting landmarks that didn't seem to exist. In Southie, the streets were laid out in a grid, numbered or lettered and labeled East or West. East Boston had none of that. Finally, afraid that she was going to be late, Jessie pulled into a parking lot and texted Carmen, asking for help. She typed in the street name and Carmen texted her to stay where she was.

I'll come, she wrote.

And, within minutes, Carmen appeared, seeming somehow smaller in her faded sweatpants and bright yellow blouse, her gray hair pulled back tight at the nape of her neck. She leaned into Jessie's window. "Thank you for coming, Jessie. Everyone's waiting. They're happy to meet you, to tell their stories and get some help." Her words were halting and slow, as if she wanted to be sure Jessie understood her.

Jessie smiled, stepped from her car, locked it and followed Carmen along the crowded strip of sidewalk, any conversation drowned out by bleating car horns and people shouting in Spanish, Italian and sometimes English. The buildings were packed tight as teeth with little or no space between them. Carmen stopped in front of a narrow four-story brick building, a shuttered bakery on the first floor. She unlocked the metal front door and directed Jessie inside, where a steep staircase and a lingering musty smell led to the floors and apartments above.

Carmen scurried ahead of Jessie and up to the third floor, where one of two doors was open. Two children were bouncing balls off the wall, the thump echoing along the small space. The children shrieked happily when they spied Carmen and Jessie and ran inside just as a young woman, her black hair hanging loose in soft waves, appeared at the door. "*Hola,*" she said.

"*Hola,*" Jessie called. "They know I don't speak Spanish, right?'

Jessie asked. She'd always planned to take a Spanish course, but her free time had been so limited, she'd never gotten around to it.

"No problem," Carmen said, stepping inside. "Most speak at least a little English and for those who don't, I will help."

The chatter stopped abruptly as Jessie entered the apartment right into the living room. An open door led into a small kitchen, and off to the side were three closed doors, likely a bathroom and bedrooms. The furniture—two sagging couches placed across from one another and a low table separating them—filled every bit of space. A gold-colored carpet lay underfoot; a wooden cross was affixed to one wall and family photos on the other. A flat-screen television filled one side of the room, but it was the scent of spices and recent meals that hung in the air that caught Jessie's attention. This was a place that exuded warmth and comfort. A family lived here.

"This is my friend, Jessie," Carmen said, introducing her.

Jessie smiled. "Hello," she said. "Carmen has told me a little about your problems and I hope I can help."

There were pleasant nods all around, except for one woman, her arms folded tightly across her ample chest. There was a scowl on her lips, and her deep brown eyes were cold as ice.

Her glare sent a shiver through Jessie's veins.

17

The women shifted on the couch and one of them—a young woman with bleached blonde hair and skin pitted with old acne scars—patted the spot beside her and motioned for Jessie to sit. "I am Clara," she said.

"I am Ana," said a woman with shiny black hair, tipped blue at the ends just like Jane Doe's. A row of crooked, cracked teeth broke up her nervous smile.

Both women were young with bright dark eyes and soft red lips. The third woman, the older woman who had scowled, didn't add her name. Jessie looked right at her. "And you are...?" she asked, hoping her voice sounded friendly. She didn't want anyone to be afraid. She needed them to trust her.

The woman let her arms drop to her sides. "I am Lucia," she said, her voice raspy, the voice of a longtime smoker.

"Jessie has come to help," Carmen said, dragging over a sturdy wooden chair and inviting Lucia to sit. "She took care of Rosa at the hospital," she added to a low murmur of appreciation from the group.

Jessie sat forward. "You think you might know the woman who died? She may have been your friend?"

They nodded. "Rosa disappeared on Sunday, the day that woman fell. And the drawing in the newspaper, well..." Carmen sat back a little further. "Well, it looked so much like her." Her gaze drifted to Ana.

"She was my sister," Ana said, so softly that Jessie had to strain to hear.

Jessie leaned forward and patted Ana's hand. "I'm so sorry for your loss. Can you tell me about her?" She'd decided not to jump into asking how they knew for sure that it was their sister and friend who'd died, and who might have wanted to hurt her. She didn't want to scare them off. She wanted to understand who Rosa was first and maybe even what had happened to her.

There was silence for several minutes until Carmen spoke up. "You knew her best, Ana. Will you start?"

Ana cleared her throat and folded her hands in her lap, her chin falling to her chest, her eyes closed. After what seemed like forever, she looked up at Jessie and spoke. "We grew up in Guatemala side by side, always together. She was a good girl, a good friend, a good girl."

Jessie remembered Roger's assessment of a past pregnancy. "She has children?"

"Only one. And she would never leave him. Never."

"A son? Where is he?"

A well of tears misted Ana's eyes and she shook her head. "We don't know. You must help me to find him."

Jessie wondered how old the son was, and if he knew of his mother's death. If Jane Doe was his mother. But she couldn't jump to that just yet.

Piece by piece, Sam had once said. *You build your case slowly. If you go in too fast, too frantically, you could lose your witnesses, your evidence, your chance at solving a murder.*

"Start with Rosa. Tell me about her, her age, when she came to Boston." She drew a notebook and pen from her bag.

"What are those for?" Lucia asked testily.

"I have to take notes, I'll never remember what you all tell me and it's important that I remember. Don't you agree?" She looked at the group of women. "I could record you on my cell phone if you'd prefer."

Lucia looked away, but the others shook their heads. "No recording us, but the notes are okay," Clara said. "If it will help, it's okay. We want to know what happened. We're afraid it might happen to the rest of us."

"What makes you say that?" Jessie asked.

"We are..." Ana said, turning to Carmen for help with the word.

"Undocumented. Illegal," Carmen said. "That is why they will not go to the police. They are afraid they will be sent to jail and then deported. Understand?"

Jessie nodded. "Let's start at the beginning then," she said.

Ana wound a strand of hair around her finger, twirling it over and over. "We came here together, Rosa and I."

"I'm sorry to interrupt, but what is Rosa's last name?"

Ana smiled, her sparkly earrings glittering in the sunlight streaming into the room. "Suarez, Rosa Suarez, and she is twenty-three years old." She held up a blue-tipped strand of hair. "We colored our hair together last month." She paused to run her fingers through her hair. "We grew up in a..." Again, she looked at Carmen for help.

"A crowded village, just outside of a city," Carmen said. "A place of poverty and hunger. Children scrounge in nearby dumps for food and items that others have thrown away." She shook her head sadly.

"Too many people in too small a space," Ana said. "No water, no electricity, always the worry about food and crime. When you are poor, there is always someone poorer who will steal what little you have. Gangs with guns wandered through looking for trouble and girls, and they found us, Rosa and me. We both... we both decided..." Her brow wrinkled and she blinked away tears.

"Are you okay?" Jessie asked, touching her knee. "You can stop if you need to."

"She shouldn't say anything else," Lucia glared at Jessie. "She is police. Remember that."

"I'm a nurse," Jessie said, "and I work with the police to help to solve crimes. Your friend was murdered. Don't you want to find out who did that?"

Lucia grunted. "I know who did it." She looked around the room for affirmation but most of the women gathered there looked away.

"It could be the gangs," Clara said. "We haven't left them behind. They are here and they kill to remind us of that. Rosa was not the first, and she will not be the last if we talk to the police."

Ana's eyes grew wide. "But we haven't said anything to the police. We must do something. And we must find the child." She spoke with an authority that belied her small stature and trusting face.

"Ana's right, and I will do my best to help you," Jessie said. "But you have to tell me everything you know."

Ana began again. "Rosa and I had babies, and after her baby..." She paused to wipe a bead of sweat from her brow.

Jessie suddenly realized that the stagnant air in the apartment was sweltering. Whisking away a line of sweat from her neck, she turned to Carmen. "I'm sorry to bother you, but could I have a glass of water?"

Carmen nodded and hurried away, returning with a colorful plastic tray holding a pitcher of water and three glasses. Jessie quickly poured herself a glass of water, drinking it down in one swift gulp. She looked up. Despite the heat in the small room, no one else had reached for the water. Her cheeks red with embarrassment and heat, Jessie bent back to her notebook and watched gratefully as Carmen opened a window, the faint breeze a welcome respite from the heat. "I'm sorry," Jessie said. "Please go on."

"We had to get out of Guatemala," Ana said. "It wasn't safe for us or the babies. We'd seen the long lines of people passing through from Honduras and El Salvador headed for Mexico and then the U.S., and we decided to join them. We said our goodbyes, afraid to leave, but a baby changes everything. Understand?"

Jessie could only nod. "How long did the journey take?"

Frustration crinkled her eyes. "Long time." She looked at Clara. "Two months?"

She nodded. "It was a long, long journey on foot."

"From the border, we walked into Texas at night and there were men waiting to drive us to safety, they said. We climbed into the back of a big truck and came here to Boston. The man said we owed him three thousand dollars each for his help. When we told him we had no money, he said we would earn it and he would be back to collect it. He left us in a big empty warehouse, but we knew he was dangerous. We watched and waited and we prayed and finally—when he'd been gone for days—we opened the door, stepped out and made our way to a church, and the priest there helped us. He found us an apartment and jobs and fed us when we had nothing. And though we've been here a year, he still looks out for us, but the other man found us. He comes here for his money and we give him what we can. We don't want trouble from him, but when it's not enough, he threatens us. Rosa owed him the most." She paused and poured herself a glass of water, taking a sip before passing the glass around to share with the others.

Jessie filled her own glass and passed it to Clara, who was sitting next to her. Clara smiled, took a sip and set the glass back down as Jessie's phone pinged with a text. She ignored it but glanced quickly at her watch. She'd been here for over an hour. As an ER nurse, she was used to a fast pace, and a part of her wanted to ask Ana to cut to the chase, but she needed these women as much as they needed her. Getting to the truth and finding Rosa's killer was going to take time.

She needed more information about this man who took their money, this trafficker of helpless girls, but she understood that they had to tell their stories in their own time. She was here, after all, to listen. She took a deep breath and settled back into the couch.

18

Jessie bent to her notebook, determined to record the important facts. "Where did Rosa work?"

"She worked for a cleaning service," Carmen said. "They don't check for visas or documents. She cleaned mostly colleges, and to the students and people there, she was invisible. People don't pay attention to those who clean up after them."

"Do you have a picture of Rosa?" Jessie asked.

Ana reached into her bag and pulled out a small photo before passing it to Jessie with a smile. "It is of both of us before we left Guatemala."

Jessie took the photo and ran her finger along the smooth surface. Ana was smiling, her arm draped lazily over Rosa's shoulder. The other girl was laughing, her head thrown back, her lips painted a bright red, her long hair pulled into a ponytail, and Jessie wondered if the marks on the dead woman's wrists came from that hair tie. The girls stood on a dirt road leaning against an old car, a goat grazing nearby while a child was caught in midflight chasing after a chicken. The simple joy reflected in that moment was palpable. She was almost afraid to look back at Ana, to confirm her worst fears. Jane Doe's face had been too battered to see any resemblance to the girl in the picture, but as she looked closer, she saw the same type of gold chain and cross that had adorned Jane Doe's neck. She took a deep breath and leaned forward placing her hand over Ana's. "I'm sorry," she said softly, "but I don't know if this is the woman who died." She paused to allow Ana to consider her news. It was almost worse to be so unsure.

"If it is Rosa, she didn't jump," Carmen said. "She would never do that, not to us."

"We don't think she jumped," Jessie said softly. "Someone hurt her and then threw her from the roof."

Ana gasped and began to cry.

Jessie gripped her hand tighter. "We don't know yet if it is your sister, but is there anyone who might have wanted to hurt her?"

"Maybe the man who comes to take our money," she sniffled. "He is the only one."

"Do you have a name for him?"

Ana shook her head. "He uses different names—Pablo, Jesús, Bobby. He never uses the same name twice."

"Do you have a way to contact him? To let him know if you have money for him?"

"No. He comes when he comes, without notice."

"So, do you all think this is the only man who posed a threat to Rosa?" She glanced at the others in turn. They murmured agreement, except for Lucia, who sat stiffly.

"We'll need more information on him," Jessie said, "once we identify our victim. Can you describe him for the police? Do you have any pictures?"

"We can describe him, but we have no pictures."

"There is someone else," Lucia said suddenly, her jaw tight. "Rosa went to see him on Sunday, and she never came back." She shook her head, her long hair breaking free of the elastic that secured it. "I know little of the man she met on Sunday, but if it were the other one—the one who comes for our money—she would have simply said that she was going to meet him. She didn't. The man she planned to meet has hurt her. I know it."

Jessie exhaled noisily. She would have to figure this out. "Was she involved with him romantically, maybe?"

"No," Lucia said. "She had no time for that."

"I think I have to tell your story to the detectives I work with. We can get Ana's DNA right now and match it with our victim. And if she is Rosa, they will protect you, and they can help to find this man and the other one and work out what happened." She turned to Ana and nodded toward one of the unused water glasses. "Will you put your lips to that cup as if you are about to drink, and then pass it to me?"

Ana hesitated but finally nodded and followed Jessie's directions. She held the glass out and Jessie realized she hadn't brought her ME bag up from her car. She asked Carmen if she had an unused brown lunch bag she could have. Carmen hurried away and returned with the bag, passing it to Jessie, who held it out for Ana. "Please just place your glass in here," she said. Once the glass was safely in the bag, Jesse folded the top and slipped it into her bag.

Ana had been watching warily. "Will you find my... her boy?" she asked.

"We'll try. Tell me about him," Jessie said.

Ana nodded. "He was with her when she left on Sunday. To meet the man that Lucia mentioned. He said he needed her help, and she thought he might repay her with a better job."

"And she didn't tell you any more? A name or a description of the man, maybe?"

Lucia shook her head but sat in stony silence.

Jessie sighed, afraid she'd hit a wall. Maybe it was time to change tactics, to focus on the child. "How old is her son?"

"He is almost three." Ana passed a photo of the boy to Jessie.

And this time Jessie gasped. It was Julio, her Julio. "He was in the ER on Sunday," she said. "The police found him wandering on Tremont Street. He wouldn't speak, only said his name was Julio, nothing else. He's with the Department of Children and Families."

Ana stood quickly, banging her knee into the small table and spilling the pitcher of water. Carmen began to mop it up. "Sit," she ordered Ana before turning back to Jessie. "Where is he? How do we get him back?"

"Do you have his birth certificate? Any proof that he is Rosa's son?"

"No, we have nothing," Ana said. "But we have to find him. I am Julio's only family. He needs me. Understand?" Her lips trembled as she spoke.

Jessie nodded, remembering what Sam had said—that he could contact DCF about Julio if a homicide was involved. And a homicide was most definitely involved. "I'll have to tell the police." She held up her hand. "Before you say no, this is the only way to get Julio back and to track down the killer and keep all of you safe. You have to think about that."

Lucia scowled. Clara blinked and Ana's forehead puckered with worry.

"It will be okay. This is important." She held up her phone. "I can call my friend now and ask him to come to speak with you."

"No," Carmen said firmly. "The man who comes for money could see and then come after all of us. No. We will meet your policeman somewhere else."

"What about Julio?" Ana asked softly. "Is he okay?"

"He was fine on Sunday, and I've been told he is in good hands, but I haven't seen him. I'm not even sure where he is."

"Then how can you help him—help us?"

"The police will help, and they will help to find the killer. If he is the man whom Rosa went to meet, he might know, or at least have knowledge of all of you. We don't know why she was killed and any one of you could be next. I'm sorry to say that, but it's true. This isn't just for Rosa and Julio. This is for you."

She plucked her phone from her bag and stopped. The screen was lit up with texts from Sam.

We have another jumper. Boston University, Commonwealth Ave.
I know you're on a day off but we need you here ASAP.

There were several more—all along the same lines. She was needed, and where was she? Roger had sent a text as well.

I am not able to get to Commonwealth Ave. Please get there. I need your eyes on the scene. Roger

Jessie's eyes were glued to her phone.

"What is it?" Carmen asked, sensing the change in Jessie's demeanor.

"I hate to do this, but I have to leave. There's another woman. I have to be there with the detectives." She stood and quickly gathered her notebook, pens and phone.

"Another one like us?" Clara asked, her eyes wide with fright.

"I don't know," Jessie said, moving toward the door, gripping her bag. "I just don't know."

19

As soon as she was in her car, Jessie texted Sam that she was on her way, and in just over twenty minutes she pulled onto Common-wealth Avenue and slowed when she saw a bevy of police cars, their blue lights whirling, the black ME van pulled to the side of the road. A flock of eager reporters with cameras and news vans hovered at the periphery of the yellow crime scene tape. She pulled up next to the ME van and a uniformed officer glared at her angrily.

"See that yellow tape? You can't park here. Get moving."

Jessie fished through her bag for her red police ID and her ME ID and held them up to the open window. "I'm with the police and the ME. They asked me to be here."

He grunted approval, wrote her name in the scene ledger and motioned her to pull in closer. She reached for the ME bag that Roger had given her just weeks ago. It held the tools of her new trade—latex gloves, small plastic evidence bags and tags, a tape measure, a flashlight, a camera and, because old habits die hard, she'd added a stethoscope.

"Hey, Jessie," a familiar voice called. "We've been waiting for you."

She turned to see Tony, Roger's assistant, as she lifted the yellow police tape and scurried under. "Hi, Tony, sorry I'm late. I didn't get the messages." She stopped to pull on a hairnet, booties and gloves.

Tony huffed out an impatient sigh. "You're here now. The body's over there. I can't touch her until you have a look."

She nodded and started for the site, where a white plastic tarp lay over the body, a broken window screen nearby. She didn't see Sam or Ralph, or any other detectives she knew, just a few uniformed officers. "What do you know?" she asked Tony as they headed to the body.

"Not much. A young woman, college student, Sam thinks, jumped from that middle building."

Jessie looked up to see three high-rise buildings blocking the sun.

"Dorms," Tony said. "Hundreds of kids live in there."

"What floor she was on?"

"I'm not sure. Sam is up there. Better to ask him. I'll let him know you're here."

Jessie nodded and bent to the body, gently lifting the plastic away. The girl lay splayed on her right side, a puddle of blood surrounding her. Her legs were bent at impossible angles, her left arm and face unmarked. Her left eye, the blue of it almost opaque, was open and staring. Instinctively, Jessie felt for a pulse but there was nothing, no signs of life. This girl was dead. Jessie swallowed the lump in her throat and focused on her responsibilities—evaluating what she was seeing.

The woman's long blonde hair was spattered with blood. Jessie pulled out the camera and took several photos before moving to turn her onto her back. "Tony," she asked, "will you give me a hand?"

Tony squatted down and helped to ease the girl onto her back. Jessie squeezed her eyes shut to get her bearings and moved in for a closer look. The right side of the girl's face, head and arms were saturated with blood, the tissue lumpy and blue with new bruising and broken bones. Her eye was lost in the swelling on her face, but it was easy to see that she'd been beautiful. Jessie took more photos, stopping only when she realized the woman was wearing spandex running gear, one sneaker on, the other likely nearby.

She felt that familiar unease, the feeling that something just wasn't adding up. Would you get ready for a run and instead jump from a building to an agonizing death? She moved in for a closer look, surveying the girl from head to toe. Although it was difficult to examine her face and neck with the splash of fresh blood, Jessie couldn't make out any pre-fall trauma. At least, nothing that was obvious. She'd have a better look in the morgue. Her eyes drifted down to the woman's arms and sleeveless running top. Again, no injuries that the fall wouldn't account for.

And then her eyes fell on the girl's hands and wrists, and she saw faint circular bruising. Several of her fingernails had been broken off as well. She lifted the camera and snapped away, thinking that the bruising resembled the marks she'd seen on Jane Doe's wrists. This couldn't be a coincidence. It had to be something more, a clue—finally. She made a mental note to get a closer look at those marks once the body was at the morgue.

The sun caught something shiny clutched tightly in the girl's right hand. Jessie leaned forward onto her hands to examine the sudden bit of shimmer. It was some kind of chain, or bracelet, perhaps. She held the camera close to the girl's hands and took more photos.

"Hey, Jessie," Sam called from behind her. "What have you got?" He stepped up next to her as the Forensics team moved in. "I had them upstairs going over her room. They came up with one sneaker. The other's on her foot?"

She nodded. "Do you think she's a jumper, or another homicide made to look that way?" she asked, looking up at the building.

"Not sure yet. But a girl in the dorm said she just came in from a run. What did you find?" He jerked his head to the body.

"She has those same circumferential marks on both wrists as Jane Doe—or Rosa Suarez, as she could be."

His eyes crinkled in confusion. "Rosa Suarez?"

Jessie took a deep breath. "I might have an ID on Jane Doe."

"You *might* have an ID?" He scratched his head. "How? When?"

"Some women who recognized the woman in the artist's sketch that was released to the press asked to meet with me. I was with them when you were texting. That's why I was late answering you."

"You went off chasing down information on your own without telling me?" he asked icily. "What the hell, Jessie? We've had this discussion before. You're a member of a team. You do not go out on your own."

"They didn't want to speak to the police. They're afraid to, but they got in touch with me through a housekeeper at the hospital. The thing is, they're undocumented, and they're afraid they'll be deported if they speak up. They ID'd the little boy I told you about as the victim's child. And if I remember correctly, he was found on Tremont Street, which isn't too far from that garage." She knew she was rushing through her words, but she wanted Sam to understand. "They think they know who killed her." Jessie paused to give Sam time to cool off. "I think they'll talk to you now."

His jaw clenched, Sam turned his attention to the body on the ground. "Alright," he said, "let's finish up here, and then we'll have to get back to the office to work through some of this information."

She touched his shoulder lightly. "You told me once that to do this job well I had to follow the facts and the story and the evidence. I know you're not happy with me, but these women didn't want anything to do with the police. I've convinced them that they would have to speak with you and that you would keep them safe. I'm trying to help sort this out, not create problems."

Sam stuffed his hands into his pockets and nodded. "I know, Jessie. We'll talk about that later. But for now, this young girl is dead. Her dorm room is a mess—hard to say if it was ransacked or the result of a struggle or, as Ralph pointed out, it was just always like that. No witnesses, but luckily the security guard closed off the area as soon as he heard the shouting and the commotion. He didn't see anyone running away." He leaned down by the body.

"Forensics is still up there brushing for fingerprints or anything else, and Ralph is having a look for cameras, but they're not likely to be there. It's a dorm. Student privacy is paramount."

"What's her name?" Jessie asked, bending to her knees once again. "I hate to think of these girls as unknowns. I want to know who she is. Was," she corrected herself.

"Her name is Alison McCray. She was twenty-four years old and finishing up her master's degree." He passed her the girl's ID. She was smiling, her eyes a bright blue set against the clean shine of her blonde hair. Jessie held onto it, staring into Alison's eyes.

"Beautiful," she whispered, passing the ID back to Sam.

"She was the dorm assistant. Lived there only this last semester. Poor kid. So, tell me what your impression is."

"There's a lot of blood, so unlike Jane Doe, she was alive when she fell. Forensics is here already, yes?"

Sam nodded. "They did a quick look at the body. They wanted you to see her the way she landed. They'll be down shortly to collect evidence."

"They probably took pictures, but I did, too. Tony and I turned her over. That's when I noticed the marks on her wrists and her missing fingernails. Same as with Jane Doe."

"Jesus, if this is the same guy," Sam said, huffing out a noisy sigh. "Anything else that connects this to Jane Doe?" He stretched his neck as if working the tension out.

Jessie pulled the tarp back over the body and stood, brushing away the bits of debris from her pants. "No, not yet," she said softly.

"Let's get back to the office and talk."

"I'll meet you there. I'll call Roger and see when he plans to do the postmortem." She picked up her ME bag and turned to go until Sam's hand on her shoulder stopped her.

"I'm not angry, Jessie. I'm not, but we have to be a team. You can't go off on your own anymore."

Jessie nodded in what she hoped appeared to be silent agreement. "See you at headquarters," she said, slipping under the yellow crime scene tape. Tony was standing by the ME van, his arms crossed, his impatience showing. Tony was conscientious as ever and his aim was always to get the body back to the morgue ASAP. "Forensics just have to have another look, Tony. I'll see you at the morgue shortly."

He sighed and leaned against the van, a pained expression on his face. "I can only hope," he said.

20

He stood away from the window and watched. He didn't want to attract attention from the police below, though probably everyone in the building was peering out watching the circus unfold. The body was covered with a white plastic sheet, but the blood was seeping out around her. He adjusted his glasses and moved closer to the window. He was in the stairwell—the safest place to watch. He'd hear if a door opened, and he'd have time to move.

A familiar figure suddenly moved into his line of sight, spoke to the man standing by the ME van and then she bent to the body, lifting the covering away. And his breath caught in his throat. This was beautiful to watch. The girl was still on her side as though she was sleeping. The woman touched the girl's neck and wrist and he smiled. She was checking for a pulse. They just couldn't help themselves. They were desperate to save everyone, but this girl was dead. The woman below looked everything over, pulled a camera from her bag and began to take pictures of the body. He wished he'd thought of that—a picture was a far better souvenir than a fingernail. He watched as the woman nodded to the morgue technician and together they rolled the dead girl onto her back.

And suddenly he knew who the woman was. She was the one from the garage roof. The one who'd found his glove. His first and only mistake. He'd gone back after the police left. He'd needed to *reassure himself that he'd left nothing behind. And then, he did just what he'd feared. He'd left the damn glove. He hadn't realized it for another day, and when he went back, she was there, bent over it. She'd chased him down the stairs, but there was nothing like the fear of being caught to put speed into one's step. She had the glove, but it didn't matter. They'd never figure out who it belonged to.*

He shook his head to clear his thoughts. He couldn't let this stuff distract him. He had to let himself savor these moments. The thrill was still there. Oh, it was still there. The satisfying but sickening thud as they fell, the splash of bright red blood against the gray concrete. They rarely screamed. It all happened too fast, and he was too good.

He smiled and adjusted his glasses as a door opened somewhere above.

21

"And that's it, Sam. I wasn't trying to hide anything." They were at headquarters, in Sam's office with the door closed, and she was recounting her meeting with Carmen and her friends. "They wanted to speak only to me, and I had to give my word." She held out the paper bag that contained Ana's DNA. "This may help us to identify Jane Doe, and if it does, we need these women. I know they'll speak with you. And the link is the little boy I told you about. One of the women is his aunt. His mother is missing, or maybe she's Jane Doe."

"For the life of me, I don't understand why you wouldn't have just told me this morning. I trust you, and I thought that you trusted me."

"I do, Sam, I do, but I had to convince those women to trust you. They said they would discuss it and let me know. As soon as they do, I'll tell you. In the meantime, I want to get this DNA to Forensics."

"Next time, you have to come to me first. What if you'd walked into a trap?"

Jessie dropped her head. He was right, of course. She'd taken too many chances in the past, and she'd promised that she wouldn't do it again. But the truth was, she probably would do it again if it involved a chance to help solve a case.

"Either way," Sam continued, "if the DNA proves who she is, they won't have a choice. They'll have to help. They'll need to give us a positive visual ID and share what they know even if they don't want to be involved. And they owe it to her and her child." He raked his hand through his hair and sighed. "Alright, let's get back to Alison McCray and the case at hand. We know that she was a dorm assistant working on her master's degree and scheduled to graduate soon."

"Has her family been notified?"

"We just got the contact information from the college. Seems she was adopted and the only child of a couple in San Diego, a much-loved daughter, from their notes. I'll put a call out to the California police in her town…"

But Jessie wasn't listening. Her mind was already on Alison and the word *adopted*. Sam said she was twenty-four years old, the same age her own half-sister would be. She'd only recently learned that her mother had had another child out of wedlock. She felt a heavy weight pressing on her chest. Her half-sister had been put up for adoption. She was out there somewhere. Was she in college? Was she happy? Did she ever wonder if she had other family? A bead of sweat ran along her forehead and she reached to swipe it away. What if this girl had been her own sister? She couldn't even imagine how she'd deal with that kind of pain.

Sam had stopped speaking, his eyes focused on her, his brow raised. "What is it?" he asked.

"You said she was adopted. And she's twenty-four years old, about the same age my half-sister would be. It just… Never mind. Let's get back to work."

Sam leaned back. "I hadn't even thought of that. Sorry, Jessie. Do you want to take a break?"

"No. Let's keep going. So, it seems to me, after seeing the body, that this was a homicide made to look like a suicide. Agree?"

He nodded. "Looks that way. It's still early. But she's the third college student to jump—if that's what happened—this year. On the heels of Jane Doe, we have to be careful. You were the one to notice the marks on her wrists, same as Jane Doe. We have to take a very close look at this one."

"Did Alison leave a note?"

He shook his head. "The others didn't either."

"Any witnesses?"

"None that we know of. Apparently, most students had finals today, others were out enjoying the warm weather, the few still in the dorm were napping until they heard the sirens. Only one saw her, and she said Alison had just come in from a run."

"And she didn't see anyone else?"

Sam shook his head.

"And you mentioned that a security guard kept everyone away?"

"He was doing rounds on the seventh floor. Heard some shouting right after she fell, and when he looked out, he saw someone on the street pointing to the body and the window screen on the ground. He wasn't sure which room she'd come from, but he knew the floor, so he stayed there and called nine-one-one, then secured the area until we arrived."

"So, we need to get the autopsy ASAP. I'll call Roger." He picked up as soon as she tapped *call*.

"You're calling about young Alison McCray, I assume," he said.

"Yes," Jessie answered. "There are some similarities with Jane Doe, though this girl died on impact, not before. I want to share my findings and photos from the scene with you. Will you be starting on her this afternoon?"

"I will," Roger answered. "Tony just brought her in. We're getting some x-rays and preliminary testing. You on your way?"

"I am," she said, standing. She looked at Sam, his eyes creased with worry and fatigue. "I'm going to the morgue. I'll keep you posted." She paused and looked him in the eye, the shimmer gone, his gaze flat. "Are we okay?" she asked.

He stood and pulled her into his arms. "As long as we're both honest, we are."

"I promise," she whispered.

He tilted her lips to his and planted a quick kiss there. "I promise too, Jessie."

She made the trip to the morgue in record time, arriving just as Roger and Tony were finishing up with x-rays and collecting blood and body fluid samples. The autopsy on Alison McCray should have been routine but for the unsettling thought that the death of this girl might just be connected to Jane Doe's murder. Jessie donned her PPE quickly and had another look at Alison. She pointed out the broken fingernails to Roger along with the marks on her wrists and the gold chain clutched so tightly that Roger had to pry it from her hand.

Roger tapped the foot pedal and began to record his findings as he worked. "Significant bleeding from her aorta and her pulmonary artery," he said, nodding to himself as he went. "Multiple broken bones and blunt chest trauma. Her open skull fracture and fracture of her spinal column at C-5 contributed to her death, but the injuries and exsanguination secondary to the trauma to her aorta and pulmonary artery were the immediate causes of death. The brain and c-spine injuries were likely suffered simultaneously. You were right, Jessie. She died on impact."

"What about those circumferential marks on her wrists?" Jessie asked. "And her broken fingernails?"

"The red areas on her wrists are similar to those on Jane Doe, who is still here. I'll have another look at her. But there's nothing under this girl's remaining fingernails, no evidence of blood or tissue, nothing to indicate a struggle."

"What about her broken fingernails?" Jessie asked. "Doesn't that indicate a struggle?"

"It could," Roger said, "but it could have happened in the fall. The wounds are fresh and the nails clearly torn off, so that's the one sign that perhaps at some point there was a struggle. But there's no forensic evidence yet to support that."

Tony nodded. "There was nothing, no fingernails at the scene. You saw it, Jessie. Just a lot of blood and that chain she was gripping."

"Can you get DNA from that chain?" Jessie asked. "See if it was hers?"

"I've already put it aside in an evidence bag for Forensics," Tony answered, holding the plastic bag up. "They'll be by soon, but did you see it? A chain with a cross?"

And she peered closely. Jane Doe had worn a cross on a chain around her neck. She supposed that half the women in Boston wore the same type of chain, but why was this one in this girl's hand? Maybe she was just putting it on, but it seemed like one more strange coincidence to Jessie. She made a mental note of it.

Roger stepped back from the table, pulling his goggles from his face. Snapping his gloves from his hands, he exhaled noisily. "This has been a tough week. These young women dead. And those college girls in the winter. And it seems to me..."

"The college girls' deaths were listed as suicide, right?" she asked.

"Yes, there was no evidence at all to suggest otherwise, but I have to say, three suicides in a matter of months in college girls with no history of depression or problems that we were made aware of, seems a bit too coincidental. Likely worth another look."

"So, will you be able to document a manner of death on this girl, or is it too soon?"

He shook his head. "Too soon. We'll wait and see what the lab tests and histology show, and I'll have a closer look at those wrist marks, compare them to Jane Doe's. I'll pull the reports and photos on the other girls. Seems to me at least one of them had similar marks. Friends of another girl reported that she'd often worn those tight cord bracelets, if I'm remembering correctly, and we matched the cords to those marks." He turned to Jessie. "I'd like you to find out if Alison had any of those type of bracelets. It could be due to something else, but I'd like to rule out the bracelet first. This could be the third girl with those marks, maybe from hair elastics, maybe bracelets, but worth a closer look." He began to peel his PPE away. "We'll see where the facts take us. I'm not ruling anything out just yet. And that includes murder."

A cold finger ran along Jessie's spine.

Jessie texted Sam from the locker room. *Dr. Dawson is interested in seeing if Alison had any cord bracelets that would cause the marks on her wrists. Has anyone searched the room?* She quickly showered, changed and checked her phone.

Something's come up, Sam had replied. *Can it wait until tomorrow? I'll see you then.*

Jessie felt a stab of disappointment. His reply seemed curt. Had she misunderstood him earlier when he'd mentioned seeing her tonight? She sighed. He had other cases that he was working on. That was probably it. Something had come up for him and there was nothing she could do about it. Her stomach grumbled, reminding her that she hadn't eaten all day and she was famished. It was already after six. She'd pick up some dinner and get home.

An hour later, she licked the last bits of takeout fried chicken from her fingers and tried to relax, but her mind was still on the oddly similar marks that both Alison and Jane Doe had on their wrists. She rubbed her own wrist and considered Roger's question about bracelets. She needed to get into Alison's room sooner rather than later, and if Sam was involved with another case, it might take days. Jessie had no interest in waiting. She picked up her phone and texted Ralph: *I'd like to get into Alison McCray's room,* she typed. *Could you arrange that for me for tomorrow morning? I could go before I come to headquarters.*

Ralph texted back right away. *Absolutely. Crime scene tape still up. I'll let the uniformed officer on duty know you'll be by and to let you in. See you in the morning. Ralph*

Jessie heaved a satisfied sigh. Tomorrow couldn't come soon enough.

22

THURSDAY, DAY 5

Jessie couldn't say if it was the ping of her phone announcing a new text or the rays of sunshine leaking in through her window blinds that nudged her from sleep, but either way, she was awake. She inched her eyes open, stretched, and reached for her phone, confident that the message would be from Sam. It wasn't.

Morning, Jessie, she read. *A uniformed officer will meet you at the dorm at 8:30 and let you in. She can assist you with your search as well. Don't know how many evidence bags you have but she will bring some as well just in case. See you later. Ralph*

There was no time to waste. It was already seven thirty, and traffic on Commonwealth Avenue would be hellish. She sprang from her bed, took a quick shower, and peered into her closet. The detectives all wore suits and ties, while she'd been wearing jeans or scrubs. To truly be one of them, she needed to fit in and to do that, she had to mirror their attire. She reached for a pale pink fitted blouse, a pair of black pleated pants and a pair of beige pumps. She pulled her hair into a loose ponytail, swiped a dash of color on her lips and almost inhaled a cup of instant coffee before heading out.

She pulled into a spot on Commonwealth Avenue, right by Warren Towers. A police cruiser was already parked just ahead. Jessie fished out her red police ID, slipped it around her neck and reached for her ME work bag, looping it over her shoulder as she walked toward the cruiser. The door opened and a policewoman stepped out, her dark blue uniform crisp, her black hair trimmed neatly, which made her skin—the color of caramel—stand out against the sparkle of her almost golden eyes. A pair of handcuffs dangled from her belt; a holster nestled by her hip. She exuded professionalism and confidence. "You're Jessie Novak?"

Jessie smoothed the front of her slacks and smiled. "I am," she said, extending her hand. "And you are?"

"Officer Asia Lincoln," she replied, taking Jessie's hand and gripping it firmly. "But call me Asia. Detective Thompson told me what we were looking for, said to bring extra evidence bags. Just in case." She reached into her cruiser and retrieved a stack of brown paper bags and a black marker. "Ready?"

Jessie nodded and followed Officer Lincoln to the middle tower. Asia spoke quickly to the guard at the desk, a few students watching warily and backing away as she pressed the elevator's call button.

Asia chuckled. "I have that effect on people," she whispered conspiratorially. "By the way, you probably already know this, but the guard said students can bypass this front reception area and the guards by slipping in through the back door. They just need their passkey."

"Interesting," Jessie said, filing the information away in her mind.

On the seventh floor, they walked straight down the hall to room 713—Alison's single room, the perk of being a dorm assistant. Asia lifted the yellow crime scene tape and unlocked the door. Though the room had already been processed, they both paused to pull on booties, hairnets and gloves.

Jessie stepped inside cautiously. The room was small, maybe twelve feet by twelve, making Jessie's apartment seem spacious in comparison. An industrial gray rug covered the floor, and the furniture, consisting of a twin bed, a banged-up four-drawer dresser, and a no-frills desk, was pushed up tight against the walls. Wires and USB connectors for a laptop, which had likely already been taken by Forensics, lay haphazardly on the desktop, a notebook and pens off to the side. A small cubbyhole of a closet took up a corner. Alison's clothes spilled out: a pile of shoes and boots on the floor, an umbrella hung on the doorknob. A bicycle was fixed crookedly on one wall while a framed Renoir print offered a splash of color to the otherwise drab interior. A large window, secured now, took up much of the third wall. The heating unit was tucked in beneath the window, the bulky control panel creating a ledge. Fingerprint dust dotted the top of the unit. Jessie leaned in, careful to avoid disturbing the dust, to peer through the window to the alley below where a broken screen and crime scene tape still blocked the area.

"If she climbed up here," Jessie said softly, "there'd be shoeprints. She had running shoes on—well, at least one." She crossed her arms and sighed.

Asia looked at her quizzically.

"Sorry," Jessie said. "Thinking out loud. I'm a runner, too. Sam said she'd just come in from a run. Hard to believe she'd jump just then. But I guess we should get to it. I'm looking for a bracelet—bangle, probably, or maybe one of those string bracelets girls wear these days, a thinnish bracelet that might leave marks. I'll start with the bureau."

Asia nodded and turned to the closet. "I guess I'll look in here."

The surface of Alison's dresser was cluttered. A small hand mirror, a pair of hoop earrings, a rolled-up sock, a hairbrush with long blonde strands peeking out, and a handful of hair elastics. She picked up the hair elastics, pulling one onto her own wrist and wincing as it pinched her skin, a small red mark blossoming. She pulled it off, snapped a photo, and dropped it into an evidence bag, labeling it with the date and time, and her initials. She moved on to a small tray filled with soap, skin cream, a tube of lip gloss, and a sleeve of crackers. The stuff of Alison's life, all there as though she thought she was coming back to it. At least it seemed that way to Jessie, who was sure that Forensics had looked through all of this yesterday. But she wanted to get a sense of who Alison was as a person, and not just her things.

Jessie sighed and ran her eyes again over Alison's dresser top. There were no bracelets, no necklaces, no other earrings.

She moved on to the first drawer, which held underwear and socks, some spandex running pants and tops rolled up in the corner. The second drawer was filled with jeans and sweatpants, and the third with sweaters, t-shirts, and casual shirts. Jessie nudged the drawer shut with her knee, turning her attention to the desk, where a day planner lay open. It held Alison McCray's appointments and schedule for the week—she'd planned to meet friends for dinner the day she'd fallen, and the rest of her week was filled with classes, a party, a meeting with her advisor. But she still had time to run, charting her daily mileage and time. She'd planned to run a 10K race on Saturday, and the event was surrounded by red exclamation points. This was the room of a young woman whose life was full, and happy from the looks of it. So why would she dress for a morning run and instead, leap to her death? It didn't seem likely to Jessie. She pulled out her iPhone and took a photo before turning back to Asia. "Anything in the closet?" she asked.

"No jewelry," she answered. "A couple of dresses, a coat, a rain slicker, shoes. Nothing in any of the pockets and nothing like the wrist bands that you've described."

Certain that she was missing something, Jessie tapped her foot anxiously on the floor, the rug swallowing any sound, her eyes drawn down. "I'm just going to check the floor," she said as she bent to her knees and swung her flashlight under the furniture, the light sweeping the area. But aside from her cluttered dresser top and closet, Alison was neat. There was the tiniest bit of dust and nothing else. Jessie sighed. Maybe it was the hair elastics after all. Most women who used them kept one or two on their wrists, and that would definitely account for the marks. But it was just too easy. It couldn't be that straightforward.

She leaned a hand on the edge of the heating unit to help pull herself up when she realized she hadn't looked under there. She bent down and angled the light into the one-inch gap between the heater and floor. The light caught something white stuck in the nubs of the rug. A piece of plastic or, more likely, trash. She'd learned enough to know that a picture was worth a thousand words. She pulled out her iPhone and took a quick photo. If it turned out to be nothing, it would be an easy delete. She reached in to retrieve it, and her mouth fell open as she got a good look. It was a piece of a zip tie. She held it out to Asia. "Part of a police-type zip tie, yes?"

Asia nodded and held open an evidence bag. Jessie labeled it, initialed it, and placed it, along with the other bag, into her work kit.

"Do you think a police officer would have dropped this when they were looking yesterday?" Jessie asked.

Asia shook her head. "Not likely," she said. "Crime scene techs and the detectives are notoriously fussy, and I don't know how you could drop a zip tie under a heater. That one was broken, either pulled apart or cut. Is that what you were thinking might have made some marks on the girls?"

Jessie nodded. "I hadn't even thought of that, but..." The scenario was chilling. "I'm ready to go," she said, "if you are. Do you mind locking up? I want to get to headquarters and get this checked."

23

Jessie texted her findings to Ralph and let him know that she was stopping first at the morgue, so that Roger could compare the wounds to the plastic tie. If this tie and ones like it were the cause of those wounds, then at least two women, and maybe three, had been murdered; their deaths made to appear as suicides.

At the morgue, Jessie took the stairs two at a time looking for Roger, hoping that he was still in his office and not in the middle of an autopsy. When she passed Tony, he raised a hand as if to slow her down.

"Hey, Jessie, where are you rushing off to? No emergencies in here," he said with a sly smile.

She held up her ME work bag. "Evidence, I hope. It's an emergency to me."

"He's in his office," Tony replied. "Lunch later? I'm meeting Al. I think I told you he used to work with us. Left a couple of years ago to go back to school and take care of his mom. He's back now and looking for work, at the BPD maybe. I thought you could add your thoughts or advice."

"Al?"

"The guy who stopped by during Jane Doe's autopsy. He used to work with us. Dr. Dawson never much liked him, but he's not a bad guy. What do you say?"

"Not today," Jessie answered. "Another time."

She hurried up to the third floor and along the hallway where the light from Roger's office spilled into the hall. She could see him hunched over papers, his computer in front of him, clearly deep in thought or research. "Morning, Roger," she said. "I hate to disturb you, but I've got something very interesting."

"Good morning, Jessie. You never disturb me. What do you have? Something to do with our Jane Doe or that young girl, Miss McCray?"

Jessie zipped open her bag and retrieved the two small brown paper evidence bags. "I was just at Alison McCray's dorm room to see if there was anything that might match those wounds, and I came across a couple of potentials. You know more about how to handle this than I do, so I'll pass the bags to you so that you can look at them, and then maybe we can go down to the morgue and check them against the body's wounds, if that sounds okay."

He nodded and motioned for Jessie to place the bags on a side table. He opened the bags and took the first sack that held the hair elastics. He pulled on a pair of gloves, peeled open the folded corners and looked inside. "These are the elastics that women use to hold their hair back. This could be it."

"Hold on," she said. "There's something else as well." She gestured to the bag with the broken zip tie.

Roger took the bag and gently reached for the tie. He squinted before pushing his eyeglasses back on his head. "Well, this changes everything, doesn't it? Let's go downstairs, Jessie. I'll ask Tony to pull the bodies and we'll check these against the wounds."

Jessie's palms were slick with the sweat of anticipation as she gripped the handrail and followed Roger down the stairs where Tony was checking off equipment orders. Roger filled him in on the new evidence and asked him to get Jane Doe and Alison McCray and bring them both to the main autopsy room.

"I'll need you in there too, Tony. I'll need measurements and photos."

Within minutes the bodies, still in their closed body bags, were lined up on the metal stretchers. Tony unzipped Jane Doe first, slipping both of her arms out of the bag, the red wounds on her wrists still visible. Roger stepped up, holding the hair elastic in one hand, a tape measure in the other and compared the wounds to the elastic. He nodded to Tony to take photos, and the only sound was the click of the camera. Jessie watched it all intently, folding her hands behind her back to prevent herself from reaching out and touching anything. Roger paused and took out the broken zip tie, again measuring it and holding it up close to the wounds. To Jessie's inexperienced eyes, the wounds seemed a perfect match to the zip ties. He repeated the comparisons on Alison McCray. Roger was silent as he replaced the tie and elastics back into the bags and initialed and timed them.

"What do you think?" Jessie asked.

"Hmm," Roger said. "The elastic is rounded at the edges. Both victims' wounds are flat, which corresponds to the zip tie. I'd say we definitely have something here. Preliminarily, my opinion is that the zip tie caused those marks on both women. I think you may have found the key to this case, Jessie, and I'm wondering about the cases in western Massachusetts now. We may have to consider exhuming those bodies. You might have given us just the break we need in this case. Nice work, Jessie."

"Western Mass?" Jessie asked.

"Three young girls jumped to their deaths near colleges out there just last year. Two from college buildings, the third from a bridge in Springfield over the Connecticut River. She didn't surface for days, and since she couldn't swim, it was assumed she jumped to her death."

"Or was pushed," Jessie said, thinking out loud.

"Hmm," Roger said. "I'm sure they looked into that possibility. Can I assume you'd like to have a look at those reports?"

A flush of satisfaction warmed Jessie's cheeks as she nodded. "If we can get them."

Roger smiled. "I'll look them up later today."

She slipped the bags back into her work case. "I'm going to

bring these to Forensics. Tony, do you mind emailing them the pictures and measurements so they can get a clear picture of what we found?"

He nodded. "Lunch another day, Jessie?"

She smiled. "As long as you're paying."

Tony laughed. "The story of my life."

Roger shook his head in mock disgust.

At headquarters Jessie bounded into the main detectives' area. Ralph was standing alone at the whiteboard, black marker in hand, his back to her. "Morning, Ralph," Jessie said. "I think we've got a link to both recent so-called jumpers, and maybe others. I have to bring it to Forensics first, but do you want to come with me so you can see it?"

He nodded and adjusted his tie. "Asia Lincoln called, too. I've asked her area sergeant to check back at the dorm periodically to see if our killer returns. I wish we could have someone there around the clock, but we don't have the resources." He shook his head. "Anyway, he went back to the garage. He just might go back to the dorm."

Jessie nodded distractedly, her gaze sweeping the large room and the entrance to Sam's office, searching for a glimpse of him. "Is he in yet?" she asked.

Ralph shook his head. "Not yet. I haven't heard from him either." He glanced at his watch. "He should be in soon. I suppose he could be at court, or with the DA, but he usually lets us know." He seemed to read the concern in Jessie's eyes. "Don't worry, Jessie. He'll be here soon."

But Ralph's words did nothing to untangle the knot of unease in her gut. Sam had said he'd be working with someone he'd been "involved" with. Something was up. She was sure of it.

24

He stood across the street. He'd come to have a look, to make sure he'd left nothing behind, but as he stood outside of the building, his forehead wrinkled. Why was that yellow crime scene tape still up? And the police cruiser parked in front—why was that still here? He stuffed his hands into his pockets, his fingers catching on one of the broken fingernails he'd taken. He should have placed it in a plastic bag by now, but losing his neck chain and cross had unnerved him.

Alison McCray had killed herself—maybe not directly, but it had been her own fault. The snotty bitch. He'd heard people yesterday saying it was a suicide, and the newspapers had reported it that way, so why were the police still hovering around?

He darted through traffic to the other side of the street and stood in front of the dorm. Most students were finishing up finals or had already left for the summer break. He stood nervously, his eyes on the entrance. He wore jeans and a t-shirt today. To a casual observer, he fit right in. He'd even slung a backpack over his shoulder, the way so many undergrads did. He moved toward the building just as a policewoman, her light brown skin a perfect counter to the deep blue of her uniform, swung the door open and stepped outside, her eyelids flickering against the bright wash of sun as she held a cell phone to her ear. She was the same one who'd been with that other woman, the one he'd seen at the garage and then yesterday looking over Alison's body. They'd been there this morning, and the other woman had left with a smug smile. He couldn't let that rattle him. She wouldn't have found anything of his. Zip ties are too small, and she didn't look that smart. Still, it was a worry.

The policewoman smiled as he approached and held the door open for him with her free hand. He nodded politely, grasped the door and tilted his head, trying to catch her conversation.

"Nothing," she said into her phone. "Aside from Jessie's find, nothing else. Forensics were here again..."

She continued walking, out of earshot, and he hesitated. Should he take the chance and follow her? Try to hear what else she was saying? Learn who this Jessie was? No, he thought. He'd taken too many chances already, and at least he had a name now. Jessie. He filed it away in his mind. Besides, she'd hardly glanced at him, and with the sun in her eyes, she'd never remember him, never be able to describe him. Best to leave it that way and not attract attention.

He let the door slide shut and headed for the stairwell. He'd just have a quick look to satisfy his curiosity. But he knew he might just to have to kill again to bring that Jessie into his sights. She could be a threat to him. She was already making him sloppy, leaving things behind. It was her fault. It was all her fault.

If there was one thing he couldn't abide, it was a threat from a snotty girl. She'd just have to pay for her actions. He had to stop her before she stopped him.

25

The Forensics team took the evidence and confirmed that they'd received the photos and emails from Tony. Ralph leaned in for a closer look and whistled. "Any way to know if this is a police-issue zip tie?"

"We'll do our best, but just so you know, police use flex ties, very similar but they're able to be ratcheted tighter." The technician focused his gaze on the bag's contents. "We'll have a better look and see if this is a flex or a zip tie," he called after Ralph and Jessie as they headed out.

"Hey," Jessie turned back. "Any matches to Jane Doe on the cup I dropped off yesterday?"

"Nothing yet. Give us another day or so."

Ralph raised a brow. "You have DNA?"

"I'll explain later," she said, and turned back to the tech. "Can we get a rush on it?"

The tech smiled wryly in reply.

"You do know we have some credible leads on our first victim, right?" Ralph asked.

Jessie shook her head. "No, I haven't heard anything."

"Sorry, I assumed you knew. Some of the other team members are chasing them down—reports on two missing women who match Jane Doe's description."

"I have a lead as well, which has to do with the DNA I just asked about."

"Really?" he asked, his tone surprised.

But Jessie's brain had already connected to her next train of thought. "Not to change the subject, but Sam said you were going to get information about Alison McCray's adoption. Anything there?"

"Not really. It was one of those open adoptions. Her mother was a teenager and the adoptive family agreed to allow her to stay in touch with her daughter. I think all three of them will be coming to town later today or tomorrow. I warned them that we likely won't be able to release the body, but they want to be here. Need to be here, I guess." He shook his head sadly. "Heartbreaking. I can't imagine what they're going through."

Jessie nodded in silent agreement.

"Jessie?" Ralph said.

"Sorry," she said. "I was just thinking."

"Sam just texted. He's still tied up."

Her phone pinged with a message, and she reached for it. *I'll be in soon. Sorry for the confusion. I'll explain later. Xoxo, Sam.* She sighed with relief, a smile draping her lips, the knot in her gut untangling.

"Roger mentioned there were three other girls who were assumed to have jumped to their deaths in western Mass, one of them from a bridge," she said. "I know about the whole copycat theory but I'm not buying it. Women don't jump. They choose less bloody ways to die—pills usually. Anyway, he's going to get the reports for me."

Ralph smiled. "You are something else, Jessie."

Within minutes her phone pinged again, and she smiled all the wider, certain it was Sam once more. But this message was from Carmen.

Some of the women have agreed to meet with the police. But you have to be there, Jessie, and we don't want you to come to East

Boston. We don't want anyone to see us with the police. There's a small diner across the street from the hospital on West Newton St. —Bernie's Café—we can meet you there at 11:00 AM. It will be quiet before lunch, and we should have privacy. Can you make it? Carmen

We'll be there, Jessie typed, looking at her watch. It was almost ten. Waiting for Sam might mean missing the women, and she couldn't let that happen. She turned to Ralph and filled him in on what she'd learned.

"Jane Doe may be Rosa Suarez, an undocumented refugee from Guatemala. And if it is her, she has a little boy—the police found him wandering on Tremont Street not long after she fell. They dropped him off at the ER, and DCF picked him up later. We never made the connection to Jane Doe, and according to Sam, DCF still has custody of him," she said breathlessly. "It's kind of a long story." She shared what little she knew. "I got a DNA sample from the girl who said she is Jane Doe's sister. But you heard Forensics—not done yet."

"Okay, so, these women want to tell us their story. On the record?"

"Yes. They're ready to talk, but I need a detective with me, and I can't wait for Sam, and I'm afraid if I wait for the DNA results, they'll get skittish. Will you come with me?"

"Sam knows about this?"

Jessie nodded. "He does. We were just waiting to hear from the women to learn if they would come forward. They've just texted me. What do you think?"

"That's all I need to hear. I'm in," Ralph said.

"They're afraid they'll be arrested, but they want to find out if Jane Doe is Rosa and they want to get Julio back. And I want to help."

"But we don't know if Jane Doe is this woman," Ralph said. "Let's hope this doesn't turn into a colossal waste of time."

"My gut tells me this is our best bet."

· · ·

Ralph and Jessie arrived at Bernie's Café across from the hospital ten minutes early. "Should we wait in the car?" Ralph asked.

Jessie shook her head. "No. If it were me, and I saw us sitting in a car, I'd think it was a setup. Better if we go in and get a booth."

They headed inside and slid into a large booth at the rear of the dimly lit eatery, the harsh scent of grease, burned coffee and sweat hanging in the air. It wasn't long before Jessie spied Carmen, dressed in her uniform of blue pants and beige blouse, blinking away the sudden darkness as she entered. She was alone. Jessie took a deep breath and nudged Ralph.

"Where are the rest of them?" he whispered.

"I don't know," she said as she waved to get Carmen's attention.

Carmen approached them slowly, her eyes darting over the surroundings before landing on Ralph, who stood and held out his hand, introducing himself.

"I promise you that we're both here to listen and to help," he said, and Carmen visibly relaxed, a slight smile of acknowledgment on her lips.

"Are the others coming?" Jessie asked, motioning Carmen to sit.

"Only Ana and Clara. Lucia is too nervous." She slid into the seat next to Jessie. "She knows more than she's saying. I think that's why she was so angry when you came to talk with us. She's still afraid that we'll all be in trouble, and the others are afraid as well. I have a green card, so I have some protection."

Ralph leaned across the table. "We want to find out if our Jane Doe is your friend. The first step will be to get the DNA results to confirm her identity. Once that's done, we'll notify DCF that we've located the boy's family and we'll use whatever information you can provide to track her killer. He may have been involved in at least one more death. We want to stop him."

Carmen nodded nervously as a tired-looking man, his belly spilling over his pants, his t-shirt stained with grease, approached. "Too early for lunch," he said, wiping his beefy hands on a grimy towel that hung from his belt. "I can get you coffee and muffins. Okay?"

"Yes, thank you," Ralph said.

A shadow crossed the doorway and Jessie looked up to see Ana and Clara standing there, their eyes sweeping the small space. "They're here," she said to Carmen, who went to collect them. They slid into the booth, sitting crushed tight together as Jessie made the introductions. "Ana believes that Jane Doe is her sister," she added.

"This is an unusual situation," Ralph said, leaning back as the food and coffee were set down. "The DNA comparison that will tell us if the woman who died is your sister is not completed yet. I understand how you must feel, and you know that we need your help." He cleared his throat and took out his notebook. The women eyed him warily. "Let me explain," he said. "I'd like you to tell me everything you know, and I'll need to take notes, so I won't forget a word. You are safe. We promise." His gaze tracked to Jessie, who nodded.

"You remember that I took a few notes as well, but please tell Ralph everything you told me, so it's on the official record, and then you can tell us the rest of Rosa's story."

Ana repeated the story of how she and Rosa escaped from Guatemala with little Julio. "A man charged us three thousand dollars to bring us here from Texas. What could we do? We had to get further away from the border to be safe, and so we took his offer. He said we could pay him a little every month, but that changed. He wanted more money and then more, and sometimes he wouldn't come for a month, but mostly he came every week or so and it was hard to have enough to give him to keep him happy. But we all tried. We all worked and saved. Rosa had been doing cleaning at the colleges. She worked in the dormitories and class-rooms, sometimes at night and sometimes during the day. She taught herself, and then us, English, by reading the books the students left around."

She paused and blinked away the tears that rimmed her eyes.

"She took Julio to work with her when none of us could watch him." She coughed nervously. "I thought—we all thought—it was the man who brought us here from Texas in his van who hurt her. He's not a good man, and he seemed the only one who might kill. Maybe as a message to the rest of us."

"Can any of you describe this man?" Ralph asked.

"Yes," they whispered together.

"He's from Guatemala," Carmen went on. "He's one of us, but he's not a good man. His hair is dark, his eyes are dark. His mood is always dark."

"That's not much to go on. We'll try to have an artist work with you to see what we can get. What about the van?"

"Just white, that's all."

"No signs, no lettering?"

"No."

"License plate? Have you noticed the state?"

"I have," Clara said. "New York. It says New York."

Ralph nodded. "So, you all think he's the one?"

Ana shook her head. "I don't know. Lucia says it is someone else. Rosa had confided in her—shared a secret that she kept from the rest of us, probably afraid that we would not believe her. She told Lucia that she'd seen something bad a few months ago. A girl was pushed from a window and she fell to her death. Rosa kept quiet about it, afraid to say anything, afraid that she'd be arrested or blamed or worse. Finally, she spoke to Lucia about it and told her she was going to meet a policeman who said that he'd seen her the day the girl fell, and he needed her help to solve the crime." Despite the full heat from the grill and ovens just a few feet away, Ana rubbed her arms as if to ward off a sudden chill.

Jessie and Ralph locked eyes. *The zip ties.* "Policeman?" Ralph asked.

Ana nodded. "He promised her a green card and she believed him. Lucia can tell you more, but she said Rosa planned to meet him on Sunday, God's day—the safest day of the week, we all believed—and she took Julio with her." She looked to the others and they nodded their agreement. "We were all working on Sunday, and we didn't notice until the next day that she and Julio hadn't returned. When Carmen saw the news story with the description of the woman who'd fallen, we worried that it was Rosa, but what could we do? And where was little Julio?" She sank a little in her seat, breaking off a piece of muffin and crumbling it between her fingers.

Carmen placed her hand on Ana's shoulder. "When I saw the small notice about the missing boy, I knew that it was Julio and that we had to speak with someone." She turned to Jessie. "You see how bad this is? If the police are involved, we are all in trouble."

"Did Rosa tell Lucia what the man looked like?"

Clara shifted in her seat. "Only that he wore the uniform of a policeman and he had a badge."

Ralph scribbled in his notebook before looking up. "I understand your fear, but we will find..."

Jessie's pulse quickened as Ralph continued, but her mind was already churning out possibilities. Was it a policeman who was involved, or maybe a security guard? That would account for the zip ties. She remembered Sam saying a security guard had closed off the area around Alison McCray's room. Was that the connection? But Sam would know the difference between a policeman and a security guard. Still, they were getting close. She could feel it. Rosa was the connection to the college girls.

"You understand how we feel?" Ana asked. "A policeman is a policeman to us. If he can kill Rosa, he can come after the rest of us." The three women looked away.

"We can protect you, but the best way to do that is to find this man, and to do *that*, it sounds as though we need Lucia's help," Ralph said. "You have to speak with her. The only way to stop him is to find him before he hurts anyone else."

But he already has, Jessie thought. *We have a serial killer out there somewhere.*

26

Ralph had stepped outside to call his contact at DCF and see what he could find out about Julio. It wouldn't be easy, but with any luck, they could help to reunite this little family. "We can trust him?" Ana asked when he'd left.

Jessie leaned forward, her elbows on the table, her eyes on the three women who sat across from her. "You can trust him with your lives. I promise you that he is a good man and a good detective, but I'll be honest, everything depends on the DNA results."

"But can't I just see her? I'll know if it's my Rosa," Ana said, her voice cracking.

Jessie gripped her hand and swallowed the lump in her throat. "You may not recognize her even if it is Rosa," she said softly. "She was banged up pretty badly in the fall."

Ana's hand flew to her mouth as if to catch a cry that hovered there.

Clara pulled Ana into an embrace. "Maybe it's not Rosa. You have to be positive."

Ana forced a small smile and dabbed a tissue at her eyes.

"As soon as we have the DNA, we'll talk about you seeing her. Fair enough?"

Ana nodded.

Carmen checked her watch. "I hope you understand but I have

to get back to work," she said. "I only get thirty minutes for my break. I must get back before someone misses me. I can't afford to lose my job."

"It's okay," Jessie replied. "I'll take care of Clara and Ana, and we'll get them back home after we've figured some things out. And I know the detectives would like to speak with them a little more." She gripped Carmen's hand. "Thank you, Carmen. Thank you for everything."

"We thank *you*," she said, slipping her hand from Jessie's and heading for the door. "*Adiós*," she called as she left the small place.

Ralph slipped back into the booth shaking his head. "Bad news. DCF has legal custody, and they won't let us see him without some kind of proof that Ana is his aunt."

Ana swiped her hand across her red-rimmed eyes. "But how?"

"They've agreed to consider submitting a sample of his saliva for a DNA test. I told him our lab was working on Ana's sample to see if it's a match with our victim. The child has a legal advocate assigned to him. I'm going to meet him now and put forward our case. If he agrees that this is compelling and we can help identify the child, we can get started today. If not, I'll need a court order. So," he began to stand as he spoke. "I'll get going. Jessie, can you get back to headquarters on your own?"

"Don't worry about me," she said. "I'll be fine. Just keep me posted."

Once he left, Ana turned to Jessie. "I... I have to tell you something. The woman who fell is not my sister. My DNA will not match hers. But it will match Julio's. He is my child."

"What the...?" Jessie began.

"The rest is true. She is my friend and I had to work in a kitchen on Sunday. She was to watch my son, and then when she was called to work, she took him with her. She'd taken him before. It had never been a problem." Ana's voice quivered as she spoke, her hands trembling as she pushed back the hair from her face.

Jessie sighed heavily and shook her head. "I don't understand why you would lie about this."

"When we left Guatemala, we decided to say that we were sisters. That way, if anything happened, we thought that we would be able to stay together."

"I don't understand why you wouldn't have said that from the start," Jessie repeated. "And you're Julio's mother? Why couldn't you just come forward and say that?"

"Because I'm here without papers," Ana said, tears streaming down her face. "You could take my child away and send me out of the country. I was terrified. I decided it was best to tell you that I was his aunt. I knew that my DNA would prove that connection. I need to have Julio with me, and if Rosa is not the woman who has died, we need to find her. Will you help us?"

"And where is Rosa's child? You said you were both pregnant." *And the woman in the morgue gave birth at some point.*

"Her baby died. She was tiny and she couldn't breathe on her own. She was beautiful, a perfect angel of a baby, but she died three days after she was born. Rosa's heart was broken and she saw that as a sign that she had to leave Guatemala."

"Do the other women know that she is not your sister?" Jessie asked.

"Only Clara," Ana said. "I told her last night. She said I had to tell you, that when the DNA came back you would know anyway that Rosa was not my sister."

"So, we don't have a way of confirming ID on the woman who died?" Jessie asked angrily.

"But we do. Clara watches those crime shows. We have Rosa's toothbrush with us." She passed her a small plastic bag, a toothbrush inside. "You can test that. She is Rosa Suarez, and I am her best friend. Please, can we see her?" she asked in a trembling voice.

Jessie reached out and took Ana's hand. "I'm sorry you've had to go through this, but you have to promise from here on in to tell us the truth. Agreed?"

Ana nodded.

Jessie knew she'd have to tell Ralph about this right away. At least they could probably prove that Ana was Julio's mother. The lies would still be a problem. If Jessie wanted to work full-time with the police, and she was certain now that she did, she had to recognize lies when she heard them. Some people had perfectly good reasons to protect themselves, and Ana was surely among those. Early on, when she first started with the police, Sam had warned her. *Everyone lies*, he'd said. He was right, but Rosa Suarez —if that's who she was—still deserved to have her questions answered and her killer found.

She stepped outside once again to call Ralph to fill him in.

"Damn it," he said, irritation evident in his tone. "Are you certain she's telling the truth now?"

"I am, Ralph. I know they've told me the real story just now. And they still say her name is Rosa Suarez. That hasn't changed. They brought her toothbrush. I can drop it off at Forensics. If Ana turns out to be Julio's mother—and after hearing her story, I believe she is—that will give us more leverage with DCF. And if he was with Rosa, he may be a witness to what happened."

"I guess so," he said. "I'll keep my appointment with the advocate and push that end of it."

"They still want to see the woman in the morgue. What do you think?"

"No. We aren't sure yet who she is, or who they are. Our other leads, by the way, fizzled. Descriptions, stories, nothing matched." He paused and she could almost hear his mind spinning theories. "Call Tony," he finally said, "and see if he can get a couple of photos they can see. But I don't think they should see her body, not until we get an ID on her. Maybe they can connect us with her family in Guatemala. That would be a start."

"I hadn't even thought of that, but you're right. I'll check with Tony to see if I can bring Ana and Clara to the morgue to see photos. I'll see you later at headquarters?"

"Yeah," he muttered, his mind already on something else.

When she slid back into the booth, Ana fixed her gaze on Jessie. "I want you to know we just hoped to make a better life. We didn't mean to lie, and I never meant to hurt anyone."

"I know," she said softly. "But here we are. And I have to ask—do you think that Rosa saw something that put her in danger?"

"I believe Lucia," Clara said. "She was nervous about telling us, but she finally did and now she's nervous about telling you and the police. You must remember—Rosa told her the police were involved. And you are the police."

Jessie looked away and drummed her fingers on the table, trying to control her anger. She couldn't understand why they'd lied. But she'd never been in their shoes. She took a deep breath. "We're not going to be able to see the woman in the morgue, but I'll call Tony, the man who works there, and see if he can come up with some photos."

Ana nodded, a tear streaming along her cheek. "If she is my friend, I'll know."

Jessie hesitated. "I'll make a call," she said as she slid from the booth and headed outside to call Tony to explain the situation.

"No problem," he said. "I can find the least shocking photos, maybe a couple from the less damaged side of her face."

"Okay. Can I bring them now? We can meet you in the family room."

"Give me five minutes."

Jessie headed back inside and smiled. "We're all set," she said. "But photos only. At least for now."

The three of them darted across the street through traffic and into the morgue, where Jessie swiped her ID on the card reader and stopped at the reception desk. She held up her ID. "I'm Jessie Novak. I work with Tony and Dr. Dawson. I'm here to see Tony."

"He told me you'd be coming. The family room is ready and if you follow me, I'll show you where it is." They followed the woman, her heels clicking on the freshly polished floor. They turned a corner into a large room furnished with a comfortable couch, a couple of club chairs and a small table that held several bottles of water and a box of tissues. The soft light of a lamp cast a warm, comforting glow on the space. "Just have a seat," Jessie said. 'I'm going to find Tony. I'll be right back."

She headed back to the reception area, running right into Tony. "Hey," she said, "the two young women I told you about are here. Got the photos?"

He slipped a small stack of black and white photos from a manila envelope. "I thought black and white would be best, less blood and gore."

Jessie flipped through the photos, peeling off the grimmest, leaving only three photos which showed the left profile of the woman's face. "This looks pretty good, Tony. They might be able to ID her from this. If she does, can she see her?"

Tony shook his head. "Sorry, Jess. Not yet, anyway. I'll have to check with Dr. Dawson." He followed Jessie into the family room and introduced himself before sharing the photos.

Ana held the photos in trembling hands, tears rolling along her cheeks as she stared at the images. She looked up, her eyes red and swollen, her face blotchy with tears. She opened her mouth to speak, but a racking sob escaped instead. She pulled herself forward, clutching the photos close to her chest. "It is my Rosa," she said. "Rosa Suarez."

Tony stepped back, allowing them a few moments, before nodding to Jessie. "I'm sorry to say this," Tony said, "but I'll need the photos back." Reluctantly, Ana passed them back. She sniffled and turned to Jessie. "What next?"

"Forensics. We have to wait for the DNA results once I drop the toothbrush off."

"But what about my Julio?"

"Ralph is working on that." She placed a hand on Ana's shoulder. "Just have faith, and I promise we will do our best to get him back to you once the DNA confirms everything. I hate to rush you, but we can't stay here. Are you ready to leave?"

"Not yet," she said, clutching a gold chain at her neck. "Rosa has a chain with a cross just like mine, a gift we gave each other. Where is that?"

Jessie looked closely at the cross. It was almost identical to the one around Rosa's neck. "The detectives have it. We'll get it back to you or her family at some point." Jessie moved closer to Ana. "It's important that you talk to Lucia. Please tell her that she must share what she knows with us. From what you and Carmen said, it sounds as though Rosa confided in her, and if she has any information about the killer, she has to share it. Please talk to her tonight and tell her how vital it is for all of you to help us find this man. We cannot let him kill again."

Ana nodded and gripped Clara's hand so tightly, her knuckles went white with the effort.

27

Jessie arranged an Uber to take Ana and Clara home, and once they were safely on their way, she called another to get back to headquarters. "Hey, Ralph," she said, turning into his cubicle, "Ana ID'd Rosa Suarez."

"From the photo?" he asked.

She nodded. "And I've been thinking about the connection between Rosa and Alison and the others," she said, "and I believe that college is the common denominator. I think just as Lucia told them, Rosa saw something at her work. I don't think she would have been targeted otherwise."

"Yeah, makes sense. I'm hoping that Forensics was able to get something—fingerprints or DNA from that glove and that piece of zip tie. I'm not convinced our perp is a cop, but I think he may be a security guard who floats to campuses wherever he's needed. I'll ask Sam to put someone on that—find out which agencies cover colleges. That's our best start for now," he said.

"Any news on Julio?"

"His legal advocate has agreed to a DNA swab. He's sending it over today. So, we'll see if it matches the woman who claims to be his mother. Her DNA, by the way, didn't match Rosa Suarez, or whoever she is."

"But that supports Ana's story. And she said it would match

Julio's. I think we're still looking at Rosa Suarez and some kind of college connection. Which reminds me, I wanted to check my email to see if Roger sent me the reports on the three alleged suicides in western Mass." Jesse slid into an empty chair, logged on at a computer and smiled when the email from Roger appeared. She clicked on the attachments and hit *print*. She quickly scanned the reports, searching for the evidence of red marks. She exhaled noisily and leaned back. "Ralph," she called. "Come and look at this."

"Whoa," he said, looking at the autopsy reports Jessie had found. "Definitely too similar to be a coincidence."

"Is Sam in?" Jessie asked, trying to keep the excitement from her voice. She hadn't seen him last night and he hadn't been in the office that morning. And the fact was—she missed him. Her heart raced a little at the thought of seeing him.

"He must be back by now," Ralph said. "At least, I hope so. We have a lot to catch him up on."

Jessie made her way through the main detectives' workroom and turned the corner into Sam's office, but it was dark. Where was he? She turned back to one of the detectives sitting at a desk. "Hey," she called. "Any word from Sam?"

He looked up and smiled. "Still with the Feds, I guess."

"The Feds?" she asked. *Still?*

"FBI," he replied as Ralph stepped up behind her.

"Forensics just called," he said. "We've got a break. Fingerprints and DNA from that glove you found, Jessie, and some touch DNA from the zip tie. Looks like the zip tie is going to have only Alison McCray's DNA, and the glove fingerprints and DNA likely comes from our killer. Forensics is trying to see if we have a match on him anywhere, and some good news—it's not a police-issue flex tie. It's the kind you can get at Home Depot or any hardware store." He paused and looked around. "Sam back?"

The other detective shook his head. "Not yet. Popular guy today, I guess." He stood and gathered a pile of papers into a folder. "See you two—I'm covering a dangerousness hearing for Sam."

"I'm going to go over to Forensics. I want to meet Julio's guardian when he gets here. Are you going to wait for Sam?"

"I guess I will. I want to bring him up to date. Maybe I'll call Roger and see if he has any other information on the three girls from western Massachusetts. I'd also like another look at the two college girls from the last few months. We have seven dead now. Hard to believe that they're all suicides."

She leaned forward to pick up the desk phone and called the ME's office. Roger was at a meeting, but Tony said he could help. "No problem, I'll call the Westfield office and get the detailed reports and photos. And you want the copies of the recent girls' autopsies? You think these are all related?"

"I do."

Tony chuckled. "You were meant for this job."

"Thanks, Tony. You're the best."

"You aren't telling me anything I don't already know," he said. And she could almost hear the laughter in his voice.

She hung up and was about to start an internet search on women's suicide when she heard footsteps approaching along the hall. She sat up to listen. Someone was humming. She smiled. That was a happy tune if ever she'd heard one. The humming drew closer and then stopped. She looked up to see Sam in the doorway, a look of surprise on his face.

Jessie jumped up. "Hey," she said, standing on her toes to plant a quick kiss on his lips. "I've missed you. Where were you?"

"I... I was working. The old case I told you about." He ran his fingers through her hair. "I missed you too, Jessie. Seeing you just now made me realize how much."

"I heard you humming. You sounded happy."

"I did, didn't I? I guess I was."

"Care to share the reason?"

"The reason is you, Jessie Novak. It's all you."

But Jessie was certain she'd heard some hesitation in his voice, as though he'd paused to think of what to say. She took a deep breath. She had to stop questioning things. Sam loved her and she loved him, and that was enough.

Or was it?

28

Jessie brought Sam up to date on the investigation. "I think the three college girl deaths here are related to Rosa and the ones in western Massachusetts. Similar red wrist marks. I think we have to get out there, or at least get their police reports. Tony's going to get the photos and complete autopsy reports and email them—maybe you could request the police investigation notes. There are just too many coincidences in these cases, seven of them now. We need to combine these investigations. Don't you agree?"

He pulled her into his arms. "I agree and I'm glad you remember. There are no coincidences in homicide investigations. I'll get on it. I wish I could see you tonight, but..."

"The federal case, right?" she asked, nestling her head into his shoulder. "It's alright, Sam. Actually, it's perfect timing. I want to look through all the autopsy reports and photos, mark up all the similarities, and I want to do it sooner rather than later."

"But you still love me, right?"

"I do love you, Sam."

He sighed dramatically. "It's so good to hear that."

"I'm famished," she said, kissing him lightly on the lips. "So, I'm gonna head out. I can get something to eat and maybe stop by the morgue to pick up the photos and reports so I don't have to print them out at home. I'm sure that Tony will have better quality than my crappy printer can deliver. I'll see you tomorrow," she whispered.

Sam pulled her closer. "You will see me tomorrow, for sure. You'd see me tonight if I could manage it."

She smiled, pushed him gently away and gathered the reports that she'd printed and turned back to Sam. "If you see Ralph, tell him I'll see him tomorrow."

She headed out and stopped quickly at the morgue to pick up the reports and photos that Tony had requested.

"You just missed my friend, Al," he said, a wrinkle lining his forehead.

"Your friend?" And a light went on in Jessie's brain. "You're trying to fix me up with this guy, aren't you?" She laughed as she said it.

"Yes, I am. Just say yes."

"Tony, I have a boyfriend, but if I didn't, I'd say yes. If you like him, I know I would."

He shrugged. "You can't blame a guy for trying to help out a friend."

"Thanks, Tony." She held up the folder he'd given her. "I know I've said it before, but I really do owe you."

"Don't think I won't collect one of these days," he said with a wink.

Once home, Jessie peeled off her clothes and pulled on her running gear. It was a perfect day for a run, not too warm, the sun fading already. A run was the only thing that really cleared her head, and she needed a clear head to go through the reports and photos she'd brought home. She'd been so involved in the cases, and with Sam, she hadn't had the time, but today, there were no excuses. She pocketed some money and her keys, slipped her sunglasses on and headed out.

She knew she'd likely have company today, for surely there'd be more people walking and jogging—those runners and walkers who only ventured out in the late spring and early summer, never in the heat of full summer or bitter cold of the long winter or even the cooling days of fall, but they added a welcome vibrancy to the scene. Another layer of life was emerging from the long, dark days of winter, set against the soft blooms on the trees and tiny budding flowers, all under the warming blush of the sun. This wonderful new season was a welcome contrast to the death and misery in the morgue and the ER, and Jessie knew that, soon, on the first really balmy day, people would be shoulder to shoulder at the local beach, eager to soak in the full heat of the sun on their pasty winter faces. The sun was just beginning to fade as she crossed to Day Boulevard and the stretch of road along the beach, the mist which always seemed to hover at the ocean's edge curling off the shoreline.

She pumped her arms, her feet flying over the road, the nearby caw of seagulls and the hum of traffic the perfect accompaniment to her almost Zen-like state of mind. She ran loops around Castle Island, stopping only when the scent of fried clam and burgers reminded her that she hadn't eaten all day. She retrieved money from her pocket and stood in line at Sullivan's ordering a clam plate and a bottle of water, carrying both outside to one of the small tables along the water's edge.

She sat and ate and watched as a group of laughing young boys struggled to slide wriggling worms onto fishing hooks before throwing their lines over the pier and dropping to sit cross-legged, their eyes fixed on the water, to wait for a bite. A sudden shriek from one of the boys jolted Jessie from her reverie. "I've got one," he shouted, standing up and pulling on the line, his little back rigid as he worked furiously to reel in his catch. A small crowd had gathered and watched as the boy pulled his line up, revealing his catch —a soggy old running shoe. The crowd groaned; the little boy frowned.

Jessie sat up straighter, an idea taking hold in her mind. Once the endorphins kicked in, running was like dreaming. The runner's high was real, so real a runner didn't always notice what was going on around her. And that, she was sure, was how Alison McCray's attacker had gotten into the dorm. If she'd entered through the back exit after her run, she'd bypass the front reception desk, and someone could easily slip in right behind her and Alison had likely never even noticed.

Until it was too late.

29

FRIDAY, DAY 6

Obsessed with figuring this case out, Jessie had stayed up late going over the autopsy reports and photos that Tony had provided. Of the girls in western Mass, all three were college students, all pretty, smart. Two lived in dorms, the third in an apartment. The first one—whose death was only listed as suspicious—was said to have fallen or jumped from the ninth floor of a college dorm. The second was reported to have jumped from the twelfth floor of the UMass library. The third was assumed to have jumped from a bridge in Springfield during a run. None of the deaths made sense, but the last one especially bothered Jessie. Runners ran, not just for the exercise and fitness benefits, but for that runner's high—that burst of feel-good endorphins that kicked in at about the third mile and lasted long after the run was finished. Jessie knew it well. And just as with Alison McCray, this was a red warning light. None of these girls had jumped. She'd bet her life on it. She finally crawled into bed sometime after two in the morning, the photos and reports spread out around her.

She woke with a start, her sheets bunched at the foot of her bed, her skin slick with the night's humid air, but despite the heat seeping into her apartment, she felt a sudden and unmistakable chill. She had an eerie feeling that someone was watching her. She pulled her sheets back up and around her and peered through the blinds. The neighborhood was just shaking off the long, hot night, people stirring, nothing out of the ordinary, no one suspicious. It must have been a bad dream.

It was seven a.m. when she pulled herself up and out of bed, stretching before heading for her shower. Once she'd dressed, choosing a straight skirt to pair with yesterday's pink blouse and pumps, she took one last look in the mirror and smiled. Her days of wearing jeans and t-shirts at headquarters were over. The detectives all wore suits; Sam's tie was often loosened but otherwise he was perfect, and Ralph's polished look was hard to beat. Jessie smoothed her blouse and leaned closer to the mirror. The woman who smiled back was far more confident than she'd been just months ago. Love could do that for you. Well, that, a slim skirt, a pair of heels, a swipe of lipstick, and a job that she loved.

She called Roger as she walked to her car to fill him in on the potential ID on Jane Doe, the progress in the investigation and the decision to include the alleged suicides in western Massachusetts in their investigation. But as she was speaking, a shadow off to her side caught her eye. She stopped. Someone was following her. Her eyes scanning the street, she turned slowly but there was no one there. The shadow had faded as well. God, was she imagining things now?

"Are you there?" Roger asked.

"Yes, sorry," she said. "I think Sam is going to contact the state police detectives for their reports, and Tony requested the photos and other documents, but it might help if you'd speak with the ME in the Westfield office—let him know about the zip ties, see if he'll have a second look."

"Will do, Jessie, and thanks for keeping me posted. Any final decision on doing this with us full-time?"

"To tell you the truth, I've been too busy to finally decide, but I'm pretty sure..."

"Well, I have to say that sounds to me more like a yes than a maybe."

She laughed and asked if he wouldn't mind calling her once he'd spoken with his colleague in Westfield. "If he has anything else, he can probably send it electronically, right?"

"Absolutely. I'll ask my secretary to email them as soon as they're in."

"Secretary?"

"Her office, sad to say, is in the basement. But she says she likes the quiet. She transcribes my dictation and does the paperwork for death certificates. You'll have to meet her one of these days. She can likely do reports for you as well."

At headquarters, Jessie slipped in quietly and approached Ralph. "Any word on Julio and the DNA?"

"Just heard. It's a match. Ana was telling the truth. She's his mother, and the DNA from the toothbrush you brought in matches our victim. Seems she is Rosa Suarez."

"Did you tell Ana?"

"I did. She'd already resigned herself to the identity of our victim, so, though she's sad about Rosa, she's grateful for finding Julio."

Jessie smiled. "Can we pick him up? Reunite them? Talk to him?"

"Whoa, slow down. Not yet. But Ana said that she's found her government-issued ID from Guatemala. She has Rosa's, too. She found them hidden away in the bottom of her dresser. She's on her way with the IDs."

"So, that's it, right? We can just pick him up, reunite them."

Ralph shook his head. "No, this is a process. I've called the state-appointed guardian. We're going to see him this morning at DCF. We'll bring the paperwork and Ana, but remember the state still has custody. The guardian's going to speak with their child psychologist to get a handle on how to proceed, and I've put a call in to our Crimes Against Children Unit for assistance."

"Why all the hoopla?"

"To protect the child. Right now, the state believes the child was abandoned. The onus is on us to prove otherwise."

Jessie groaned. "Does Ana know?"

"She will when she gets here."

"Oh damn, I hate waiting. Julio and Ana need to be together. It's been days."

"And a day or two more to confirm everything won't hurt."

Jessie sighed. "I know." She sank into one of the chairs and told him about the three cases from western Mass. "All three had fingernails broken off and all had those red wrist marks. I'm certain these cases are related to ours. We definitely have a serial killer on our hands."

"If we're sure it's the same killer, we do."

"I'm sure," Jessie said. "Have you spoken to Sam this morning?"

"He came in right before you," he replied playfully. "Go on in."

"Let's both go and fill him in."

They filed into Sam's office. He was sitting behind his desk, engrossed in reading printouts. "Hey," he said, looking up. "You're just in time. I read your reports and spoke to a homicide detective in the state police about the three college students in their jurisdiction.

"They haven't closed their investigations yet," he continued, running his fingers through his hair. "And these seven deaths have all occurred within the last year. But the last two have happened within a week, and if it is the same guy, his behavior is escalating. We have to find him fast before he does it again. I have a meeting with the commissioner to discuss the possibility of putting out an alert for female college students to keep an eye open for strangers."

"But what if he's not a stranger?" Jessie asked. "What if he's somebody they know? I'm hoping Lucia comes in today. She has information about a possible security guard or maybe a policeman, the man Rosa met up with. And what if he is a security guard or a policeman? Of course they'd feel safe with him."

"I'll bring that up," Sam said.

"Just got a text," Ralph said, looking down at his phone. "Let me make a quick call and I'll be right back. I want to check something out."

"What about you, Jessie?" Sam asked. "Anything from Roger?"

"The autopsy reports on the three girls outside of Boston all describe the same red wrist marks and broken fingernails. Did you see anything else in that report from the state police?"

"Nothing more than what I just said. No real evidence at the scene. I think at this point the autopsy reports are our best evidence that these deaths are connected."

Ralph strode back into the room. "Sorry about that." He turned to Sam. "Jessie and the Guatemalan women told me about a man in a white van who comes to collect money they allegedly owe him for getting them up here from Texas. I alerted the patrol cars in East Boston to be on the lookout, and he actually showed up late yesterday just hours after I put out the word. They picked him up for questioning and it turns out he drives between Boston and New York to collect money from the women and kids he's brought up from the border. Anyway, he's under arrest now for extortion and human trafficking, but his alibi for the murders checks out. He's been in New York for a week. He was arrested there Saturday for threatening a man at a bar. He was released on Monday, but he stuck around for his bail hearing which was the day before yesterday. He only arrived in Boston yesterday morning and thought he'd hang around here for a while. He wasn't happy to be picked up so quickly, but it doesn't seem likely that he was involved in the murders. He claims to know nothing about the students, or their deaths, and I believe him. The detective who questioned him said he couldn't even pick out Boston University or UMass Amherst on a map. He claims he's been in Texas shuttling other asylum seekers and refugees up to the northeast. They're checking on that now, but I think we've pretty much ruled him out, unless something comes up to rule him back in."

Jessie nodded. "Well, there's still that man who showed up at the ER to ask about Rosa. I don't think he ever called you guys, did he?"

Sam shook his head. "Only calls we got were complaints about the garage. A couple of calls from women about the victim. One caller asked if we were setting up a GoFundMe page for any survivors. Other than that, no information, no queries about whether she survived or not."

"What about that doctor at the scene? The press put out that request for him to come forward to help. Did he?"

"You're right," Ralph said. "We never heard from him, and we did speak to the EMTs. Just as they told you, they were too busy to really identify him. Do you think you could identify the man who presented to the ER asking about her?"

Jessie shook her head. "Not really. Average, I guess. Brown hair, jeans, yellow teeth and the scent of old cigarettes on him. Nothing else. It had been a really busy day, so I wasn't paying attention to him beyond the fact that I was probably a little irritated that he came to the ER to ask how she was. I'm sure he picked up on my irritation. I remember he left pretty quickly when I suggested he call the police."

"What about the girls' friends? Did they have anything to add? Any old boyfriends who had held grudges, or were angry? I mean, there's got to be a motive somewhere, or are these murders random? It just doesn't seem that way."

"I don't think they're random," Sam said. "But of the girls, four had steady boyfriends, all of whom had alibis. The other two were single—they were apparently focused on studies and school. I mean, it could be a college student, but he's hit six different colleges now. We're missing something."

Suddenly the door swung open and a patrol officer poked his head in. "You guys have a couple of visitors. You ready?"

Jessie turned to see Ana and Lucia in the doorway, their eyes wide, their mouths turned down, their faces pinched.

30

"Lucia, I'm so glad you came," Jessie said, moving to Lucia's side.

Ralph stepped forward and stuck out his hand, introducing himself.

"Thank you for coming. Are you ready to help us, to tell us what you know about Rosa Suarez?"

"But what about my Julio?" Ana asked before Lucia could speak. "I want to see him. I thought he'd be here." She was almost shouting, her eyes darting around the room.

Jesse took her hand. "Not yet, Ana. He's safe, and we're working on getting you to see him and helping to bring you both back together. It's hard to understand, but we have to take it one step at a time. If you have your IDs, we can make copies and fax them to DCF and keep copies in our file as well. I know this has been very hard—losing your friend—but Julio is okay. This will all be okay."

Ana closed her eyes and offered the faint nod of someone who's been disappointed and let down at every turn.

"Why don't we get those IDs copied?" Ralph asked. "And then we can sit and talk to Lucia and get to work on finding out what happened."

Ana and Lucia followed Ralph silently while Jessie held back with Sam. "I'll be right there," she called, before turning to Sam. "You look tired. Is it your federal case?"

He sighed. "It is. I just want to get it finished and get back to my own work." He stood and leaned down, brushing his lips against Jessie's.

"Are you going to join us on this interview?"

"No, you guys go ahead. Just keep me posted."

"Will I see you tonight?" she whispered.

"I wish I could, but not until this other case is done." He kissed her forehead and sat back behind his desk.

Her shoulders slumped. "I'll miss you." She blew him a kiss and left his office, wondering why this damn case took so much of his time. She grabbed a pen and notebook and hurried to the interview room where Ralph and Lucia were just settling in.

"Is Sam joining us?" Ralph asked.

Jessie shook her head. "He's still wrapped up in that federal case. He said for us to go ahead without him. Where's Ana?"

"Speaking with our Crimes Against Children officer and faxing her ID to Julio's guardian," Ralph said. He turned to Lucia, her brows knitted, her eyes angry slits, her arms crossed tight across her chest. Her body language told Jessie that Lucia still didn't trust them, and her words confirmed that.

"Before we start," Jessie said, "I just want to say how sorry I am that you've lost your friend. You've been a good friend to protect her, but now it's time to speak up, to help us, to help her."

"I agreed to tell you what little I know to help," she said, "but I don't know much."

"You might know more than you think," Jessie said. "And as you believed, we've confirmed that the man in the white van who extorted money from the women has a solid alibi, so the other man that you told me about—the policeman or guard—is someone we're interested in. Anything that you can tell us will help."

Lucia looked around nervously as though searching for an exit. Finally, she uncrossed her arms and looked down. "I'm just afraid. What if he knows about me? About all of us?"

"That's where we come in," Ralph said. "We need to track this guy down and stop him."

Lucia nodded, and began. "A few weeks ago, Ana came to me and said she wanted to tell me a secret. She said she had to tell someone, that she couldn't hold it in anymore. She said that one of the girls who had jumped to her death from a college classroom a few months back hadn't jumped at all—she'd been pushed, and Rosa saw it all. She was afraid to speak up, to tell anybody, because she had no papers, no visa, nothing, and she knew she was the one who'd be in trouble, not the man. She saw his profile only quickly when she tried to slip away but she was sure that he had seen her, that he knew who she was. She saw his uniform—a police uniform, she said. A man to fear. So, she kept it to herself and she tried to stay away from that college."

"Which college?"

"Northeastern," Lucia whispered.

"Close to the garage where Rosa fell," Jessie said softly.

Lucia sat a little straighter. "After a few months, her boss told her that she couldn't pick and choose where she went to work, and so she had to go back, and that very first day there, a man approached her while she was working. He wasn't in a uniform, she said, but he told her he needed her help, that he worked with the police, and they knew the girl hadn't jumped and needed Rosa's help to trap the man. She was afraid, but he told her that she would be rewarded with a green card and her immigration problems would be over. When she told me about it, I was suspicious, and she reminded me that I am suspicious of everything. Rosa was determined and said this might be her only chance to get a green card." Lucia hesitated and wiped away the tears that had begun to pool in her eyes.

"Take your time," Jessie said.

"He asked to meet her last Sunday, somewhere downtown. I don't know where, but it was to be late Sunday morning and Rosa thought, what could be safer than a Sunday morning? Ana had already left for work, and none of us was able to watch Julio, so Rosa took him with her."

"What time did she leave?" Ralph asked.

"I left at nine thirty, so she left sometime after that. She said she had to take a train and two buses. She left a note that she would be back in the afternoon, but she never came home, and we thought she was working and had Julio with her. But on Monday—after the news reported a woman had jumped from that garage—I told the others. Carmen promised to speak with you, Jessie. She said you were an ER nurse who worked with the police and we could trust you."

Jessie nodded. "You can trust all of us."

"But what if this man really is a policeman, will you still help us?" She turned to face Ralph, her eyes boring into him.

"Yes. I can assure you that we will help," he said. "We want to find whoever is responsible for this murder. We will do everything we can to find him. Do you have any questions for us?"

She shook her head and mumbled to herself before looking back to Ralph. "Just find the man who did this. Rosa was a good woman and someday, Julio will want to know what happened." She stood then and turned for the door, her hand on the knob. "Thank you for helping to return him to his mother," she said as she opened the door and headed back to Ana.

"Her information is a start at least," Jessie said.

"I agree. And I think that a policeman would just use his standard-issue flex ties, not zip ties, though I guess I might be wrong. Still, I think Sam was right. We need to check on companies that supply security guards to the colleges in question."

"Sam said a security guard was on the scene at Alison's dorm. He apparently helped to secure the scene, but I wonder..."

"I'll check and make sure we have his name and contact information."

They went in search of the women.

31

They found Lucia and Ana sitting with a plainclothes female officer who stood and held her hand out when she spied Ralph. "Good to see you, Ralph," she said with a hint of a Spanish accent. She was small, not much taller than Jessie's five foot three. Her dark hair was pulled back into a neat bun at the nape of her neck. She wore jeans, a blouse, and running shoes—the kind of clothes designed to put children at ease. She turned to Jessie. "I'm Paulina."

"I'm Jessie," she said, sticking out her hand. "Nice to meet you."

Paulina nodded. "We've copied the IDs and faxed them to the legal guardian. He's going to let us know if we can come to the DCF offices. If all goes well, we'll try to get an emergency hearing to get Julio home. Just so you know, a child psychologist who works with DCF and with us here in the children's unit will be there as well. We hate to have things be this crowded, but better safe than sorry."

"No problem," Ralph said. "We're ready when you are. Do you think there's any chance we could talk to Julio today—maybe show him some pictures?"

"Let's see how it goes, and we'll hear what the child psychologist says. We've done criminal checks on both of these ladies, and they check out fine. They understand we're not interested in their immigration status, only in solving this murder and reuniting this mother with her child."

At those last words, a trace of a smile brightened Ana's face.

Paulina's phone beeped with a message. "Be right back," she said as she hurried away, holding her phone to her ear. Within minutes, she returned and nodded to Jessie and Ralph to join her in the hall. "DCF has received the DNA results and Ana's ID, and I've discussed that he may have witnessed the woman's fall. So, they will allow us to come in with Ana. Their child psychologist will introduce Julio to Ana to see what happens. The rest of us will only be allowed to watch through a viewing window. It would be too confusing for Julio if there's a crowd in the room. So, we'll take this one step at a time, and if he reacts positively to Ana, they'll start legal proceedings to reunite them. They may ask for an emergency hearing."

"I have photos I'd like the boy to see. Any chance of that?" Ralph asked.

"Not graphic, I hope?"

"Not at all, no views of the victim. The photos have been scrubbed so they are just views of people from a distance."

"Alright. The psychologist will speak with you both and if she deems it safe, we'll proceed from there. Just be prepared, this could take all day."

Once they arrived at the DCF office, they were joined by Linda, the child psychologist, and Gerry, the guardian. Ana sat nervously tapping her feet on the tiled floor, her eyes searching for Julio.

They sat around a low table and listened as the DCF team explained the process. "Julio knows you are here, Ana," Gerry said. "We showed him your photo ID and he shouted *mamá,* so we are going to bring you to a room where you can see him."

Ana let out a soft cry, her hands clutched at her chest. "Now?"

"Yes," the psychologist said, leading her from the room.

Gerry directed Jessie, Ralph and Lucia to another room where a large window revealed the room next door where Ana was just settling in, sitting alone, her feet tapping the floor. Just then, a door opened, and Jessie watched as Julio entered, his head down, his little hands scrunched deep in his pockets. He was shuffling in the way of an old, sad man. Jessie's heart broke and she rested her palm flat against the window as if she could reach out and hold the little boy to her own chest.

They all watched as Ana gasped and Julio looked up, his mouth dropping open, his eyes wide. "*Mamá!*" he screeched. Ana reached for him, pulling him so close there seemed not a millimeter of space between them.

Jessie's own heart fluttered with the joy of that moment. She leaned her forehead against the glass and wiped away the lone tear that streaked along her face. And she wondered, for the hundredth time, how a mother could willingly leave a child.

"Are you alright?" Ralph asked, interrupting her thoughts.

She hadn't even realized that she'd been holding her breath. Inhaling deeply, she turned to him. "I'm fine. Seeing this makes a lot of things worth it, doesn't it?"

Ralph nodded. "Not sure we'll be able to speak to him today, though right now, this reunion is more important."

"We'll see what the team thinks," Gerry said from the doorway. "But it will be a while. You might want to go out for lunch, or coffee, or go back to your office, and we'll call when—and if—you can speak with the boy."

Lucia cleared her throat as if to remind them that she was still there. "Lucia," Gerry said, "of course, you should remain here. Ana will need you, perhaps Julio as well. He may need the security of another familiar face."

"I would like..." Jessie began, hoping to see Julio as well. But she was interrupted when the psychologist entered the room.

"Things are going well," she said, smiling. "But Julio is asking about Rosa, where she went that day. Ana has tried to explain that Rosa is in heaven, but he's clearly got more questions, and Paulina and I think this might be the time to ask him what he remembers, to get him past the worry."

Ralph heaved a sigh of relief. "Can we go in?"

She shook her head. "Absolutely not. This requires an experienced child investigator. Paulina will fill that role, and I will be there as support and to stop the questioning if Julio seems upset. I'm sure you understand."

A ripple of unease settled in Jessie's gut. "Any chance I could see him? I took care of him..."

"No, we want to keep new people, strangers, to a minimum. This has been a tough time for the child."

Jessie was about to speak up, to say that she wasn't a stranger, that they'd bonded in the ER, that he'd remember her, but she caught herself. This wasn't about her. This was about Julio.

Ralph passed the photos to Linda, who flipped through them to be sure they were child-friendly. "As you can see," Ralph said, "they are just crowd shots, the victim has been filtered out."

The psychologist took the photos and they all crowded around the window to watch as Julio, snuggled onto Ana's lap, began to answer the questions in the natural way of a three-year-old. He seemed to remember very little, only that he'd taken a train with Rosa, and she'd told him to wait.

Jessie's eyes were riveted to Julio. He must have been terrified that day; no wonder he wouldn't speak. Her heart broke a little more. She watched as he shook his head at the first photo and Paulina moved to the second photo—a close-up of the back of the man who was doing CPR, the man who'd told the EMTs that he was a doctor. At the periphery, a couple of other men stood alone. One youngish man with a backpack slung on his back, the other an older man in a suit.

Paulina spoke softly in Spanish and they watched as Julio's index finger circled the men and then he stopped and smiled. "Him!" he shouted.

Jessie and Ralph exchanged glances. "The doctor," she whispered. Ralph nodded and they watched as Paulina turned the next picture face up. Julio chose the physician again but on the next photo, he hesitated before pointing to the young man with a back-pack. On the final photo, his little finger landed on the old man in a suit, a shopping cart at his side.

Ralph exhaled noisily. "He's too young to remember. I was afraid of that, but maybe it's for the best that he doesn't remember."

Julio nestled further into Ana's arms as Paulina left them to join Jessie and Ralph. "Gerry's gone to arrange an emergency court hearing to get Julio back to his mom," she said. "But I'm afraid there's nothing else for you guys here."

And Jessie sighed, relieved, but maybe a little disappointed that Julio was fine without her.

32

"What do you think?" Jessie asked Ralph as they slid into his car for the ride back to headquarters. "Should we re-interview the witnesses at the scene, see if anyone remembers the doctor or can identify him?"

"We did ask. No one could describe him. We never did speak with the doctor, or whoever he was. He left before anyone could get his name, and he hasn't responded to any of our public requests to come forward to help. He certainly might just be a busy young doctor, but we still need to find him." He fastened his seat belt and backed up. "Can you track down the medics again and speak with them? Maybe they can add something about that doctor for us. Which reminds me, that man who showed up at the ER to ask about Rosa. Could you identify him? Maybe he's the young man with the backpack in the photo."

"I don't know. Maybe. They both have brown hair, but the young man with the backpack just doesn't look familiar to me at all."

"We still have loose ends. The gold cross—Rosa had one around her neck, Alison had one clutched in her hand. Coincidence? I'd hoped Julio could give us more, narrow this down." He heaved a sigh and tapped his fingers against the steering wheel.

"Sam was going to contact the team in western Mass that

worked the cases there. Think he's finished with his FBI work? Maybe we can..."

"We'll see," Ralph said as he pulled into the parking lot at headquarters.

They headed upstairs to fill in the rest of the team. Jessie dropped her bag and turned toward Sam's office just as his door opened. He stood there, rubbing his back, his white button-down shirt rumpled, a bead of sweat tracking along his forehead, his eyes crinkling with a smile. Jessie smiled in return. How she wished she could throw her arms around him, but this was work and their relationship was a well-kept secret. Only Ralph knew that they were a *thing*. "Hey," Sam said, "got anything new for me on our murders?"

"Yes, we do," Jessie said as Sam and beckoned them inside.

"Give me ten minutes," Ralph said. "Got a couple of things I want to follow up on." He winked at Jessie before heading for the hallway.

Jessie followed Sam inside, closing the door quietly with her foot. He turned and pulled her into an embrace. "What a day already," he said. "I'm so glad to see you, to hold you."

"Nice to see you too," she whispered. "Maybe dinner tonight?"

"Oh God," he said. "I wish, but the team is planning meetings with the US Attorney to prep for the trial which starts on Monday."

"Is it a case I might know about?"

He shook his head. "Old case, murder and terrorism charges dating back about three years. But fill me in. How did your little boy do?"

"Ahh, he's back with his mom, so that's good. I don't think he can identify anyone for us, but he'll be okay. He's a well-loved little boy."

"Which raises the question—have you been in touch with your mother?" Sam asked as though he could read her mind.

She hesitated. Though Sam knew the story of her mother, she'd shared little else. He'd always known his mother, he'd had that close relationship, and the very word likely evoked homey, loving images for him. But for Jessie, the whole mother thing was complicated, and she'd kept her deepest feelings close, separate from Sam and everyone else. She wasn't even sure she needed a mother now. The world was full of haves and have-nots where mothers were concerned, and she was long used to being a have-not. That was likely the root of her insecurities, her anger, her impatience. Maybe it was just too late to create a close relationship with her mother. Or maybe she should just stop feeling sorry for herself and allow her into her life. She was torn, afraid that allowing her mother in was a betrayal to her dad who'd worked so hard to raise her alone. But he'd died several years ago, and Jessie was left without a family. It was all just too much, too complicated to think about. At least for now.

She rubbed the back of her neck and offered a faint smile. "A text here and there, but no calls yet. I've needed time, I guess, to accept her and her story. And... I know I should call her. I will. Once this case is over, I will."

A rap on the door interrupted her thoughts. "Okay to come in?" Ralph said as he joined them, taking the chair next to Jessie. Together, they filled Sam in on what they'd learned from Lucia and Julio.

"So," Ralph said, "aside from an ID on Jane Doe, we don't have anything new. Could be a thousand guys or could be one of the men the boy pointed out. We're getting in touch again with the young man with the backpack. He was a witness to Rosa's fall, and he stayed to speak with the officers who responded. Same with the old man in the suit. The doctor, however, is another story. Still hasn't responded to public requests to come forward to assist us. I'm putting my money on him."

"You're thinking he wasn't a doctor?" Jessie asked. "That he started CPR and pushed the EMTs to get her to the ER right away as a cover? Hmm. I wonder if that means someone saw him and he was creating a diversion that allowed him to get away. He kept his back to the street cameras, so we never got a view of his face."

"I wondered," Ralph said, "if perhaps he wasn't the man who

showed up at the ER to ask you about the woman's condition? Though I suppose if he knew she was dead, why would he ask? Still, it's something to consider. Once he saw the EMTs start working on her, he might have worried that she was alive after all. So, we have the presumed doctor, the security guard and the man who came to the ER, but at least we've eliminated the trafficker. That's one down. We'll have to focus hard on the others."

Jessie cleared her throat. "I got the autopsy reports on the three deaths from western Massachusetts, and they all had those red marks on their wrists—impressions, really—from what were assumed to be due to the elastics that many of us wear on our wrists." She snapped the one on her wrist to prove her point. "Sam," she asked, "any word from the state police on those girls? Anything to link them to ours?"

"Eerily similar to the girls here," he said. "No connection to one another at all. Different schools, different majors, totally different lifestyles. One girl was a partier, another a pre-med, the third had no major yet. No friends in common, no activities in common, nothing. I know that the wrist marks, in retrospect, are red flags, but at the time they were so faint they weren't even considered."

"Any with gold chains?"

Sam gave her a puzzled look.

"Rosa was wearing one and Alison was clutching one in her hand. It may be just a coincidence, but... I don't know."

"So, no drugs on board, or any other injuries?" Ralph asked.

Jessie shook her head. "No. Just as with the girls here, all negative. They all died on impact from the blunt force trauma suffered in the fall. Rosa was the only exception. She was dead when she fell, and I think that Lucia was right—Rosa knew something about the other deaths, or at least one of them."

"I have another detective on that," Sam said. "He's with her supervisor now trying to get her assignments for the last year. It's been tricky. Our warrant is in process, but that will take time, and I want to get this information quickly. We know that she witnessed the murder at Northeastern, so we can focus on the list of security guards who were at Northeastern on that day."

Jessie leaned forward, her elbows on his desk. "What about the security guard you spoke with at Alison's dorm after she fell? Did you get his information or his name?"

"I pointed him toward one of the officers and asked him to leave his information. To tell you the truth, I don't know if he did or not. I was too focused on everything else. Ralph, will you check the witness file and see if we have his information?"

Ralph nodded and jotted in his notebook. "We'll need to talk to this guy and to the young man with the backpack at the scene of Rosa's death."

Jessie leaned back, running her fingers through her hair. "It is absolutely chilling to think that some bastard would kill all these girls. But there's got to be something we're missing, someone maybe connected to each of them but peripherally, so he's escaped notice."

"You're right. We've got to work out a motive," Sam said. "Why these girls? Aside from Rosa, they were all college girls, all young and pretty, did well in school, had lots of friends, so why target them?"

"Maybe that's exactly why they were targeted. They were all pretty and popular and sometimes people envy that," Jessie said.

Ralph shook his head. "Envy enough to kill?"

"People have killed for less," Sam said. He pushed back from his desk and stood. "But the state police are going to have another look at their cases and they'll be in touch. On that note, I have to get to the US Attorney's office." He slipped into his suit jacket, his gaze sliding to Jessie. "I'll call about dinner. Okay?"

Ralph stood and headed back to his own desk. "I'll see you out here, Jessie," he said, striding from the office and allowing them another private moment.

Jessie nodded and stood, smoothing her skirt. "You're beautiful today," Sam said softly.

A flush of color warmed her cheeks. "Thanks," she said,

blowing him a kiss. "See you later." He drew his hand along her back as he moved towards the door, his touch making her skin tingle. She took a deep breath and headed back to work.

An hour later, she and Ralph had made no headway in reaching the backpack man from Rosa's scene. Ralph had left a message, while Jessie checked on the scene notes from Alison McCray's death to see if there was any information on the security guard that Sam had mentioned. But she'd had no luck either and considering how late in the day it was, and a Friday to boot, Ralph decided it was best to wait. "Maybe we can catch up with them tomorrow. Are you available?"

Jessie nodded.

"We'll talk soon," he said as he checked his iPhone. "I'd like to get home at a decent hour for once." He waved as he headed out, and Jessie soon followed, her thoughts on dinner with Sam and a cool shower to offset the stifling heat that still lingered in the air.

She pulled onto K Street and into a spot right in front of her house, marveling at her luck as she locked the car and started up the stairs. Before she could push open the front door, Rufus appeared.

"Oh, Jessie," he said breathlessly. "I'm so glad you're home. Something bad has happened."

His hand went instinctively to the raw spot on the back of his neck where she'd broken the chain when she'd pulled. How could he not have noticed? That damn girl had what his mother had always cherished—her gold chain and cross. She'd valued that more than she did him, her only child. She'd been the one to tell him he'd never amount to anything and to stop mooning after those pretty, popular girls. "They'll never give you a second look," she'd said with a sneer. He laughed. They're looking at me now, Ma. He wished he could see her reaction, but she was dead and buried and just where she belonged. Six feet under.

And her cross didn't matter anyway. Maybe he'd replace it, but it wasn't urgent. What was urgent was that bitch, Jessie. He wondered how much she'd figured out already. She was a smart cookie, that one, but he was smarter still. He needed to flush out her details—where she lived, her habits, her routine and how to use that to his advantage, so that when he turned the tables, he'd be in full control.

To do that, he had to move quickly. He hadn't been in any rush to kill again, but now he had to, not just for the thrill, but to bring Jessie into his sights once more.

Jessie stood perfectly still, her eyes quickly surveying Rufus to check for injuries or obvious illness, but aside from the glaze in his eyes, he seemed fine. "What is it?" she asked, a tinge of worry in her voice. Rufus was her dearest friend, her protector, her voice of reason. She took his hand, the skin weathered and thin, almost translucent, the whorl of his veins showing through.

"It's Fluffy," he said, his lip trembling. "Oh Jessie, she's gone."

"Gone?"

"She passed this morning. One of the neighborhood boys took her and buried her in the yard for me."

"I'm sorry, Rufus." Jessie's heart ached for him and she held his hand tightly, not sure what else she could say.

"A part of me thinks Mary probably wanted Fluffy with her after all this time. I knew I had to be ready to let go. It's just that she's been a good companion for me all these years." He wiped away the tears from his eyes. "I'm lucky I have you, Jessie."

Jessie swallowed the lump in her throat. "You'll always have me. I'm sorry I wasn't here for you." She headed for the kitchen. Despite the heat, she knew that a cup of tea and her company was just what he needed.

Jessie's phone pinged with a text from Sam as she set the kettle to boil. *Ready for dinner?* Her shoulders slumped a little, knowing that she couldn't leave, but there'd be other dinners.

She texted back that she'd have to cancel. *I'm so sorry, something's come up with Rufus. Maybe this weekend you can sneak away from your meetings to see me.*

I'll try, he texted back. *I miss you already, Jessie.*

"You're sure you're not supposed to be somewhere?" Rufus asked.

She placed her hand over his. "I'm right where I'm supposed to be, Rufus. I'm not going anywhere." She reached for the cups and teabags and set them on the table, missing the swish of the cat's tail and the soft padding as she wandered through the rooms, often settling on a chair in the kitchen.

"You're a good friend, Jessie. I don't know what I'd do without you."

35

SATURDAY, DAY 7

What was that? And there it was again—an insistent buzzing. Jessie sat upright, her eyes adjusting to the dim glow of the television. She'd fallen asleep, still dressed, on her couch. She began to stretch when the buzzing seared through to her brain. Her phone. She reached for it, a familiar number blinking on the screen.

"Hello?" she said groggily.

"Hey, Jessie, it's Ralph. Sorry to wake you," he said. "But I pulled the short straw and I'm the detective on call for Homicide this weekend. I just got a call that we have another jumper, so we really need you at the scene."

"Oh, no," she answered, suddenly wide awake. "What time is it? Where is it?"

"It's almost three a.m., and she's in an alley off of Washington Street, right behind one of those student apartment buildings," he said. "Right by those clubs the kids go to—and a block or so from your ER."

Jessie was already on her feet and in the kitchen, splashing water on her face. "Give me five minutes," she said. "I don't live too far from there."

"Medics on the way, too," he said. "Just in case."

"Like Rosa," Jessie whispered.

"What?" he asked.

"Nothing," she said. "I'll see you there."

She grabbed her keys, her ME bag, and a bottle of water and took the stairs to the street two at a time. The neighborhood was quiet, the Friday night partiers long gone. Jessie threw her things into her car and sped along the deserted streets to the scene on Washington Street. A bevy of patrol cars and an ambulance, all with lights flashing, told her she'd arrived. She pulled in by the alley and stepped out, grabbing her bag before following the two EMTs who'd also just arrived.

"Over here," a patrolman called. He was perched atop the roof of a car, where a body lay, hanging over the edge. A crowd of detectives and patrolmen hovered nearby. Someone turned on the klieg lights, putting the scene and everyone, including Jessie, into full, clear view. "Get a stretcher," the cop shouted. "She's alive."

The EMTs ran for their equipment as Jessie raised her arms so she could be hoisted to the car's roof. The girl was on her side, one leg bent under her, one arm dangling over the side of the car, shiny blonde hair covering her face. Jessie leaned down and pushed the hair back as she felt for a pulse. The patrolman was right—the girl was alive. Jessie's own pulse quickened. The girl was breathing, and as Jessie leaned closer, her eyes, wild and frightened, snapped open momentarily before closing again. She opened her mouth as if to speak, but the effort proved too much and only a heavy sigh escaped her lips.

"We're going to get you to the emergency room," Jessie whispered. "I'm a nurse. I promise you you're safe."

"Hey, Jessie," one of the EMTs shouted as they arrived with the gurney. "Help us move her, will you?" With the help of the policemen, Jessie and the EMTs managed to get the girl onto the stretcher. Jessie slid from the car's roof and ran behind, jumping into her own car as they loaded the woman into the back of the ambulance.

"Hey," she called, holding up her phone. "I'll call it in and ask them to page Tim Merrick."

"Thanks, Jessie," an EMT called out as they secured the stretcher in the back of the ambulance. "See you there."

Jessie made a quick call to the ER, alerting them that a critically injured patient was on her way. "Please page Tim Merrick, stat," she added.

"He's already here," the nurse replied. "We had a gunshot wound."

Jessie groaned. "Is he going to the OR?"

"No. He just pronounced the poor guy. He's in the lounge, drinking coffee. I'll tell him you called and asked that he stay."

"Thanks," Jessie said, hanging up and yanking open her car door.

"Hold on, Jessie," Ralph shouted, jogging toward her.

He looked especially rumpled, as though the heat and the ungodly hour had affected him too. "She's still alive?" he asked.

"Just barely, but alive," she said, sliding into her car.

"Anything else?" he asked, whisking away a pool of sweat from his neck.

"Not yet. I'll keep you posted," she said as she closed the door and pulled into the street, her foot leaning heavily on the gas pedal. Minutes later, she steered her car into the ambulance bay and raced inside.

"Trauma One," a security guard shouted as she hurried past.

She pushed open the door to the trauma room and stopped. The team was already working quietly over the girl. Someone had started an IV, another was hooking her up to a monitor. The respiratory technician was placing an airway and oxygen mask over her face and the x-ray tech was setting up his portable machine. Tim Merrick was overseeing it all.

"Ortho on their way?" he shouted without looking up. He was examining the girl's abdomen and thinking out loud, as he always did. "After we get some films of her extremities and neck, we'll get a CT scan to assess her belly and chest before we take her to the OR. I'm not sure if she has any internal injuries yet. She might be lucky—it seems like that car roof broke her fall."

Jessie felt herself heave a sigh of relief. Tim looked up and nodded when he saw her. "Do you ever have a day off?" he asked.

"I could ask you the same," she answered, smiling.

"Well, then, make yourself useful. She'll need another IV and labs, and maybe you could check her hemoglobin?"

"I'm on it," she answered, pulling on exam gloves and reaching for the equipment she needed. She moved to the patient's right side and placed a tourniquet on her arm, looking for veins, and then she froze. A familiar red indentation circled the girl's wrist. Jessie reached over and lifted the other wrist and saw an identical mark. Several of her fingernails had been torn away as well. A chill ran up her spine.

"Tim," she said softly, "I'm just going to get a quick photo of the marks on her wrists and her fingertips, and then I'll do the IV and labs, okay? I'll explain later." She slipped her iPhone from her pocket and quickly snapped a few pictures, making sure to have the girl's hospital wristband visible in the photo. Jessie looked closer. The girl was still listed as an unknown female. She slipped an IV catheter into the girl's arm, withdrew the necessary blood samples, attached a bag of fluid and headed to the small lab by the trauma room to check the hemoglobin, which would give them an estimate of her blood loss.

"Six point zero," she read aloud. She hurried back and informed Tim of the hemoglobin level as he and an orthopedic surgeon looked at the x-rays on the lighted viewing box.

"Her c-spine looks good," Tim said. "A couple of long bone fractures and a pelvic fracture," he added.

"Any signs of sexual assault?" Jessie asked.

"No, clothes and underwear were intact," Tim said as he directed the team to ready the patient for transfer. "We're heading to CT scan, and then the OR. Will you make sure the blood bank has six units ready, and let the OR know we'll be up soon?"

"I will," she said, lifting the phone and watching as the team hurriedly bundled the patient up and rushed her through the door to CT scan. Once she'd made her calls, she peeled off her gloves and surveyed the room, the debris clear evidence of their efforts to save the girl. Jessie said a silent prayer, hoping that she would survive and let them know what had happened, and even perhaps provide a description of her attacker.

She called Ralph next to fill him in. "She'll need a guard to keep her safe," Jessie said.

"I'll send someone down. Can you stay until I can assign someone?"

"No problem. I'll watch over her."

Jessie hurried to her locker to change into scrubs and make her way to the OR waiting area. She left a message at the front desk to overhead-page her when the patrolman assigned to watch the victim arrived. She grabbed a cup of coffee from the staff lounge and headed to the OR, the elevator and hallways eerily quiet. She glanced at her watch. It was four fifteen. The sun would be up soon. She swiped her ID to gain access into the OR area and slipped into the waiting room, sinking onto one of the bizarrely bright orange vinyl couches. She sipped her coffee and flicked through a magazine, but nothing held her interest. Her attention was drawn back to this girl and to the others. This last girl made number eight. There had to be a connection, or maybe he was just taunting them—a catch-me-if-you-can killer. She sighed and threw the magazine down. They'd find him. They had to.

"Hey, what are you doing here?" a familiar voice asked, breaking into her thoughts.

36

He stood back, making sure to stay hidden in the darkness, and he smiled. This was definitely his favorite part, watching them all scurry about. He may have been rushed, but it had worked out alright, at least so far. It was never good to get ahead of himself. He needed to calm down and think and just enjoy this moment and remember. It was their eyes he remembered best, the way they looked to him for help, for mercy. The power was all his. Just as it should be.

As he was watching, a steady surge of light filled the scene below—an artificial burst of daylight—though he was still safely hidden in the darkness above. He moved on his belly a little closer to the edge of the roof, the roof opposite the one that he'd pushed tonight's girl from. They'd never look up, not until the body had been taken away and the fluorescent lights dimmed. He'd learned that much.

But for now, the light illuminated everything and everyone in the alley. He recognized a detective and a patrolman from another scene. And then, just as he'd hoped, Jessie appeared. He recognized her dark brown curls, the soft sweep of her shoulders and the teasing, sultry way she moved. When someone called her name, she turned, almost in slow motion, and he was riveted. And then he froze.

It was her—that nurse from the emergency room, the one who wouldn't share any information about Rosa as though it was a damn state secret. He recalled that smug look in her eyes when she told him to call the police for information. The bitch. He made sure to memorize the curve of her lips, the porcelain skin, the same smug look in her eyes. Were they blue or green? He couldn't tell, but he kept his eyes on her as she turned to the body, her fingers on the girl's neck, her ear over the slack mouth, and suddenly Jessie was moving again and shouting.

"She's alive! Get the medics! We need to get her to the ER."

He watched the ambulance back into the alley, Jessie shouting that she would call it in and meet them in the ER.

Damn it! That was what happened when he moved too quickly. This girl had landed on the car instead of the pavement and that had likely saved her. But it wasn't his fault. It was that miserable bitch, Jessie.

But he knew her first name, what she looked like and where she worked. It would be easy enough now to make her pay. They weren't his mistakes, after all. They were hers.

37

Jessie looked up to see Tim Merrick, his scrub mask pulled down, bits of hair sticking out of his surgical cap. She sat up straight. Had she fallen asleep? She checked her watch. Almost five a.m. The color drained from her face. "I'm waiting. What are you...?" she asked.

Has she died?

"Are you alright?" Tim asked.

She bit back the lump in her throat and stood. She wanted to face the news, bad as it might be, head-on. "Is she..." But she paused, the words unspoken.

"Dead?" Tim asked, his brow furrowed. "No, she's actually doing okay, considering what she's been through."

"Why are you out here then?" Jessie asked. "Doesn't she need a trauma surgeon?"

Tim shook his head. "No, her only injuries are orthopedic. Complex bilateral leg fractures, a pelvic fracture, some bruises and lacerations, but that's it. Orthopedics is managing those injuries, and she has nothing else. No brain injury that we can see on CT, and her abdomen and chest are clear. Believe it or not, she's stable and holding her own."

Jessie sank to the couch, a bead of sweat trickling along her forehead. "You're sure, Tim?"

He nodded and sat next to her. "Sure enough that I'm going to go home for a shower and a nap. What about you? Are you heading out?"

"No, I'm here to keep an eye on her until a police guard arrives. She's the first survivor. We have to keep her safe."

"First survivor?"

"The presumed jumpers? Like the woman on Sunday? They're not jumpers, they're murder victims."

Tim pulled his surgical cap off and ran his fingers through his hair, smoothing down the unruly tufts. "Wow. Want me to stay?"

"No. The police will be here soon. And our guy likely thinks she's dead. I'm betting the police won't release any information that might let him know she's still alive. But we need to be safe, and we also have to ID her and inform her family."

"Can I at least get you some coffee?"

She shook her head and pointed to her cup. "I'm all set, and with any luck I'll be back in bed in a few hours."

Tim stood. "Alright, I'll be back later but I have my beeper if you need me."

"Thanks, Tim," Jessie said. He raised a hand as if in salute and she watched as he turned and walked through the swinging doors to the main corridor. She leaned back, a kind of relief sweeping over her. *This girl was going to be okay!*

She wanted to text Sam, but it was probably still too early. She'd call him in a few hours. She texted Ralph with the update.

Great news! Patrolman Cyr is on his way in. Go home and get some sleep. I'll call you later.

Not on your life, she replied. *Are you at headquarters? I'll be in as soon as the patrolman gets here. I want to see everything we've got on this case. I'll sleep later.*

Just then, the overhead speaker crackled to life, breaking through the almost eerie quiet and asking Jessie to call the ER front desk. She grabbed the hospital phone and dialed. The clerk advised that the patrolman had arrived.

"Can you ask him to just check in with Security and they can bring him up? I'm in the OR waiting room. Thanks," she said, and hung up.

The patrolman arrived and showed her his ID while Jessie introduced herself and explained the situation. "So, we just have to be really careful," she said. "I don't think this guy realizes that she's alive, but I'm going to stop at the admissions office and speak with the administrator on duty and make sure that she's just designated *patient X*. We need to protect her and block any information from being released."

"Got it," the officer said. "I asked Security to keep an eye on all entrances and exits as well."

"She'll be going to Recovery once she's out of the OR, and then likely the ICU. I'm going to get over to headquarters. I'll make sure Detective Thompson arranges relief, so you get a break and then get to go home at the end of your shift."

"Thanks, Jessie," he said. "I'll take good care of your girl."

She headed out just as the sun was nudging up over the horizon. Jessie made the drive to headquarters in record time, arriving before six. But as early as it was, the parking lot and corridors were already bustling. She guessed it was true. *The city never sleeps.* At least, not in ERs and police stations. She found Ralph and several other detectives hunched over computers, discarded coffee cups all over the desks and every available surface.

"Hey," Ralph said as she approached. "Nice work tonight, Jessie. How's our girl?" He crushed a Styrofoam coffee cup and lobbed it into a nearby wastebasket, smiling when it hit its mark.

Jessie smiled. "Holding her own so far," she answered. "Do we have any ID on her yet?"

"We do. Sarah Gorman, twenty-two years old, just graduated from Boston College and moved into that apartment. She's been waitressing at a nearby bar, and that's where she was earlier. We tracked down a friend of hers who was at the bar."

"Family?"

"Still working on that. Her friend thinks her family live in New Hampshire, but she wasn't certain. I've got a call in to the college to see if they can help, but I'm sure they won't even get the message until later. I might just send a car over there in a while to light a fire under them. I know it's Saturday, and most students have left for the summer break, but I don't want to wait until Monday for this information."

Jessie smiled. "Anything else? Any evidence at the scene? Any witnesses? I know that's too much to hope for, but I have to ask."

"Nothing so far on any of those fronts. Her friend didn't notice anyone bothering her or following her later. We're checking the neighborhood cameras to see if we can pick anything up. This case is still early. We don't know if she has an angry boyfriend or anything along those lines, and it doesn't seem like it was a robbery. She lives in that building but her apartment was still locked. Her keys and a bag with her ID were on the stairs as though she'd dropped them. Somebody lured her or forced her to the roof. But, as you can see, we don't have much else."

"It's only been a few hours," Jessie said. "In the ER, I noticed the same red marks on her wrists that the other victims had. She had some missing fingernails, too. I got some photos of the marks and her fingers. So, somebody restrained her wrists, broke off a couple of fingernails and got her up there before she was pushed off. I think it's the same guy. Any chance Sam will be in today?"

"I don't think so. He's still involved in prepping for that federal trial." He pushed away from the desk and reached for his suit jacket. "I think we should both be getting home for some shut-eye. What do you say? See you later this afternoon?"

"I'll be back," she said, and reminded him about arranging relief for the policeman watching Sarah Gorman.

"Already taken care of."

"If it's okay with you, I'd like to go back to the scene later. I think he's returned to at least one scene, and I'm just wondering if he'll do it again. And just so you know, I've made the girl a *patient*

X, which means no information is to be released at all. It's as though she doesn't exist. There's no information anywhere that she's a patient at BCH."

"That's great—thanks, Jessie. I'll see you back here later. Go home and get some sleep."

She nodded and headed to her car, coming to a stop when she stepped outside. Despite the early hour, the sun was almost too bright, the air already thick with heat. Today was going to be a scorcher.

38

Jessie slept fitfully, her windows open, a fan running, but the unrelenting heat and city sounds still seeped in and clung to every corner of her apartment. Her sheets were soaked, her skin slick with sweat when she finally gave up. After a cool shower, she pulled her hair into a topknot, pulled on a light sundress and a pair of sandals, and brewed a pot of coffee. She grabbed a sweater just in case, as she dared to hope that the air-conditioning was working at headquarters. She knocked on Rufus's door on the way out to see how he was faring. When he pulled open his door, a cool waft of air wrapped around her.

"You have air conditioning?" she asked.

"I sure do. It's the only luxury I've ever allowed myself. You want to come inside?"

She swiped away a fresh line of perspiration from her back. "I do, but I'm on my way to headquarters, and since there's no AC in my car, it's better if I don't get used to it."

"You don't have it upstairs, Jessie?"

"I don't. Maybe I should price a unit. They just always seemed too expensive—a luxury that I couldn't fit into my budget."

"Don't be putting things off, Jessie. You got to be good to yourself. If you need an air conditioner, you should get one. We can ask your friend Sam to put it in."

Ahh, Sam, she thought, a new wave of heat surging through her. She could only nod.

"Well, until you get one, you're welcome to sleep here. I have a second bedroom. It's filled with stuff, but I can clear it out."

She leaned in and planted a kiss on his cheek. "You are the best, Rufus. Since you're doing okay, I'll get going. I'll see you later but let me know if you need anything."

At headquarters, the air conditioning sputtered to life only intermittently; a refreshing blast of cool air was soon followed by stagnant heat. Jessie fanned herself with Sam's file folder as she pored over the reports. She leaned back. There just wasn't anything new. She wanted to text or call Sam. What she really wanted was to hear his voice, feel his touch, lie next to him. She didn't understand why she couldn't see him for even an hour. She sighed. Ralph wasn't in yet either. She felt lost without her team.

She walked over to Forensics to see if they'd got a DNA or fingerprint match to the glove she'd found on the roof. "Nothing yet," the technician replied. "He's not in the system, but trust me, he'll make a mistake. We'll get him. Sometimes, you've just got to be patient."

She thanked him and wandered back to the detectives' area. She sank into one of the chairs.

"Hey, Jessie, get any sleep?" Ralph asked as he arrived looking refreshed in short sleeves, perfectly groomed hair, and a comfortable smile. He carried a bag of donuts, the grease leaking through.

"Not much. Too damn hot," she said, fanning herself with the file folder. She was tired, but it was a good kind of tired. It wasn't from the heat or the exhaustion of being woken up in the middle of the night to be called out to a scene. It was the fact of changing the case from a homicide to a rescue. She smiled. She was good at this. No, she wasn't just good at this; she was really good at this. Maybe this last case was the sign that she should leave the ER, maybe work there part-time and become a full-time member of the Homicide unit. She did seem to have a knack for it. But now Ralph was standing over her, waiting to discuss the investigation. "I spoke with Forensics," she said, her eye on the bag of donuts.

"I remembered your love of donuts," he said, placing the bag before her. "Got these for you."

Jessie leaned forward and plucked a frosted cruller from the bag. "Thank you," she said through a mouthful of sweet dough. She hadn't even realized how hungry she was until she'd spied the donuts.

He sat down next to her. "Anyway, I asked about last night, too. The only fingerprints and shoeprints we managed to get were from the girl. Our man scrubbed that scene, or just took great care. We have one smart guy."

Jessie raised a brow. "Not smart enough. She's alive. We can outwit him with that. As long as he believes she's dead..."

"Good point. How is she?"

"I haven't heard anything, but she was stable. I think I'll stop by to check on her. Has anyone reached her family?"

"Yes, the police in New Hampshire reached them and told them that we weren't releasing any information and asked them to please keep it quiet for now, but to get down here to see her. He was blunt, told them that her attacker believes she's died, and that might just give us the upper hand. And God knows, we need a break in this case. That glove and tiny bit of zip tie that you retrieved are all we have so far."

"We do need a break. I think I'm going to head to the hospital to see her. Want to come along?" She licked the last of the glaze from her fingers and pushed her chair back from the desk.

"I do. I'd like to speak with her family, and maybe with her if she's awake and able."

Ralph insisted on taking his air-conditioned car to the hospital and Jessie happily acquiesced. At the hospital, they took the elevator to the fifth floor where she swiped her ID to gain access to the ICU.

"This is great, Jessie," he said. "Makes a difference working with you, avoiding the protracted negotiations to get in to see a victim."

On the fifth floor a patrolman was speaking to an older man and woman, both agitated and tearful. Ralph moved closer and held up his gold shield. "Detective Ralph Thompson," he said. "Are you Miss Gorman's parents?"

The woman leaned heavily against the man, who wrapped his arms around her. "Shh," he said. "We are."

"I want to see the doctor," the woman cried. "Please tell me she's okay."

Ralph turned to Jessie, who stepped forward. "Jessie Novak is a nurse here in the hospital and she works with us as an investigator," he said. "It was Jessie who realized last night that your daughter was alive..."

It wasn't lost on Jessie that he'd left out the word *homicide*, but she didn't want any of this to be about her. And besides, it was the patrolman on the scene who'd first shouted that the girl was still alive. She stepped back. "If you'll excuse me, I'm going to find the surgeon and I'll be right back."

She stepped into the ICU where the hum of voices, cardiac monitors, ventilators and medication pumps made the place seem noisy and chaotic. But on this Saturday afternoon, there actually seemed fewer patients than usual. The surgical ICU was likely readying for the steady stream of the usual victims of the Saturday-night gun and knife club. Jessie spied Ellen, the nurse in charge, and waved to get her attention. Ellen bobbed her head in greeting and gestured with her hand for Jessie to join her. "Good to see you," Ellen said. "How are things in the ER?"

"Busy," Jessie answered, "but I'm working a case with BPD, and I'm here about Sarah Gorman, our *patient X*. We're wondering how she is."

"Wow, you're involved in that one? Were you there last night?"

"Yes," Jessie said. "Her family's here, so we're hoping to get whichever surgeon is in charge to speak with them. And if she's awake and able, we'd like to speak with her as well, but I'm getting ahead of myself. Is Tim Merrick in charge of her case?"

"Of course," Ellen said. "The surgical ICU is command central for him. But right now, he's in the Recovery room checking on a patient. I'll send him a quick text page and let him know you guys are here."

"While you're doing that, is it okay if I peek in on her?"

"Yes, she's actually in the room right across from the nurses' station."

Jessie turned and surveyed the area, her stomach twisting in knots. "Where's the policeman who's supposed to be guarding her?"

"He's right inside the room with her, just by the door. We didn't want to scare any other patients or family members. And if he's in there, he can definitely keep an eye on her."

"Thanks," Jessie said, a swell of relief easing her stomach's woes. "I'm just going to poke my head in." She moved quietly into the room. The patrolman stood and eyed her suspiciously. Jessie held up both her hospital and police ID badges. "I'm Jessie Novak. Her family and one of the detectives are here, and before we bring them in, we wanted to know if anyone's been around looking for her or asking about her."

He shook his head. "It's been quiet, aside from hospital staff. You're the first."

"So, no activity?"

"No. From what I was told, she's designated a *patient X*, so she doesn't exist. No information anywhere that she's here. And she's been asleep since I've been here, but you can see for yourself that aside from the IVs and monitor and those wires, ropes and pulleys for her legs and those bandages, she looks pretty peaceful."

Jessie nodded and looked up at the monitor, which revealed a stable pulse, blood pressure, and vital signs: all of them good indicators for this young woman, but she was most interested in Sarah's brain function. Would she wake up? Would she remember? Could she help them find this son of a bitch?

A tap on her shoulder interrupted her thoughts, and she turned to see Tim Merrick standing there.

39

"Good to see you. Want to step out so we don't disturb her?" he asked softly.

"Absolutely," she said as they moved into the hallway. "How is she?"

"She's doing well. She's asleep because of sedation and pain meds, but she's certainly been responsive between doses. We're just trying to keep her quiet and let her get as much rest as she can, hence the sedatives."

"Her family's outside. Could you come out and speak to them?"

"Yes, of course, and then we can let them in to see her. They understand what happened?"

"I'm not sure if they know all of the details. One of the other detectives is with them, likely filling them in."

"Okay, we can speak to them outside."

Jessie smiled. Despite his reputation as an impatient, prickly surgeon, he really was a good guy. He followed her to the main corridor where the Gorman family stood with Ralph. They all turned expectantly as Jessie and Tim walked toward them. Mrs. Gorman's hand flew to her mouth as if to hold back a cry. Jessie reached them first. "This is Dr. Merrick," she said, turning toward Tim. "He's the surgeon in charge of Sarah's care, and he has good news." She said the last placing her hand on Mrs. Gorman's shoulder.

"I've explained what we know to the family," Ralph said, "and also advised them that we're keeping her condition and all information about her private. Absolutely nothing is to be released. As you can understand, they are anxious to see her and to know how she's doing."

Tim folded his arms and smiled. "I'm happy to tell you that she has no injury to any major organs—her lungs, heart, everything looks good. Her injuries are to her lower extremities, and she does have complex bilateral leg fractures and a pelvic fracture. She's had surgery, and she has pins and wires sticking out of both legs with bandages and casting around them, so that might look a little overwhelming, but she's stable."

The older woman heaved a worried sigh. "But is *she* okay? Will she be our Sarah when she wakes up?"

"She's asleep now, but she's been awake, and I have to say that so far things look very good for your girl. Of course, until she's fully awake, we won't know for sure. Do you want to come in and see her?"

"Yes," they replied in unison, a sudden smile lighting up the woman's face. They followed Tim into the ICU and into Sarah's room.

Jessie and Ralph held back to allow the family some privacy. The patrolman who'd been sitting by Sarah nodded, stood up and came out and joined them. Ralph shook his hand and they all watched through the glass as Tim seemed to be explaining Sarah's injuries and prognosis. Her mother leaned down and pulled her into a tight embrace. Tears nicked at Jessie's eyes as Sarah's eyelids flickered before opening. Tim moved in, leaning over his patient, but as quickly as she'd woken, Sarah slipped into sleep once again. Her mother visibly sagged, and Tim said something to her before joining them in the hallway.

"Was she awake?" Jessie asked.

"Probably not, not in any real sense," Tim said. "It may have simply been an unconscious reflex to hearing her mother's voice. It's a good sign, but remember, she's still on heavy doses of sedatives. I think we'll likely start reducing that over the next few hours and days. We want to bring her out slowly and monitor her responses to see how she does."

"So, no chance of speaking with her?" Ralph asked.

"None," Tim said curtly. "She's still very fragile."

"I understand, and I'm sorry I have to ask," Ralph said, "but any idea when we might be able to speak with her?"

"I know how important it is." Tim glanced at Jessie as if looking for support. "But right now, she's my patient and my only concern is her health."

"I understand," Ralph said. "I do. But my job is to protect her and find this guy to prevent this from happening again. He's still out there, which is why I have a policeman watching over her."

Tim Merrick never took kindly to being rebuked, and Jessie winced. But to her surprise, he only nodded. "Understood," he said. "Her mother asked where her cross is. Apparently, she wore one on a gold chain. I didn't see one. Did you, Jessie?"

Jessie shook her head. A cross again. Another connection, but this was bizarre.

Tim nodded and headed back into Sarah's room.

Ralph passed his card to the patrolman who had been guarding Sarah Gorman. "Will you give this to her parents and ask them to call me? I want them to have some time with her, but please let them know it's important that they call me today. Either Jessie or I will probably be back later as well."

The patrolman nodded and pulled up a chair just outside of Sarah's room.

Jessie and Ralph headed to the ER. "I just want to check in with the nurses there and see if anybody's come to ask about her," she said.

In the elevator, Ralph flipped through his small notebook. "What do you think?" he asked. "Will we be able to speak with her today?"

"Probably not. It's pretty late now, and I don't think Tim Merrick will want us to be back to bother her."

Ralph stopped at the ER entrance. "I'll see you outside," he said as Jessie swiped her ID against the reader and pushed open the door, running right into Donna.

"I was just going to call you," Donna said, tucking a few loose strands of hair into a bun at the nape of her neck.

Jessie groaned. "Before you ask, I'm not interested in doing any overtime," she said. "I'm here about our *patient X*."

"I heard about her, and I suppose if she's a *patient X*, that's a good sign. The news stories only reported that a woman fell or jumped from the roof of an apartment building and was presumed dead at the scene. Nothing else."

"That's good then," Jessie said. "So, why were you going to call me?"

"I'm not sure how important it is, but someone came in here asking if Jessie was working."

"Well, that's not so unusual, is it?"

"I suppose it wouldn't be if he'd said your full name, but he only asked if Jessie was working. Carol was at the front desk, and she asked if he was looking for Jessie Novak. She said he smiled in an odd way before he said that he was looking for a Jessie Sullivan, thanks anyway, and then he just left."

"That's not such a problem, is it? Is there a Jessie Sullivan who works here in the hospital?"

"No," Donna said. "I actually checked the whole staff directory. It just struck Carol as creepy. She said it was as though he was just fishing for your last name. Just be careful. Let Sam know, or whoever you're working with today."

"Does Carol remember what he looked like?"

"She said he had brown hair and lousy teeth. You know Carol and her fixation on teeth."

Jessie laughed. "That description fits so many people who come through here. Nothing else?"

"I'm not sure. She's gone home, but you can call her. I'll give you her number if you want," she said, scrolling through her phone's directory.

Jessie copied the number into her phone. "Thanks, I'll call her later."

"So, back to Sam. How is he? How are things going?"

Jessie smiled. "He's good, though I don't see him nearly as much as I'd like to."

"Well, that's a good thing, isn't it? To miss being with someone who probably misses you too?"

"It is a good thing," she said, deciding to text him later to tell him just that. "Let me know if anyone shows up asking about our *patient X*."

Donna nodded.

Jessie headed outside, the day still warm, though cooling a little. She lifted her face to catch the soft breeze as she opened the door and slid into Ralph's car. "We just got a call," he said.

"Not another...?"

"No, our doctor at the scene just showed up. Turns out he's a medical student, third year at Boston University. He was too embarrassed to come forward earlier. Said he thought he felt a pulse, but it was probably his own. One of the detectives said he was red-faced and contrite."

"And his story checks out?"

Ralph nodded as he sat a little straighter and tossed his notebook onto the dashboard. "Ready?"

She nodded. "He was the one that Julio picked out, though he pointed to others as well. We're back to square one." She sighed. "Can we just stop at the scene? I'd like to see it while there's still some daylight. Everything looks so different at night."

"Sure," he said, pulling out and into traffic. "The patrolmen are still there. I think Forensics is still scouring the site, and some of my guys are around, knocking on doors to see if we have anyone who heard or saw anything. Crime scene tape is up. We can have a look at her apartment as well, and see if we can spot anything. I just want to call in and see if any of the guys have spoken to her friends or anyone else in the building. I want them to speak to everybody while Sarah is fresh in their minds."

Ralph pulled onto Washington Street and into the alley behind Sarah's building—the area still dotted with police vehicles, media vans and onlookers. He parked and they exited the car, both heading to the spot where the young woman had landed. A group of forensic technicians and detectives hovered by the car. One technician was squatting on the roof taking photos, while others scoured the alley for any clues.

One of the detectives shook his head as Ralph approached. "We're waiting for a tow to get the other cars moved out. This alley is too damn cramped."

"Looks it," Ralph said. "Anything else?"

"Nothing," the man said. "No one really knew her. Apparently, she just moved in last week. Most hadn't even seen her. One woman waved to her in the lobby. That's it."

"Did anyone hear anything last night?" Ralph asked.

"No. There was a party in one of the apartments, but by two a.m. everybody was gone and the people who stayed were passed out. No one heard anything until the sound of that car alarm when she landed on the roof."

"Cameras, anything?"

"Nothing, no gloves, no zip ties, but it does look like there was something of a struggle. A couple of plants were kicked over on the roof. We don't have all the video yet. Not everybody in the neighborhood has a camera and there were no cameras in the alley. Figures, right?"

"Are you running background checks on the building's residents and guests?" Ralph asked.

"We are. One of the guys has gone back to get started on that. We just collected the last of the partygoers' names."

"Okay," Ralph said. "Have you been into her apartment again? Anything in there?"

"No, same as last night. She clearly hadn't been home. Her keys, you remember, had been found on the stairs along with her bag and phone. I would guess that someone surprised her and she didn't have time to scream for help."

"Unless she knew her assailant," Ralph said.

"But if she did, why not continue into her apartment?" Jessie asked. "It doesn't make sense just to go to the roof and drop your keys and bag on the stairs if you're with someone you know and feel comfortable with."

"You're right," Ralph said. "It makes it more likely that she didn't know this person and she probably dropped her keys and bag in a struggle. The access door to the roof was propped open, and she was likely brought up there."

"Yeah," the detective said. "Nothing on the roof. And he had to have moved fast once that car alarm went off. But he left nothing— and no prints anywhere."

Ralph nodded, his eyes surveying the scene and the crowd just outside of the crime tape. "Anyone out of place show up?" he asked.

"Look around. Most of those people look out of place, but do I think he's here, watching? Maybe, but we can't haul them all in."

"I think it's the same guy," Jessie said.

"It fits the pattern," Ralph said, "but he's generally pushed them or thrown them off a roof where they've landed on hard concrete. This time a car likely saved her. If it's the same guy, was he in a hurry? Did she land on the car by accident, or was this something else? An angry boyfriend? We really need to speak with her."

"How's she doing?" another detective asked.

"Holding her own for now," Ralph said, "but we'd like to keep that quiet."

"Understood. I'm back to the neighbors," he said with a wave as he walked on through the crowd.

"We're going to have a look inside her apartment," Ralph called.

They headed to the front of the building and retraced Sarah's steps to the roof. Jessie looked down and exhaled noisily. "She was lucky to have survived at all."

Ralph nodded. "Let's have a quick look at her place. See if there's anything there."

They stepped under the yellow police tape and pushed open the door to Sarah's studio apartment and stood there. From the doorway, they could see the entire space. It was tiny, an entire home cramped into a space the size of Alison McCray's dorm room. Sarah was apparently still moving in. Three large boxes stood in the middle of the room. A futon against the wall and a small desk in the corner were the only pieces of furniture. Her kitchen was the size of a closet and held a dorm-sized refrigerator and tiny stove. The bathroom was equally cramped: a stall shower and a small sink littered with her toiletries filled the space. One smaller box lay open on the kitchen floor. Jessie sifted through the photos, notebooks and day planner. Just like Alison McCray, she had her days and nights planned. At least Sarah might have a chance to do the things she'd planned. A chance to apply for the social service job she'd circled in a job list, or to RSVP to the wedding invitation in her pile of opened mail. A promising young life interrupted. But, mercifully, not ended.

They headed back outside. "I'm just going to run to the back for a minute to check something with one of the detectives. We can get going after that," Ralph said.

"Okay, I'll be here," Jessie said, studying the groups of people clustered on the sidewalks watching the continuing drama that had unfolded in the night. Suddenly, she had that eerie feeling once again. Someone was watching her.

A sudden buzzing noise made her jump. It was her phone.

Can we meet for a quick dinner? I really miss you ♥ *Sam*

The eerie feeling faded and she smiled at the simple lovely ordinariness of that text.

40

He was lost in the crowd, just another nobody peering into someone else's misery. No one would even notice him as he stood there, trying to keep a smile off his face. But damn, he wanted to smile. He'd gone to the ER. He knew she wouldn't be there. She'd likely been up all night at the scene, but he had to find out who she was for sure. So, he took the chance and went in and asked, in his most sincere voice, "Is Jessie in?"

The clerk, a middle-aged, dowdy-looking woman who'd probably been forced to attend those pathetic customer service seminars, gave him a stupid smile. "Who are you looking for?" she'd asked as if she hadn't heard him the first time. She was using those steps that they'd given her. Be sure to clarify a request—let people know you're listening. Blah, blah, blah.

"Is Jessie working today?" he'd asked again, and this time the woman gave him a bright smile.

"Jessie Novak?" she'd asked.

And he stood there dumbfounded for a minute. Part of him hadn't expected it to be this easy. He almost burst out laughing but he bit his tongue, the coppery taste of his own blood calming him down. He shook his head. "No, I was looking for Jessie Sullivan."

The woman's forehead creased, making her look even older.

"There's no Jessie Sullivan here," she said, her voice softer, almost confused. "Are you...?"

She was speaking again but he wanted to get out—to get away before she remembered him, before she could describe him. When he turned away to leave, she hadn't even noticed, she just kept chattering away. He almost bounced out of there, happiness putting a spring in his step.

And now as he stood there by the alley, watching, Jessie Novak arrived with one of the detectives from the previous night. But it was Jessie who had his full attention. He watched her walk the length of the alley, her bottom swinging as though she knew he was watching. It was all he could do not to reach out and grab her right then. She was just like the others—full of herself and thought she was too good for him. But he'd show her who was too good.

He fingered the cross that hung from his neck. It was his now, and try as they might, they had nothing to connect him to this.

His gaze was drawn back to Jessie Novak once again. She and the detective she was with were looking very pleased with themselves. That was what was wrong with these guys—they were happy just standing around looking incredibly satisfied with their work. But he was the only one who should be proud of himself. He'd left nothing behind, and he'd gotten what he wanted: Jessie Novak's last name. It would be easy enough to find out where she lived and easier still to see her fall from a roof.

He felt a rush at the thought. She had it coming.

41

Jessie smiled as she read Sam's text. *Yes! I'll be home soon. Call me!*
♥

She felt almost desperate to see Sam. She hadn't realized until just then how much she missed seeing him, though it had only been a day. And of course, there was this case. She couldn't wait to tell him about it.

"Not much to do here," Ralph said, emerging from the alley. "We'll be waiting on Forensics to see what they can come up with. We've both had a long day. Come on, Jessie. I'll get you back to headquarters so you can pick up your car and go home."

At headquarters, she jumped into her car, which had sat in the sun for hours and was stuffy and hot, the vinyl seats and steering wheel burning her skin. She got out and opened all the windows to let the car breathe before slipping back inside, pulling into traffic and turning for home.

Once home, she checked on Rufus, who was looking cool and comfortable in his air-conditioned apartment. He invited her in, but she declined. "I'm hoping to see Sam later," she said, "but let me know if you need anything."

Upstairs, she showered and pulled on a t-shirt and shorts. She was just brushing her teeth when she heard a knock at her door. "Who is it?" she mumbled through a mouthful of toothpaste.

"Me," Sam said. "I have dinner."

Jessie spit out her toothpaste, tugged at her t-shirt and opened the door. Sam stood there with a bag of food, a wide smile, and his silver eyes glistening with pleasure. She pulled the door open wide and he entered, dropping the food on the table and turning to pull her into his arms. "Oh my God, I missed you," he murmured as his lips found hers, and his hands pulled her closer. "I know it's only been a day, but I needed to see you." He kissed her then, so deeply that her toes tingled as she stood on them to reach him.

"I've missed you too," she said. It was then she noticed he wasn't wearing his usual work suit, and was instead dressed in blue jeans, a button-down shirt with the sleeves rolled up and a pair of running shoes. "The US Attorney doesn't have a dress code?" she asked.

"Oh, he does. But we're in meetings just for trial prep, getting us ready so we're all on the same page." He glanced at his watch. "I'm sorry to say that I have to go back in a while, but at least we can have a quick dinner."

"Time to talk about our serial killer?"

"I heard we have a survivor."

"We do. We haven't spoken with her yet, but we will. Soon, I hope. We also have another odd link—a cross." And she filled him in on the details of the last three cases and the curious missing cross. "Rosa Suarez had one on her neck, Alison McCray was clutching one in her hand and Sarah Gorman was missing one. I've read the other case reports, and there was no mention of a cross in their possession or at those scenes. What do you think?"

"I'm not sure," Sam said. "Maybe it's someone different, a copycat killer."

"But how would he know about the zip ties? We've just discovered that. What do you make of it?"

"Not sure," he said dropping onto the couch, reaching for a sandwich and popping open a can of soda. "Might be a coincidence."

Jessie raised a brow and sat down next to him. "Aren't you the one who told me there are no coincidences in homicide?"

"I did, but there are exceptions to every rule, and we don't know everything yet about the other victims."

"What about getting a profiler to look at this case?" Jessie asked, choosing the hot pastrami sandwich and almost moaning with pleasure as she bit into it.

Sam used a napkin to dab at the mustard that pooled at the corner of Jessie's mouth. "We could, but we'd have to go through the higher-ups for that, and that takes time, and I can tell you— based on what I know of the case—they'll say he's a loner, probably lives with his mother or by himself, has no real friends, no girlfriends, stuck in a dead-end job, angry at the world. At least, that seems to be the profile for all the serial killers. It doesn't really help much." He turned his attention back to his turkey sandwich.

Jessie washed down a bite of hers with a large swallow of Diet Coke. "We have his DNA. What about a genealogy profile?"

"It's a pretty new science, and will only work if one of his relatives has sent in a DNA sample to one of those ancestry websites. It's a possibility, I suppose, if we get nowhere."

"I don't actually mean that. There's a fairly new science of doing a physical profile down to eye color from DNA."

"Pricey, and only works in retrospect. They find similarities once they have their suspect. Not much help in a working case."

"Damn it, Sam. There's got to be something we can do."

"Let's go over what we do have. Seven dead, one survivor, all clustered near colleges in two city areas—Springfield and now Boston. All with zip tie restraint marks, broken fingernails. I think we're looking at a security guard. A police officer would use flex ties—they're more reliable and easier to maneuver onto a struggling suspect."

Jessie nodded. "And zip ties are available just about everywhere. So, we're looking for a security guard?"

"Or someone impersonating one. I wish I'd paid more attention to the guard at BU. I directed him to a uniformed officer but he apparently just kept going. That's on me. On top of that, turns out he wasn't the one who called nine-one-one. It was sloppy. No excuses." He shook his head and huffed out a sigh, placing his sandwich down and sinking back into the couch.

Jessie rested her head on his chest and listened to his heart pounding against his ribs. "We'll get him," she said. "I'm sure of it."

He leaned down and lifted her chin up, brushing his lips against hers before kissing her more deeply, his tongue probing her mouth, his hands cupping her head. Her skin tingled at his touch. Suddenly, he pulled away.

"I have to go," he finally said. "Or I'm never going to leave." He pulled her close once more, his lips finding hers. "I wish I could stay, but I can't." He stood and pulled out his keys. "I'll see you soon."

"I hope so," Jessie said as she pulled the door open and watched him bound down the stairs and out her front door. Something was different with him tonight. And then it hit her.

He'd forgotten to say he loved her.

And she'd forgotten too. It wasn't the end of the world, just something else to wonder about.

42

It seemed an eternity since Rosa had died, though it was only a week. They needed to get this case solved. And Sarah Gorman just might hold the key to finding the killer.

Jessie ran her fingers through her hair as she dressed and wondered if Sarah was awake yet, and if she had any memory of the incident which had almost killed her. The only way to find that out was to get to the hospital and talk to Tim Merrick. He was likely still there since it was his weekend on. She microwaved a cup of instant coffee and sent a text to Ralph.

I'm on my way to BCH to see if our girl is awake and ready to talk. Any chance you can meet me?

Yes. Give me twenty minutes. Ralph

Jessie replied that she would see him then and she headed out. At the hospital, she found Tim drinking coffee at the nurses' station in the surgical ICU. "Morning, Tim. How is she?" Jessie asked, bobbing her head toward Sarah's room, the blinds drawn, the door closed.

"Very stable. She probably doesn't need the ICU, but we're going to keep her here for safety's sake."

"Is she awake?"

"She is," Tim answered, "but still drowsy from the pain meds."

"Has she said anything about the incident? Does she remember anything?"

"I don't know. She asked me what happened, and I told her that she'd fallen. She seemed confused about that, and I didn't want to get into details without you or one of the detectives here. And luckily, she drifted back to sleep. But that was late last night after her parents had left. I think she slept through the night."

"Do you think we can speak with her this morning?" Jessie asked.

"Sure, as long as I can come with you," Tim said. "It's still important that we do our best to keep her quiet, and not upset her. These are critical hours for this young lady, and we want her to recover to her fullest."

Jessie nodded. "I understand," she said as she checked her watch. "I'm waiting for Ralph." Just then he stepped through the door.

"Morning, Jessie. Dr. Merrick."

Jessie nodded. Tim stood and shook Ralph's hand. "We're ready if you are."

Tim knocked on the door before the trio stepped into Sarah's room. The policeman on duty sat a little straighter, clearly recognizing both Ralph and Jessie. "Morning," he said softly.

Jessie smiled in reply. "Has she been awake this morning?" she whispered.

Sarah's eyes flickered open in response. "I'm awake," she said, turning toward them. "Who are you?"

"Do you remember me?" Tim Merrick asked. "I was on your surgical team. I took care of you in the ER and then here. You asked me last night what had happened to you."

Her brows knitted as though she were trying to remember. She nodded slowly as a single tear tracked along her cheek.

Jessie moved to her side and took her hand. "It's okay," she said. But Sarah shook her head again. "It's not okay. I don't understand why I'm here or why my legs are broken or why my parents were here crying, and I don't know why a policeman has to sit next to me." She gripped Jessie's hand. "I don't understand any of this. Please, can someone explain this to me?" She pointed to her legs, held up by a series of pulleys and wires.

Jessie pulled up a chair and sat, leaning in close. "My name is Jessie. I'm a forensic nurse with the Boston Police Department. This is Ralph Thompson, a detective. We need to ask you some questions."

Sarah's brow furrowed. "Why?"

Ralph stepped to the bedside. "Friday night—well, early Saturday morning—you were attacked. Someone..."

Sarah gasped and tried to sit up.

Jessie put a hand on her shoulder and gently eased her back onto the pillow. "You're safe now," she said, "and we have the policeman here to make sure you stay safe. I promise you we will not let anyone hurt you."

"What happened?" Sarah asked, her lips trembling.

And Ralph told her the little they knew: that someone had probably followed her home from the bar, restrained her wrists, pulled her up to the roof of her building and thrown her off. "You landed on a car, which saved your life. I know this sounds horrible and hard to believe."

Sarah's hands fluttered to her eyes and she held them there as if trying to block out what Ralph was saying. She lay that way for what seemed, at least to Jessie, an eternity. "I'm sorry to ask," Jessie said, "but do you remember anything about Friday night?"

Sarah pulled her hands from her eyes, revealing a trail of tears. "I worked. We were understaffed and I worked the floor as a waitress. It was busy. I remember that, and I remember leaving and starting for home."

"You walked home?"

"I did. It's not far."

"Did you notice anything along the way?"

She shook her head.

"Do you remember if anyone bothered you or paid too much attention to you during the night?" Jessie asked.

Sarah shook her head once more. "I mean, there's always guys hitting on me—on all of us. But I can't remember that from Friday. Wait... I remember a guy saying he lost his puppy. It's fuzzy, but I think the front door to my building was open. I think he said the puppy went in there and he needed help to find it."

"Do you remember anything about this man? What he looked like, what he was wearing?"

Sarah shook her head. "Everything is a blur. I'm not even sure if what I just said happened or I dreamed it. I'm sorry."

"Don't be sorry," Jessie said.

"Any chance he was wearing a security guard or policeman's uniform?" Ralph asked.

"I don't think so. I think I'd remember that, but I can't say for sure. I don't even know what he looked like."

"I'm sorry that I have to ask you," Ralph continued, "but is there anyone who would want to hurt you? An old boyfriend, a friend, a customer at the bar, anyone at school?"

"No one that I can think of. My boyfriend and I broke up when he moved back to Chicago after graduation. It was his decision, not mine, and my friends have all mostly moved home, too. I stayed because New Hampshire is close. I can go home for a day or a weekend and see my family, and Boston just has more to offer me." She picked at the top sheet as if to avoid the thought that someone would want to hurt her. "I was thinking of applying to grad school, and I just wanted to earn some money while I decided. It all seems stupid now. I should have just moved home."

Jessie gripped Sarah's hand. "Don't blame yourself. This was not your fault. We will find whoever did this and you will be okay."

Ralph pulled out his notebook. "Can you tell me your boyfriend's name?"

"You don't think...?" Sarah began but stopped before she could finish the thought.

"No, I don't, but we have to check everybody and their story.

It's routine, and sometimes friends remember things that you may have forgotten—a man who was attracted to you, a friend who was angry, a long-forgotten old boyfriend. It's important that we check and rule everything in or out. Do you know Alison McCray? She was a student at BU. Or Rosa Suarez, who was a housekeeper at some of the colleges?"

"No," Sarah said. "I don't know them, and I don't know their names. Should I?"

"They were both killed in the last week, and we're just trying to see if there's any connection between you all. Maybe you knew someone who knew them."

Sarah's eyes scanned the room. "I don't think so, but everything's in my phone—friends, family. I don't even know their numbers without it. But I don't know where it is. Do you have it?"

"We found everything—your bag, phone and keys—on the stairs in your building. Will you give us permission to access your phone? I can bring it back here later."

"I'd like that. I think I'd like to tell some people where I am before they read about it. Thank you."

"They won't be reading about it," Jessie said. "We've kept your name and your condition out of the news, and here at the hospital you're listed only as *patient* X. No one knows who you really are or that you survived the fall."

Sarah nodded and wiped away the fresh tears that had gathered. "But my parents were here."

"Of course," Jessie said. "We wouldn't keep that information from them."

Sarah reached to her neck, her fingers fluttering there. "Where's my cross? Do you have that?"

"No," Jessie said. "Did you have it on Friday night?"

"I always have it on. Always," she said, her voice cracking.

"The man who did this may have taken it," Ralph said. "Can you describe it?" He held his pen ready over his notebook.

"It was simple, a plain gold cross on a gold chain. My grandmother gave it to me when I was six and I've worn it since then. I just don't understand why someone would do this to me."

"We don't either," Jessie said. "And unfortunately, as I said, you're not the first. But you are the first to survive."

"Is that why the policeman is here?" Her voice cracked as she spoke.

"Yes," Jessie said, "to keep you safe. But the hospital is keeping you safe as well. Nobody can get into this area. I promise. We're leaving but I'll get your phone. Will you give us your permission to go through it to look for contacts or anything that might help?"

Sarah wrapped her arms around herself as if to ward off a chill and nodded as Ralph passed her his notebook and pen so she could write her password down.

At headquarters, Jessie stopped by Forensics to pick up Sarah's phone before joining Ralph at his desk. "At least we've got more than we had yesterday," Jessie said. "A damn puppy ruse. I wonder if he's used that before. I'm just going to look through her contacts and make a list. But I don't think we'll find what we need. From what we know, the only thing she has in common with the other victims is that she's young and blonde and pretty. I'm not sure yet where the cross figures in, but Rosa Suarez is the outlier, and I think she was killed because she knew something about the killer."

Ralph leaned back in his chair. "Speaking of Rosa Suarez and her potential connection to the colleges, one of the other detectives found a security company that provides guards to all of the colleges. He left a note for me." He held up a piece of paper. "He called and asked them to send me a list of employees who worked there last year in western Mass. in the time frame of the three murders there, and who may have started here in Boston since January when the other murders began. Haven't heard back but it's Sunday. I guess I shouldn't expect to hear anything for a few more days."

"Unless you have something for me," Jessie said, "I'm going to copy all of her contacts and get this phone back to Sarah at the hospital. Should we try to start calling people today?"

"No," Ralph said. "Let's wait until tomorrow. Hopefully, Sam will be back, and we can have a quick conference to decide who's going to call who and where we'll go from here."

"I hope he's back, but I think that federal trial starts tomorrow."

Jessie said her goodbyes and headed back to the hospital, where she went through the phone with Sarah to see if she'd missed anyone. There wasn't anybody in her contacts that Sarah thought would hurt her or might even know the other victims. "My friends would have mentioned that they knew somebody who had jumped to her death or been killed. I think that's the kind of thing people would talk about, and nobody has."

Jessie patted Sarah's shoulder and put her number into Sarah's phone. "If you need me, I'm only a call away. The policeman is here for as long as you're here, and I think your parents will probably be in later. Okay?"

She passed the phone back to Sarah, who took it with trembling hands. Jessie slipped her notebook into her bag and headed for home.

A run was just what she needed to clear her head.

43

So, Jessie Novak, you're not as smart as you think you are. You live on K Street in South Boston—easy enough to find and easy enough to wander around and wait for you.

He hadn't had to wait for long. He watched as she'd pulled up in her crummy old car and headed into her house. It wasn't much later when she'd reappeared in running gear. He wasn't surprised, not really. She was just the type to run, to make a spectacle of herself in tight clothes. Probably headed for a long run along the beach or around Castle Island. But he wasn't stupid enough to follow her. Besides, it was too damn hot for a run. She might be stupid, but he wasn't. He could wait.

It wasn't quite an hour before she returned, a glossy layer of sweat covering her skin. He felt the hair on his arms tingle as he watched her. She had a determined spring to her step, her breasts bouncing as she slowed to a walk. She was full of herself, looking around to see if anyone was watching her. He looked away quickly, her eyes never catching his. She made him sick. She was just the type of girl his mother had warned would never look at him, but how wrong his mother had been. That type of girl looked at him plenty these days, though never in the way he'd always hoped.

He fingered the broken chain in his pocket, the cross resting there protecting him against the likes of those girls. But maybe he *should give Jessie Novak a chance. Maybe he should try to meet her. She was different from the others—well, except for Rosa Suarez, but he'd never been interested in Rosa that way. He'd only had to shut her up. Jessie Novak was different. Maybe he'd think about it; maybe he'd give her a chance, try to meet her, although he didn't want to have to take up running to achieve that goal. Maybe he would see her on the street, maybe strike up a conversation and get to know her, or he could rent a car and rear-end her at an intersection when no one else was around. Though that would be a waste of time. She'd just be snotty, like the others.*

He nodded to himself as he watched her lean over and stretch her legs. She wanted everyone to look at her. Damn! Jessie Novak had gotten on his nerves and under his skin, and it was her fault that he'd gotten too messy, and that was never good. He knew he had to get rid of her, but he definitely should change things up, change the way he did things. That would throw the cops off. They wouldn't have a clue. And a car accident late at night in a deserted area might be just the ticket.

He'd just have to watch her more closely and take his time. That was his problem; he was always too impatient. At least, that was what his mother had always said. She'd asked him time and again why he was in such a hurry. "You're never going to amount to anything anyway. Why are you always in such a rush to prove that?"

What would that old bat think if she could see him now? He was the one in charge. He was the one who controlled events and people. He was the center of everyone's world and yet he was invisible.

Which was perfect, and just as it should be.

44

MONDAY, DAY 9

Jessie dressed quickly, eager to get to work, to see Sam, to get this case solved. She paused as she stepped outside. A bank of full clouds hung in the sky; the air was heavy, a humid breeze brushing against her skin. It was going to rain, a relief, she supposed, for the wilting flowers that lined the tiny gardens along the street. She ran back inside to get an umbrella and sweater.

At headquarters, she showed her ID to the policeman at the desk, raced up the stairs and rounded the corner to the detectives' area where, though it was still early, she seemed to be the last of the team to show up. Already, Ralph and the other detectives were sitting together, likely discussing the case.

"Morning, Jessie," Ralph said as she walked in.

"Morning," she said. "Am I late?"

"I guess you haven't heard the news?" a detective asked.

She shook her head.

"The word is out that our girl survived an attempt on her life," one of them said. "The press reminded the public that she was the third to fall in the last week but the first to survive. They haven't yet connected them to the two other victims in the last six months, or the three who died in similar fashion in western Massachusetts. But they will. It's only a matter of time."

Ralph nodded. "The mayor and commissioner have released a

statement to the press and we are all on notice to get this solved ASAP."

"How did word get out?" Jessie asked.

"Probably someone at the scene. But I suppose it was bound to happen. We just have to double our efforts to stop him."

"But what about Sarah? Will she be safe?" Jessie asked, her voice rising.

"She will. We have a car outside the hospital, an officer by the elevator and another in her room—we've moved her, by the way. Nobody will get near her."

"What does Sam have to say?" Jessie asked, her gaze straying to his closed door.

"He's still holed up with one of the FBI agents," one of the team said. "We might be able to catch him before he heads to court, but he said not to disturb him yet."

"We do have some good news," Ralph added. "The security company, Tempus Security, got back to us and eight men fit the profile and time frame we're looking at. They all passed background checks that were outsourced to another company specializing in that work. None still work for Tempus Security. Five are local. One of them, a Jack Nolan, is a student at Northeastern. Another—an Allen Smith—died in a car accident after he left Tempus. A Phil Davis is living on the Cape and working at the hospital there, and the last two—a Jack Feeney and an Arnie Boone —don't seem to be working, at least not that we can find. None of the five has a criminal record."

Jessie's eyebrows rose. "Northeastern is right near the garage that Rosa was thrown from, and a student fell from a classroom there."

"Right," Ralph said. "Right now, two of the team are going to follow up on Jack Nolan at Northeastern and Phil Davis, the one on the Cape. You and I, Jessie, are going to pay a visit to the two other local men. If you're interested."

"Of course, I'm interested," she said. "I'm ready."

Just then the door to Sam's office swung open. Jessie looked up expectantly, a smile already playing at her lips. But it wasn't Sam who emerged. Instead, it was a tall, leggy brunette, her shiny brown hair draping the shoulders of a linen suit that seemed tailored to show off her curves. She raised a hand in greeting when she saw the group of men. Every eye in the room was on the woman and every inch of her seemed to know that. She exuded confidence, in the click of her high heels on the floor, the swing of her hair, the sway in her walk. Jessie sank down into her chair.

"Hallie Rose, long time no see," one of the men said, his eyes glued to her face.

"Miss me?" she asked, her voice sultry, her blue eyes scanning the room. She paused at the desk where they'd gathered.

"Every single day," another said. "How's DC? I bet it's you who misses us."

"I knew you'd be back," someone chuckled.

Hallie Rose laughed, one of those perfect tinkling laughs that make men swoon.

Two more men peered in. "Hallie Rose. I'll be damned."

And a soft murmur seemed to ripple through the whole of the second floor. "Hallie is here." The news traveled quickly; a group soon hovered around her as she moved to the center of the area.

"Did she work here?" Jessie whispered.

"Ahh," one of them said. "She was here before your time. She's Sam's fiancée."

Jessie felt the color drain from her face. *A fiancée?* A hard lump formed in her chest. Out of the corner of her eye, she saw Ralph's jaw drop.

"He's not engaged," Ralph said firmly.

"You're right," another said. "She broke off with him when she joined the FBI in DC two years ago, left him for greener pastures. Just about broke his heart. Maybe she's had a change of heart. Maybe life as a general investigation agent isn't as glamorous as she expected."

Jessie's own heart pounded in her chest. Sam had never mentioned a fiancée when he'd said that he'd be working with an ex. What the hell was going on? Was Hallie the reason Jessie hadn't been invited to meet his mother? She swallowed the bitter lump in her throat and tried to focus.

"Let's get back to work," Ralph said, probably trying to put a halt to the speculation surrounding Hallie and Sam.

"They were a great couple, though," a woman said. "I always thought she'd be back."

Ralph cleared his throat and began to summarize the backgrounds of the potential suspects. "The videos from the colleges are pretty vague. Looks like students only, but our guy could have changed and then slipped out and into the crowds. So, for suspects..."

"Suspects," one of the team said, "is a stretch at this stage."

"Maybe, maybe not," Ralph agreed, "but we have to start somewhere, and we have nothing else. We have DNA and prints that don't match anyone in the database. That rules out police officers. We have access to their prints in the database. No matches."

"Seems to me that security companies require employees to be fingerprinted as part of their background check."

"True, but the background checks were outsourced to a second company. They promise to reach out and pass along that information. And I can tell you, it was a struggle to get the names and addresses and photos. So, this is what we have," Ralph said as he passed the documents that included names and photos. "And even if prints or DNA match up, that only means someone was at the scene. It doesn't prove he was the killer. We need more."

Jessie leaned forward. "Are we just spinning our wheels then?"

"No, we're just kicking into gear," a detective said as he stood and followed another out. "We'll keep you posted," he said.

Jessie nodded, a ripple of sweat running along her neck as her eyes tracked back to Hallie Rose, who was still the center of attention, men fawning over her. She pulled her gaze away. *Get a grip*, she reminded herself.

45

"Jessie," Ralph said. "You agree?"

"Yes," she mumbled.

Sam's door opened and he stepped out, a smile on his lips when he saw Jessie. "Hey," he said, taking the chair next to her. "How's the case going?"

She only nodded and looked away, listening as Ralph filled him in.

"So, you're going to speak with these two?" Sam asked, tapping the papers.

"We are," Ralph said, shuffling the papers. "And," he continued, recognizing the unease seeping from Jessie's pores, "we should get going." He stood. "Ready, Jessie?"

Jessie nodded gratefully, glad to get away and have her mind back on the case. Hallie Rose was laughing again, and Sam seemed to suddenly realize that she was still there. He muttered something under his breath and turned to Jessie. "Can I speak with you before you leave?"

Afraid to speak, or to lose her composure, Jessie only shook her head, gathered her things and headed for the door. Hallie Rose was still laughing, giggling really, and the murmurs of appreciation echoed in the halls and followed Jessie down the stairs and outside, where she waited for Ralph.

But it wasn't Ralph who came up behind her. It was Sam.

"It's not what you think," he said gently, placing a hand on her shoulder. "I told you about her."

She shrugged his hand away. He had told her, but he'd mentioned it casually—as someone he used to see, not someone he'd planned to marry, and not that she was this gorgeous woman whom every man within a five-mile radius was fawning over. And here Jessie was, same old insecure Jessie, acting like an ass, blowing up and pushing him away. *What the hell is wrong with me?*

"Hey, Jessie, ready?" Ralph called as his car pulled up.

"Let me explain," Sam said.

"Later," she said, forcing a smile and pulling at the door handle before sliding inside, her breath catching in her throat. She could see Sam in the rearview mirror. He shook his head sadly before stuffing his hands into his pockets and heading back inside. *Idiot. I'm an idiot.*

"Are you okay?" Ralph asked.

Jessie nodded. "I'll be fine. This is my job, and this case is important to me. I have to stop just reacting to things and move on."

Ralph pulled into traffic. "For what it's worth, I know that Sam loves you. She's here for that case, and I know you didn't ask, but my advice to you is don't get caught up in that stuff. She doesn't look like his type to me."

"Ralph, I appreciate your support, but they were engaged. She's definitely his type. And the type of every man in that room. You're a good friend, but I just want to get back to our case. Where are we headed?"

"Braintree first. A city south of Boston, and about fifteen minutes on the expressway. We're going to stop first at the police department, a courtesy call to let them know we're there and why, just in case there's any trouble, and to see if they have any information for us on our guy, Arnie Boone."

"Do you think that there will be trouble?"

"Probably not, but if there's one thing I've learned, it's just to be prepared. Better safe than sorry, and all that." Ralph maneuvered his car onto the Expressway South. The traffic was manageable this morning, and within fifteen minutes they were pulling into Braintree's police headquarters, a funny-looking, square, squat building with narrow slivers of glass for windows. It looked more like one of those meatpacking companies by the hospital than a police department. She wouldn't have known it was an official building except for the big sign out front.

Once inside, Ralph pulled out his badge and ID and Jessie did the same. "Sorry to bother you, but we're here to speak to one of your residents in relation to a series of murders of young women in Boston, and—"

"The would-be jumpers? Just tragic," the sergeant said. "Got daughters of my own. Come on into my office."

They followed him into a small windowless room with a battered old desk which held a computer, printer, and a landline phone. A vinyl-covered chair stood behind the desk and two straight-back wooden chairs were placed in front. A battered metal file cabinet held a coffee maker. "Coffee?" he asked.

And Jessie remembered she'd been in such a hurry that she'd left home without her usual morning caffeine. "Oh, yes," she said. "I would love a cup."

"Milk? Sugar?" he asked.

"Black for me, thanks," she said.

He turned to Ralph who put his hand up. "None for me. Thanks."

Jessie took a long swallow of the dark brew, the aroma and the caffeine jolt clearing her head.

"Sergeant," Ralph began.

"Please, call me Pat," the sergeant said, taking a seat behind his desk. Jessie and Ralph slid into the seats in front of the desk.

"Okay," Ralph said, "we're here looking for a former security guard who worked at some of the colleges involved. There's a possibility that the man involved in our cases has worn a security guard uniform and has used zip ties to restrain his victims."

"You have his name?"

"Arnie Boone, date of birth August twenty-fifth, nineteen ninety. Worked for Tempus Security. Know him?" Ralph asked.

Pat leaned back. "Arnie Boone? I do know of him."

Jessie sat forward, her lips parting in anticipation. Catching this guy was going to be easy. "How do you know him? He doesn't have a criminal record, or does he?" And she paused. "Unless it's sealed."

"No criminal record. Grew up here. By all accounts, he was a good kid. He worked some dead-end jobs for a few years after high school before he left to attend a community college in Worcester. And you're right, he worked as a security guard for a company out there. But he left all of that, quit school and his job and came back here to Braintree about four months ago."

"That just about fits our timeline, Pat," Ralph said. "Do you have any idea where he's working now?"

Pat's brow wrinkled. "Sadly, Arnie Boone jumped to his death from the Fore River Bridge in Weymouth not too long ago. He was an only child—his death left his parents devastated. There was no death notice, nothing in the papers to mark his passing. The news reports never used his name, at his mother's request, I heard. She didn't want people to know he'd taken his own life. Sad."

"He jumped?" Jessie glanced at Ralph and shook her head. "That seems like a strange coincidence."

"Did he leave a note?" Ralph asked.

"No. No note, and no indication that he was depressed to that extent, though his mother said that he'd been skittish in the months since he'd returned. He seemed anxious about something. He hadn't started a new job yet but he'd been in touch with the security company he'd left. He'd applied to work in Boston and was waiting for a start date."

"Any evidence at the scene to indicate a struggle?"

"Nothing."

"And no signs of defensive wounds?"

"You'd have to check with the ME, but the report we received indicated the cause of death was multiple trauma as a result of the fall. He'd taken water into his lungs if I remember correctly, but not much. He died on impact."

Ralph nodded.

"I can email the investigation reports to you."

"I'd appreciate that," Ralph said as he stood and held out his hand. "Thank you for the help. If we need anything else, we'll be in touch."

"We'll be here," Pat said, taking Ralph's hand and then Jessie's.

Once they were in the car, Ralph opened the folder he'd brought. "That leaves only one for us—Jack Feeney, twenty-nine years old. Lives in Boston."

"Are you thinking what I'm thinking?" Jessie asked. "That maybe Arnie, like Rosa, knew something? That he was killed to silence him?"

"What is it that Sam says? *There are no coincidences in homicide.* So, yes, I'm thinking what you're thinking. Too much of a coincidence. We'll have to pull that autopsy report, see if there were any zip tie marks on this young man's wrists."

A chill ran along Jessie's spine. "We have an escalating serial killer on our hands, don't we? This young man makes eight if he was killed. We have to find our guy before he kills again. And we're down to three potentials, maybe four, right? The one who came to the hospital inquiring about Rosa Suarez, the one working at Cape Cod hospital, the Northeastern student, and Jack Feeney."

"Jack Feeney." Ralph smiled the satisfied smile of a man who's sure he's narrowing his list one by one. "He's next on our list."

"Doesn't this feel almost too easy, though?" Jessie asked. "Yesterday, we had nothing, today we have three or four potential suspects."

"It doesn't feel too easy—it feels like we finally caught a break."

Jessie sank down into her seat as Ralph started his car, the engine purring to life.

They were missing something. She was sure of it.

46

Ralph's phone rang and he pressed the *answer call* button on his car's console. It was another detective from the team. "Hey, Ralph, both of our potentials checked out. The Northeastern student transferred home to California three months ago. We've spoken to him and he's got an alibi. We'll check it out, and he's also agreed to submit DNA to the local police there. The kid working on the Cape checks out too. He's a medical assistant in the ER and in school full-time. He has to clock in with his fingerprints, and they confirm he was working for the last three deaths. He's also agreed to submit DNA."

Ralph filled them in on the curious death of Arnie Boone. "So, that leaves us with a man named Jack Feeney. We're going to check him out now," he added before ending the call.

"How are we going to do that?" Jessie asked.

"It's an uphill climb, that's for sure. All we have so far is the DNA and fingerprints that the killer left on that glove. But he's the last man standing of our initial four, and if that DNA matches his..."

"We both know that one glove won't prove anything."

"True. So, let's start at his address. See if it's still current. Just have a look around." He passed the folder to Jessie as he maneuvered the car onto the Expressway North. "Just let me know the address."

Jessie scanned the paper until she came to the address. "You won't believe this," she said, turning to Ralph, "but he lives on Washington Street, in a building just a few blocks from Sarah Gorman's. That's almost too easy. Do you think this address is reliable?"

"Well, that's where he asked for his final paychecks to be sent, and it's all we've got right now. There's a photo of him in that folder. Will you have a look? Maybe we'll get lucky and catch sight of him in the neighborhood. Otherwise, we'll jump out and see if his name is on the mailbox."

Jessie pulled out the grainy photo, enlarged from his work ID. "It's not a great photo, but nothing distinguishing—brown hair, brown eyes. Says he's six feet tall. No weight, but he looks bulked up. Big shoulders and arms, at least from the little I can see. If we're going to see Jack Feeney, don't we need backup?" she asked as Ralph exited the expressway and headed toward Washington Street.

"We do, but we'll just swing by, maybe ring his doorbell and see what happens. I think we should just have a look around for now, get the lay of the land and then head back to the office and try to dig a little deeper on Jack Feeney. See what we can come up with. And, I suppose, he might not even be our guy."

Jessie nodded and settled back as they headed down Washington Street, past a row of restored brownstones and into a seedier, more run-down area that had yet to be rehabbed. Here, the rents were cheaper, making this a neighborhood where people stopped on their way to something better, or where they languished forever, knowing there was no way out.

"Here we are," Ralph said, slowing in front of a particularly shabby four-story brick building. Overflowing garbage cans lined the sidewalk and a mangy dog munched on a bone still wrapped in paper. A young, heavily pregnant woman pushed a baby stroller, while an older man dragged a broken shopping cart behind him. A group of teenagers lingered at the corner, eyeing the old man before turning away. A dumpster was pushed close to the side of the building. Maybe a cleanup was in the works. "It looks more like a rooming house, doesn't it?" he asked.

Ralph continued on, turning the corner before circling back to Washington Street. "See anything? Anybody?" he asked.

"No," Jessie said. "Maybe he's at work."

"Now, that's a damn frightening thought, isn't it, especially if he's found work as a security guard. All the more reason to get back to the office and get on this."

Jessie's phone pinged with a text.

I'll be back in the office later. Please give me a chance to explain.
♥ *Sam*

"Sam?" Ralph asked.

"How did you know?" she asked wryly.

"It's not rocket science, Jessie. I think he loves you. I told you, she'll be gone in another day or two. Don't let her get under your skin."

Jessie's forehead wrinkled. "You're right, and now is not the time to think about it anyway."

"Alright. I'm sorry. Let's just change the subject," Ralph said, slowing the car in front of what they assumed was Jack Feeney's apartment building. "I don't see anybody that resembles our guy. Do you?"

Jessie shook her head, her gaze fixed firmly on the building.

"Hey," Ralph said, breaking through her reverie. "Still nothing. Do you mind jumping out and seeing if his name is on the mailbox?"

Jessie looked up. "Not at all." She jumped out as the car came to a full stop and jogged up the stairs to the building's entrance. She didn't have to worry about doorbells or trying to get in. The outer door was wide open, the hallway dingy and dark. There were eighteen mailboxes and three had been pried open. Jessie peered closely at the handwritten labels taped to each box. And there it was: scrawled on the label for number sixteen was simply *Feeney*. Jessie inhaled deeply. At least something was going right. She peered through the grimy glass top of the inner door and tried the knob, but it was secure, likely the only thing here that was. She pressed on Feeney's doorbell again and again but there was no answer.

And she wondered if maybe he was watching them. Outside, she stood and stared up at the windows, but there was nothing to see. But the day hadn't been a total waste. At least they knew where he lived.

47

A bubble of anger churned in his stomach as someone pressed on the doorbell. Again and again. He had half a mind to go down and pull open the door and wring the bastard's neck. But he stopped himself. He'd come this far. He just had to stick it out a little bit longer, and besides, who could it be?

He moved to the window, inching the blinds open the tiniest little bit and peering out. He looked down on the street where a shiny black sedan was idling at the curb in front of the building. It was a Crown Vic, an unmarked police car.

And as suddenly as the buzzing had started, it stopped. Whoever had been ringing the bell had given up. He focused his gaze on the street. And it was then he saw her. It was that damn Jessie Novak. What was she doing here? She looked up, her eyes scanning the windows. But he moved back quickly, the blinds slipping into place. He held his breath, counted to ten and moved back to the window, edging the blind open to a mere slit. She was moving away from the building, and he watched as she slid into the Crown Vic, her dress riding up, her legs on full display. He felt himself harden at the sight. She pulled her legs in without ever adjusting her dress. She was teasing him. She looked up one last time as she pulled the car door shut. She knew he was watching.

The hair on the back of his neck stood up at the sight of her, at the thought of touching her. He watched as the car pulled away before stepping back, letting the blinds fall haphazardly.

48

At headquarters, Jessie and Ralph shared what they'd learned with the team. "Feels like we're still at zero, though. Sarah's friends described a nice, quiet girl. No current boyfriend. No one they could think of who might hurt her. Same with Alison, and the other victims."

Ralph leaned back so far in his chair it teetered unsteadily on its back legs. "Sam suggested we think about planting something in the news. We've done that before. Might just smoke our guy out."

"What kind of information would we leak?" Jessie asked. "Isn't that dangerous? Puts Sarah in his line of sights once again. Do you think this will really get Jack Feeney's attention? And what about the man who came to the ER? He's still in the mix, isn't he?"

"He is. And a planted story might just be what draws whoever it is, out," Ralph said. "Or we could mention the zip ties. Say that they were found at several scenes. That might be enough to really make our guy nervous and show himself."

"But wouldn't that make him move again? I don't think we should put anyone else in danger," Jessie said, folding her arms across her chest. "He's already escalating. A total of eight deaths if we include the three from western Massachusetts and Arnie Boone, and nine if we count Sarah Gorman. He definitely intended to kill her."

"He's absolutely accelerating, but why?" Ralph said. "And we still don't know why he kills in the first place. None of these girls are connected in any way beyond being young, pretty college students or recent grads. They had no connections to each other. They just seem random."

"But they're not random," another detective said. "We just have to figure out how or why he chooses the ones he chooses."

"None has been sexually assaulted, but maybe he's come on to them and maybe he's something of a loser, someone they'd shy away from. Maybe they've turned him down for dates or drinks or whatever. The connection is there," Jessie continued. "These are young girls in college settings where security guards are a natural part of the landscape. They're there to provide protection. Most people don't even notice them."

"Which reminds me," Ralph said. "The day of Alison McCray's fall Sam mentioned that a security guard had closed off the scene on her floor. We contacted the service that covers that college, and he said there are guards only at the dorm entrances. None are upstairs patrolling the corridors. The guard at the entrance that day was alerted to the fall when several students told him minutes after it happened. He called nine-one-one and then called his supervisor, who told him to wait for assistance and to go upstairs and secure the area only after a second guard arrived. He was told not to leave the desk unmanned. The guard said he never got a chance to leave the desk at all—the police showed up before his relief did, and when he finally went upstairs to see if the police needed anything, a uniform told him they were all set, so he left."

"So, the man who spoke with Sam wasn't a legit security guard, and he simply walked away from the scene just as he has every other time but this time, he must have laughed all the way home. He was right under our noses and he got away."

"But could the guard from the dorm entrance who went upstairs be the guy that Sam spoke to?" Ralph asked.

"No," the detective said, checking his notes. "The entry guard who went upstairs is black. And he was the only official security guard who went upstairs. Sam described the guard he spoke with as white."

Ralph nodded his head slowly as if mulling it all over. "That could be our guy. Looked legit enough that Sam believed him. And he meets the criteria for a serial killer. Usually, we consider three as serial with murders taking place over at least a month or more. And the murders are similar, victims have something in common. And our guy started that way. His three kills out beyond Worcester were young college girls and their murders were spread over several months and marked as probable suicides. It likely emboldened him. He came to Boston and his first two victims followed that pattern. Until Rosa Suarez." He paused. "Does that make sense to you?"

Jessie nodded. "And he had to kill Rosa Suarez and maybe Arnie Boone, too, to keep them quiet, but what's happened since? Because now he doesn't fit the pattern, at least in the time frame. He's now at three in the last week. Well, two and one attempt."

"And it's got so it's harder for him to stop," Ralph said. "It's almost a compulsion. He just has to do it. Most serial killers find a physical and psychological pleasure in killing. The control and power they experience is addicting and after the first kill, they crave that high. That's why they shorten the kill cycle, which leads to less control, and maybe that's what's happening. He's losing control. And having to kill again and again to get it back."

"Which means," Jessie piped in, "that he's either going to choose another victim soon, or even move on. He left his last location after three kills. He has four here now including the likely witnesses, Rosa and poor Arnie. So, what next?"

"Dig into this Feeney guy. See what we have, and if we can post someone by his rooming house. Keep an eye out for him so that if he moves, we know it. I'll see if we can get a search of any email addresses we can trace to him. We can look for family, friends, Facebook, the usual."

"I think I'll actually see if I can write up an affidavit," Ralph said. "And then have an assistant district attorney sign off on a warrant to permit a search of that room. We have the glove with DNA, we have the zip tie, and we have that cross that Alison McCray was holding in her hand. I'll have to check with Forensics. The touch DNA must be back on that, but that should be enough for us to get into the room."

"What if we get the warrant, and get in, and he's there?" Jessie asked.

"We bring him in," Ralph said. "He's a person of interest and we can question him. That'll at least put a scare into him."

And Jessie's gut knotted up with the thought of coming face to face with the man who she was increasingly sure was the killer.

49

"Who's ready for lunch?" Ralph asked as he stood and slipped out of his suit jacket and draped it over a chair. He looked pointedly at Jessie as he spoke.

She shook her head. It was one of the rare occasions that she really wasn't hungry. It was this damn case that had her gut all twisted up.

Ralph's brow furrowed. "Are you sick?" He moved closer and placed his hand on her forehead. "Jessie?" he asked, his eyes crinkling with worry.

"I'm okay," she said softly. "Just not hungry."

He raised a brow slyly. "That's a first. Sam will never believe this."

"Pizza?" someone asked, interrupting them.

Ralph pointed to his crisp white shirt. "Something with a little less grease for me."

Jessie laughed, remembering the first time she'd met Ralph in his pristine suit and white button-down shirt, and how he'd held the slice of pizza away from himself as he ate before finally dropping it back onto his plate and wiping the grease from his fingers.

"Jessie," Ralph said, straightening his tie, "I have cleaning bills to consider."

"We're getting pizza," another said. "You two are on your own."

"Fair enough," Ralph said. "Come on, Jessie, my treat."

Determined not to attract any more attention, she stood reluctantly and nodded. She walked alongside Ralph down the stairs and to the first-floor cafeteria. "Can we get a warrant today, do you think?" she asked. "Maybe get into Feeney's place?"

He grabbed a tray and stood by the counter, scanning the overhead menu. He finally settled on a grilled chicken breast and a side of asparagus before turning to Jessie, who shook her head. "Honestly, I'm just not hungry. I'll grab something later."

He gave her a stern look. "We have a lot of work to do, and I won't have you feeling faint." He turned back to the line. "She'll have the same," he said, moving along the line to collect their plates, then heading for an empty table in the corner. "Just eat, Jessie," he said, placing the meal in front of her.

She forced herself to smile. "You don't give up, do you?"

"I can tell that you're distracted..." he began.

And with that, she stopped listening. She was distracted, and why shouldn't she be? It wasn't just the case, though that had consumed her. It was Sam and her damn history of choosing the wrong man again and again, setting herself up for misery every single time. She thought of her mother's abandoning her, an act of cruelty by the one person who should have loved her the most. It had set her up for a lifetime of thinking she wasn't deserving of real love. She shook her head as if to shake herself loose of those feelings. Her mother was back, all apologies and declarations of love. Jessie knew she did deserve better; she just had to choose better. And with Sam, she really thought she had.

Ralph cleared his throat to get her attention. "You haven't heard a word I've said, have you?"

"Sorry," she said sheepishly.

"At least eat so we can get back upstairs and back to work."

She speared a piece of chicken. "I'm ready to focus on this case. I promise."

He raised a brow and she wished she could talk to him about it, about her insecurities and her perpetual inability to choose the right guy. She had to get her head into that space that she could get into in the ER's trauma room where nothing else—personal or otherwise—mattered except the patient and the problem at hand. She had to bring that same focus to her work with the Homicide unit and the medical examiner.

"I swear, as soon as we're finished eating, we'll get back to work, see if we can get a warrant and see what else we can find on this Jack Feeney."

"That's more like it," Ralph said. "But if you need to talk, you can always talk to me."

"Thanks, Ralph." She reached out and touched his hand. "I'm fine, and I know that right now this case is what matters. Everything else can wait."

They finished their meal and made their way back to the second floor, where an empty pizza box and crumpled napkins were scattered on a desk. "Everyone ready?" Ralph asked.

The gathered detectives nodded and one spoke up. "The computer wizards already got some hits on this Jack Feeney. Only child of a single mother. No father named on his birth certificate. That must have been fun to bring to school and then jobs, huh?" He huffed out a sigh.

"Grew up in public housing on the outskirts of Springfield. High crime, dirty streets, gangs, tough place for a kid. He was a loner. His high school yearbook lists no activities, no special interests, made him seem like a kid who managed to stay under the radar, and except for a few incidents, he did just that." The detective leaned back, a satisfied smile on his face.

"What incidents?" Ralph asked, motioning for Jessie to sit as he sank into a chair.

"He started a fire behind the building he lived in and was suspected of killing a neighbor's cat, but he denied it and they couldn't prove it. In high school, he was a mediocre student, but he did manage to graduate and then went to a junior college, and he's been a security guard on and off since then. Has a few complaints in his file, but nothing major. Doesn't seem to have any close friends and lived with his mother in the housing project until she died a couple of years ago. He wasn't allowed to stay in the apartment as a young single working male, so it looks like he's been bouncing around sharing small apartments or rooming houses. He doesn't really have any roots anywhere and no other family. Apparently, his mother was also an only child." He took a breath. "There you have it."

Jessie sat forward. "I'm no psychologist, but that history does seem to hit all the marks, doesn't it?"

"It does," Ralph agreed. "But we still need to prove this. I'm going to write up our affidavit so we can get a warrant and have a look inside his apartment. I'm hoping I can have it in a couple of hours."

"Okay," Jessie said. "I'm going to head over to the ME's office and see if we have autopsy reports on the three deaths from western Massachusetts. Roger was going to go over them once he received them and look for any indication that the red marks on their wrists matched up with zip ties. They hadn't been documented as zip tie marks. I just want to make sure they match. I should be back in an hour or so. Maybe I'll stop in and see how Sarah is doing as well."

"Perfect," Ralph said. The team huddled to go over assignments.

"I was going to head over to his apartment building and talk to his neighbors," one of the detectives said, "but I don't want to spook him before we get a warrant. I think I'll just continue my search here online."

"I'm going to see if Forensics has anything for us—check if the security guard company still has his fingerprints on file," another said. "If they have them, maybe they'll give them up without a warrant."

"Alright," Jessie said, waving her hand as she was leaving. "I'll see you all within an hour or two." She grabbed her stuff and headed out, turning at the corner to take the stairs—and that was when she heard it.

The tap, tap, tap of stiletto heels on the tile floor, a flurry of familiar giggles and murmur of voices coming from the long corridor. She stopped and listened.

"That was great," Sam said. "Couldn't have worked out better."

"Just like old times," Hallie said, a hint of triumph in her voice.

Sam murmured something that Jessie couldn't make out and she slid out of sight, her back hugging the wall as they turned the corner, her broken heart pounding hard against her ribs.

50

She drove on autopilot to the morgue, parked in the hospital's garage and raced across Albany Street to the ME's office, swiping her ID across the reader to gain entry. She waved to the receptionist as she took the stairs to Roger's office. From the end of the hallway, she could see the glow of his desk lamp as he bent to his work. Roger—experienced, reliable, steady. And he had asked her to work alongside him full-time. She smiled at the thought. Her life was good. She had no business complaining.

"Afternoon," she said, tapping softly on his door.

He looked up, smiling. "Good to see you, Jessie," he said. "Are you here to tell me you've taken me up on my offer?"

"I haven't decided just yet," she said, wrinkling her brow. "Still on the fence."

"If I can't convince you of that just now, what can I do for you?"

"I'm here about our zip tie murders. I don't know if you've heard about the girl from Friday night?"

He shook his head. "Can't say that I have. Not around Boston, then?"

"In Boston, just a few blocks away, but this girl survived. She's in the ICU across the street."

He leaned back in his chair, his full attention focused on Jessie. "Will she make it, do you think?"

Jessie smiled. "She will. She landed on a car and has bilateral leg fractures that required surgery. She's in traction and will likely need rehab, but she'll be okay. At least physically."

"Terrifying, I imagine."

"I guess it would be if she remembered anything, but she doesn't remember much."

"And you think her attacker was our zip tie killer?"

"Our latest girl had the same red marks on her wrists. We're just trying to link all of the cases, and the only thing that we've really got, aside from similar looks—young and blonde—and lifestyles—college students—are those zip tie marks on the victims' wrists, so I'm just checking to see if you've had a chance to look at the autopsy reports, or speak to the pathologists from Westfield."

"I did. And he actually took pictures of those marks. Two of the girls had those marks, the first one didn't. So, although her fingernails were torn away, her death may be separate. Anyway, the ME wasn't sure what the marks were, and thought that they matched up with the elastic bands that so many girls wear on their wrists, just as we initially did. But from his pictures, those certainly appear to be zip tie marks." He began to rifle through the pile of papers on his desk. "I have the written reports right here, Jessie, if you want to take them."

"I do, Roger, thank you."

"It seems to me that this job suits you. I think you should carefully consider our offer."

"I will. I promise," she said, waving the papers in the air. "I'll see you later, Roger. Have a good day."

"You too, Jessie," he called as she raced down the hallway to the stairs, preoccupied with the reports she held and the warrant that Ralph was pursuing.

"Hey," a familiar voice shouted. "Where's the fire? You almost knocked my girl over."

She looked back to see Tony, Roger's assistant, leaning to pick up a small cat. He straightened, holding the cat in his arms.

"Oh, sorry, Tony," she said, reaching out a hand to stroke the tabby's soft fur. "She's beautiful. She's yours?"

"She was. Well, still is until I find a home for her."

"A home?"

"My landlady has developed an allergy and I have to get rid of her. Roger said I could keep her here in his office until I can find someone for her. Know anybody who'd like a cat?"

And Rufus immediately came to mind. "Actually, I do," she said, "but I'd have to check with him. He's my neighbor, and his cat just died of old age. How old is this cat?"

"She's just two, and she's a good girl," he said, rubbing her ears. The cat purred loudly and settled further into his arms.

"Is she a house cat?"

"She is," Tony replied. "She's house-trained, uses her litter box and likes a good cuddle."

Jessie held out her hand so that the cat could get her scent. "What's her name?"

"To tell you the truth, I never named her. I just call her Cat and she responds."

Jessie laughed. "I think I like that. Well, Cat, I'm going to see if my neighbor would like to have you. Can I check and call you later?"

"Sure. If you decide to take her, you can come back and get her. She'll be living in Roger's office for now."

"Thanks," Jessie said, continuing her run down the stairs, but now with a sudden spring in her step. At the hospital, she stopped at the ICU and made her way to Sarah's room, now at the far end of the unit, the policeman on duty sitting outside. He nodded when he saw Jessie. "Still quiet?" she asked.

"Only ones in to see her are her parents and the staff. No one else even tried. She's safe."

Jessie could see Sarah, surrounded by her parents and a therapist who was helping her stretch her upper body. She knocked softly on the door and poked her head in. "Hi, Sarah, I just wanted to say hi, see how you're doing."

She offered a faint smile and shrugged her shoulders. "Okay, I guess."

"Any word?" her father asked.

"Not yet," Jessie said. "But I promise we'll keep you posted, and in the meantime, we'll keep Sarah safe."

"Thank you," he said softly.

Jessie backed out and made her way to the garage. When she pulled out, the rain began, light, barely-there drops, almost invisible except for the intermittent swish of her windshield wipers keeping her windows clear. By the time she pulled into headquarters the rain had picked up. She grabbed her bag and Roger's reports and pulled out her umbrella, whose clasp failed to open. After a few frustrating minutes, she threw it back into her car and hurried inside, stamping her feet and shaking her hair free of the water that had flattened her curls.

Upstairs the detectives' cubicle area was empty, but Sam's door was wide open. She paused and took a deep breath before smoothing her dress and stepping inside. Sam was alone, sitting behind his desk, his fingers flying over the keyboard, a crumpled napkin stuffed inside a cardboard coffee cup on his desk. He stood up as soon as she came into his view. "Oh, Jessie," he said. "I'm glad you're here. We have to talk."

"Later. Right now, the case is the only thing on my mind. Where is everyone?" she asked. "I've just spoken to Roger. I don't know if you've had any updates on our zip tie killer, but at least two of the cases from western Massachusetts are consistent with our cases. It looks like it's the same guy. The first girl who died had fingernails torn off, so maybe..." She swallowed the hard lump in her throat, determined to keep this conversation professional, not personal.

"Jessie, we can talk about that as soon as everybody's back. I've been reading the reports. I know what's going on with the case. Ralph just called—he's got a warrant for Jack Feeney's room, or apartment, whatever it is, but you and I need to talk. There's nobody here. This is the perfect time. Please."

"Where's Hallie?" Jessie asked, listening for the tap, tap, tap of her stilettos.

"Gone back to DC."

And Jessie wanted to smile, but she didn't. "Can't we do this another time? We're at work, and I don't want to blur the lines. There was plenty of gossip and speculation about you and Hallie. I'd like to avoid being at the center of anything like that. Besides, no one here, aside from Ralph, knows about us. I'd like to keep it that way."

Sam's face crumpled. "What gossip?"

"Oh, please. You were engaged. Ring a bell?"

"We *were* engaged. For about five minutes. And that was two years ago."

"Two years is not such a long time."

"It's a lifetime and long ago to me. I'm not in love with Hallie. I'm in love with you."

Jessie crossed her arms tight across her chest. "I want to believe you, but..."

"But nothing. I told Hallie about you. She didn't blink. She has a boyfriend in DC. She didn't come back here for me. She doesn't love me—turns out she probably never did. But she doesn't matter. Not to me. It's you I love."

Betrayal—or the familiar shadow of it. She should be used to it; her mother was the first, but not the last. And was this even betrayal, or just misunderstanding? Was she overreacting again, shooting first, thinking later? But she didn't want to think or talk about that right now. They stood in silence, Jessie's thoughts too muddled to speak, Sam afraid to say the wrong thing. He reached out his hand to hers just as Ralph appeared. She pulled back.

"Okay to come in?" Ralph asked, looking from one to the other.

"Sure," Sam said, sliding into the chair behind his desk, putting a barrier between him and Jessie. He sat stiffly. "Get the warrant?"

Ralph nodded. "We have an unmarked car outside his place right now. We don't want any surprises. But there's been no sight of him. And before I forget, I have a photo of Jack Feeney." He passed the picture to Sam. "Could this be the security guard you saw this week at the dorm?"

Sam took the paper and examined it closely. "Could be," he said, nodding. "Fuzzy and a bit grainy, but maybe."

"Now that that's settled, are we going to head over to his place?" Jessie asked.

Ralph cast a nervous glance toward Sam.

"What?' Jessie asked. "Why are you looking at him?" And then she realized—they weren't going to include her. They were going to freeze her out. "I think I should be there," she said, her lips in a tight line.

"We can't allow civilians in, Jessie," Sam said. "Serving a warrant can turn dangerous in a heartbeat and we can't take any chances. Sorry. It's not personal."

Jessie simmered. Why did people say that something wasn't personal when it so clearly was? She sat perfectly still, trying to think of a snarky response, but her mind was blank.

"Sam's right," Ralph said. "We just can't take any chances. It's the same with any warrant. It's not just you, it would be any civilian and before you say it—I know that you work with us, but we have to keep you safe."

Jessie crossed her arms and huffed out an angry sigh. "I can keep myself safe, if you remember."

"That's true, and maybe once you have a little more experience under your belt, we can include you," Ralph said in a brotherly way.

She could only nod. She wasn't giving up. She knew where they were going. She just had to work out how to be a part of their search. "Well, I have some things to do. I guess you can text me later." She stood and grabbed her bag and pulled out the autopsy reports from Westfield, passing them to Ralph, purposely avoiding Sam. "These are the final reports that Roger got from the Westfield ME's office. Two of those victims had the same zip tie marks as our girls. They were initially thought to be from hair elastics, but the photos included reveal marks that Roger agrees are consistent with the zip ties."

Ralph took the report and began to flip through the pages.

"Thanks, Jessie. Are you going to wait here for us? We're going to be meeting with the team before we move."

Not on your life, she thought. *You'll be here for at least an hour strategizing and getting a team together. These things take time.* She forced a smile. "No, I'm going to speak with my neighbor about a cat."

Ralph chuckled. "That sounds like a punchline, but I'll leave it there." He headed for the conference room. "I'll see you there," he said to Sam as he left.

Sam stood and came around the desk. "Can we talk later?" he asked, an unfamiliar pleading in his voice.

"Yes. But will you reconsider letting me in on the search?"

"I wish I could, Jessie. I do. But my hands are tied." He offered a faint smile. "Later?"

She shrugged.

51

Jessie waited for Ralph and Sam to disappear around the corner before heading out. To add to her miserable day, the light rain had turned to a downpour, the fat drops pelting her as she ran for the safety of her car. *Could this day get any worse?* By the time she unlocked the door and slipped inside, she was soaked, her clothes clinging to her skin, her hair flattened against her scalp. She pulled the door shut, the rain lashing at her windshield, the wipers doing little to stem the flow of water obscuring her view. She pulled into traffic slowly, the puddles kicking up, traffic slowing to a crawl. At this rate, it would take half an hour to get to Feeney's place. She fiddled with her radio, finally settling on an all-news station. The weather bulletin described heavy rain and fog that was expected to last for a few more hours. It was apparently a slow news day, and the announcer focused on the three recent alleged jumpers.

"Do we have a serial killer on our hands?" he asked, and Jessie slammed her hand on the steering wheel.

"Damn it," she shouted. How the hell did this get out? And right after the news of Sarah's survival. Was there a leak somewhere in the department? Someone feeding the stories to the press? They were putting Sarah and every young woman in Boston at risk. She couldn't just sit idly by. She'd have to do something. And soon.

Jessie spun the button around again until she found a country music station, the love-gone-wrong ballads striking the right chord for her. After an eternity, she turned onto Washington Street and drove by Feeney's building, the sidewalks deserted in the heavy rain, the traffic moving at a crawl, her eyes scanning the street for the unmarked car. But wherever it was, it was well hidden, and that was how *she* wanted to stay.

She maneuvered into an empty spot across the street from the building. She had a clear view of Feeney's place and the windows on the top floor, all with shades or blinds drawn tight. She watched and waited. And waited.

And while she sat, she picked up her cell phone to call Rufus and ask him if he might be interested in Tony's cat. He answered on the first ring. "Hey," Jessie said. "Just checking in."

"You're a dear. I'm fine," he said, though the tone of his voice said otherwise.

"You're missing Fluffy?" she asked.

"Terribly. I hate to admit it, but that cat was good company and I miss her, but I'm happy to hear from you."

"I'm still working, but I have some good news for you," she said. "A man I work with has a beautiful tabby cat—gorgeous green eyes, dappled gray fur. She's two years old, a very friendly house cat and she needs a home. His landlady won't let him keep her."

"That is good news. What's her name?" he asked, and she could almost see his smile.

"Tony never named her, he just called her Cat and she answers to that now. I suppose if you're interested in her you could rename her."

Rufus nodded. "I have to say I like the name Cat. Keeps it simple. Where is she now?"

"Well, right now she's at the morgue."

There was a momentary silence. "She's dead?"

"No, no. I should have explained that better. She's in Dr. Dawson the medical examiner's office, with food and water and a litter box. Tony works at the morgue and had to leave her somewhere, and I said I'd ask you about her. If you're interested, I can pick her up later and bring her home. Do you still have Fluffy's cat bed and toys and food and litter box?"

"I do," Rufus said, "though I think a new cat deserves new things, don't you?"

"Tony left her things in Roger's office. She'll probably be most comfortable with those, don't you think?"

"Guess I'll clean up a bit before she gets here. She's been in a doctor's office? She's not expecting the high life, is she?"

Jessie laughed. "Rufus, I think Cat will love you as much as I do. I'll get her from the morgue and drop her off to you in a few hours, and if you like, you and I can go out tonight or tomorrow to get new things for her. Okay?"

"Sounds good to me. I'll be here."

"I'll see you later then, Rufus."

"I know I've said it before, but what would I do without you, Jessie?"

"Likewise," she said, smiling, as she ended the call.

She glanced toward Feeney's place again but there was nothing to suggest he was even there, no movement behind the shades, nothing. The rain slowed to a soothing, steady drumming on the roof of her car and as she watched, her phone pinged with a text. Certain that it was Sam or Ralph, she looked quickly. It was her mother, who had a knack for popping up at the worst possible moments. Jessie was still grappling with all of her confusing thoughts about getting to know her mother, and they'd barely spoken in the months since she'd reappeared in Jessie's life. It wasn't that she didn't want a mother; she did. She just needed time to figure out how to be her mother's daughter. Being on her own for so long had made her wary, though meeting little Julio and seeing him with Ana had made her long for that kind of special bond. She read the message.

Thinking of you and hoping we can talk soon. Love, Mom.

She set her phone down. She needed to give her mother a chance. She'd call her later. It was time for Jessie Novak to grow the hell up.

And then she decided to rattle Jack Feeney just a little. She stepped from her car and ran through the rain and the traffic, cars honking, her feet sloshing through puddles, before she reached the front entrance and hurried up the steps to the shelter of the foyer. She'd just stepped in—not sure what to do, afraid to ring his doorbell to gain entrance—when suddenly the door swung open, an older man, disheveled and smelling of stale booze, shuffled out and smiled when he saw her. "Go on, miss," he said, holding the door open.

"Thank you," she whispered, feeling as though he'd just answered her question. This was a sign, a gift from the heavens. She stepped into the main lobby—a stretch to call this dank, dark place a lobby, she thought. But at least she was inside. She decided to head up to check where Feeney's number sixteen was, to see if there was any sign that he was at home, then she could let Sam and the team know and prove she'd earned her spot alongside them.

She hurried up the staircase, the narrow hallway reeking of urine and rotting food. This place was nothing like Sarah Gorman's carefully tended building just blocks away. Jessie wrinkled her nose and when she reached the top floor, she stopped to take a breath and simply listen. But there was nothing, no sound at all from any of the three apartments up here. The place seemed deserted, and maybe it was. Number sixteen was on her left. She moved soundlessly to the door and laid her ear against the wood but heard nothing, no hint that anyone was on the other side. She took a deep, steadying breath and knocked softly, but still—nothing. No movement, no sound. No one was there. Her heart pounding, she gripped the doorknob and turned but the door was locked; the knob wouldn't budge. She tried again, but the lock was sturdy, and the door held.

"Damn it," she muttered, heading back down the stairs. She'd have to think of something else.

He'd been getting ready to leave when he'd heard the footsteps, shuf-fling almost, of someone trying to be invisible, something he knew well. He held his breath. He'd been looking outside periodically, but aside from the rain and the traffic, there was nothing to see. No police, no one watching, nothing out of the ordinary. He moved closer to the door and then he heard it—the soft tapping on the wood and for the first time he could remember, he was afraid. He held his breath, his pulse pounding in his ears, and then it occurred to him. The police didn't tap softly on your door, they shouted to open up and then they kicked it in.

He calmed himself and then he saw the doorknob twisting back and forth. Someone was trying to get in. Just his luck. A goddamn burglar. He stayed perfectly still, ready to strike if they forced the door open. He watched as the doorknob turned one more time and then he listened as the soft steps, tiptoes almost, backed away and hurried down the stairs.

He sighed with relief and hurried to the window, peering through the blinds, and watched as none other than Jessie Novak ran across the street, climbed into her car and just sat there.

And he smiled. He'd go out the back way, get his car and just follow her.

This was going to be a good day.

Jessie sat in her car wondering what to do next. Jack Feeney wasn't where they expected him to be. She considered calling Sam but decided not to let him know she'd been here first. He'd discover soon enough that Feeney wasn't there. She huffed out a sigh and shoved her phone into her pocket. As soon as she turned the key in the ignition, the rain began to fall in heavy sheets, the streets flooding quickly, the steam rising from the black asphalt. She could hardly see through her windshield. She'd just have to wait until it slowed. Once the rain had stopped, the air would be cooler, fresher. Maybe she could even go out for a run later and really clear her head. That's what she needed to do to get back to herself.

As if on cue, the rain slowed again to a soft tapping on her windshield. She switched on her wipers and headlights. The rain had turned the day dark and gloomy. She'd pick up the cat first and then head back to headquarters. They'd all meet there anyway if their search came up empty. She pulled into traffic, making her way to the morgue, where an empty spot out front beckoned her. She pulled in and checked her watch. Damn, it was already after five. She wondered if Tony would still be here. She grabbed her bag and phone and hurried to the entrance, sliding her ID against the reader and pushing open the front door. The receptionist was gone, the lights dimmed, the area quiet. She headed up to Roger's office on the third floor but from the hallway, she could see that the door to his office was closed. And she hesitated. Could he be in a meeting? She went down to the second floor to search for Tony, and instead ran into Sean, another of Roger's assistants.

"Hey, Sean," she called. "Have you seen Dr. Dawson or Tony?"

"No," Sean said. "I think that they both left for home. I'm heading out to pick up a body. Need anything before I go?"

"I'm all set, thanks," she said as she headed back upstairs, tapping softly on Roger's office door before opening it and stepping inside.

The room was bathed in darkness. It took Jessie a minute to adjust her eyes and, in that instant, she was certain that someone was watching her. She turned quickly, her eyes wide open.

54

Sam drove to Washington Street, the car almost sliding on the wet blacktop. Once on Feeney's block, it was clear that there wasn't a parking spot to be had. Ralph radioed the others to get their location.

"We're parked right in front of his building. We managed to get here just as the rain slowed a little. Patrol car parked up the street didn't see anything. We haven't either," he said just as Sam pulled up next to him. They rolled down their windows to speak.

"So, should we just go in, or wait a while, see if he appears?" Sam asked.

"We've waited too long," Ralph said. "Let's just go in and get the bastard. He's probably sitting up there waiting for the rain to stop."

"Okay," Sam said. "Let's hold on. We need to have a plan. I'll find a parking spot and be right back." He pulled into traffic. "Keep your eyes peeled, will you?" he asked Ralph. They made two turns around the block before a car pulled away and Sam was able to park. He and Ralph jogged back to join the others.

"Our plan is to keep this as quiet as possible," Sam said, pulling open the back door so that he and Ralph could get out of the rain. "I don't want any trouble from neighbors or anyone else. From what I can see that main entry door is wide open, so once we're inside the foyer, we'll just try all of the buzzers. Somebody is sure to just let us in. We'll head up to his apartment, knock quietly to see if he's in and give him a chance to answer. If he doesn't, then it's on to Plan B—we'll kick the door in. Though I hate like hell to do that. Somebody always gives us grief for that." He sighed noisily and looked at his watch. "Patrol cars coming?"

"Yes," Ralph said. "Another few minutes."

"We'll wait," he said, leaning back. "We're going to do this right."

Ten minutes later two patrol cars rolled up and double-parked in front of the building. Sam got out and directed the second car to pull in behind the building. "Alright, everyone ready?"

Ralph and the others nodded in unison and all four turned for the entrance. They took the stairs, maneuvering around the drunk sleeping it off under the eaves before stepping into the dingy main entryway. Eighteen mailboxes in all. And there was Feeney's— number sixteen, just as Jessie had said.

"This must be a rooming house," Sam said. "Too many mailboxes for this to be an apartment building." They began to press buzzers at random until finally, just as Sam predicted, someone buzzed them in. They headed up, checking the numbers on the doors.

"Damn," Ralph said softly as they headed to the fifth and final floor. "He's got to be on the top floor, right?"

Number sixteen was at the end of the hallway. Sam knocked, once, twice, three times. "Jack Feeney," he said. "Boston Police. We have a warrant. Open up."

But the sound echoed and bounced off the walls. There were no footsteps, no sounds from inside. Sam put his shoulder to the door ready to shove hard but when he put his hand on the doorknob, the door slipped open without a struggle. "I guess it's our lucky day," he said, stepping inside, where a foul odor hit him full in the face.

"Jack Feeney, this is Boston Police," he called out before seeing the body stretched out on the floor. The man's skin was gray, his wrists zip tied behind his back, a belt pulled tight around his neck, his eyes and mouth wide open as if in surprise. Sam slid his gun from the holster on his belt. "Check for a pulse," he said, his eyes scanning the small room, a closet in the corner and a tiny bathroom next to that. Two windows, blinds pulled down, covered one wall.

"He's dead," said a detective.

"Oh, Jesus," Ralph said, slipping the photo from his jacket. "This is Jack Feeney."

"Call it in," Sam said, stepping into the bathroom, his gun held out before him. He stopped cold. A photo of Jessie was taped to the mirror. "Jesus," he said, "where's Jessie?"

"What?" Ralph asked.

Sam turned, his skin blanched, a dark shadow crossing his face. "Where is Jessie?" he repeated, his lower lip quivering.

55

Jessie turned and flicked on the overhead light in Roger's office, blinking at the sudden brightness, her eyes scanning the room for Cat. But she seemed to have disappeared. Jessie peered under the desk, the chairs and around the bookcase, and though the cat's food, water and blanket were there, the cat was not. And she realized that the cat had likely slipped out when she opened the door, and that was probably what made her think someone was watching her. It was the damn cat, watching and waiting for a chance to escape. Now Jessie had to go on a search for her.

Through a morgue.

At night.

Her day had just gotten worse.

She took a deep breath as she knelt to gather a handful of nuggets from the food dish and began her search. "Cat," she called softly as she headed down the dark hallway. "Are you here?" There was no response, no scratching, no purring, nothing, which meant she'd have to go through every inch of this place to find that cat. But there was no question she'd stay and find her. She'd promised Rufus, and she wouldn't leave until she had the cat in her arms. And then she'd make her way to headquarters and join the real search.

She continued padding softly along the hallway, her eyes scanning the area, but the hallway was narrow, most doors closed; only a bathroom and staff lounge and kitchen were wide open, and there was no sign of Cat. Alone in the silence, she was startled when her cell phone began to jingle loudly in her pocket. She pulled it out to silence it and saw that the caller was Sam. She hit mute; the last thing she needed was a noise to frighten Cat. Once she had her, she'd text Sam that she was on her way back to headquarters. She shoved the phone deep into her pocket and resumed her search.

"Here, kitty," she called as she headed upstairs to the fourth floor which held a library, more offices and equipment storage—but where again, there was no sign of the damn cat. She hadn't been to the fifth floor, but she knew it held the nuts and bolts of the power grid that kept this old building going. She went upstairs and pushed on the heavy door. The room was bathed in darkness except for the blinking lights that seemed to match the rhythm of the hum and whir of the machinery. She could have kicked herself. Of course the cat wasn't there, she thought. A cat couldn't push that heavy door open.

She retraced her steps and descended to the second-floor autopsy suite, the hallway dimly lit, the main suite in darkness. Jessie flicked on the lights and called for Cat, but the room was empty except for the line of stainless-steel gurneys, side tables and dissection equipment, wrapped and ready for the next postmortem examination. The whole area was quiet, on-call staff out on a pickup and everyone else gone for the night. But she had to find Cat. There was no way she could let a small animal wander around in a morgue. There'd be hell to pay if word of that ever got out. She turned out the lights and took the stairs to the first floor, which held the reception area, the family waiting area, a room for police, another for press. But the entire floor was as empty as the whole building seemed to be.

As she stood there, the rain began again in earnest, the windswept sheets of water slamming against the frosted windows, the boom of thunder and the crack of lightning breaking through the silence. She took a deep breath and headed downstairs to the refrigerated section where bodies were stored before being claimed or picked up by funeral home employees. Some bodies, she'd learned, stayed there for as long as six months. If they weren't claimed by then, they'd be buried in a city cemetery in nearby Hyde Park. Some cities cremated their unclaimed bodies, but mercifully, Boston did not. That meant if family turned up, or the body was a victim of homicide, the police could order an exhumation and examine the body again for identification or investigation purposes. But as she descended, she saw that the whole area was in darkness, the atmosphere unsettling and even spooky. She'd been down here before but she hadn't been in the back, in the areas where the bodies were kept. And she hadn't been alone.

"Kitty, kitty. Please come out! Don't make me go through these rooms. I have dinner," she called as she turned on the lights and proceeded along the hall to the body storage area. She pushed open a door to the refrigerated section and felt an immediate chill in the air. She shivered and rubbed the goosebumps that had erupted on her arms, though the real chill was in the stainless-steel coolers that held the bodies just inside the bank of large lockers built into the wall. Handled drawers were numbered; a log, labeled with name, date of birth and date of death, corresponded to the body inside, and lay on a nearby desk. Only two were currently unidentified and labeled as unknowns, with date of death and a grainy photo on the label should a potential identification occur.

She called for Cat once more and headed to the next room— the area where funeral homes could claim bodies. Roger's secretary worked here and made sure the paperwork was in order before releasing a body. It would be the responsibility of the funeral home to get the death certificate sorted out with the hospital or primary care physician. This whole lower level was an eerie place, and Jessie just wanted to get out. She made a cursory inspection, calling for Cat all the way, before finally giving up.

She huffed out an irritated sigh. She'd just have to head back upstairs. Cat was likely somewhere on the third floor near Roger's office. If she was looking to follow Tony's scent, she'd still be upstairs. Jessie reached up to turn off the lights when a crash of thunder echoed in the hallway. The lights suddenly flickered and died. With a final groan, the whir of computers slowed and then stopped, and the refrigeration motors shuddered and heaved a lonely sigh before fading out altogether.

Her shoulders tensed with the growing darkness until she remembered that there was a generator in the back of the building. Surrounded by a rusting chain-link fence, the generator was as ancient and decrepit as the morgue building, and she assumed that it would just kick in and restore the power momentarily. She counted to ten and then twenty, and then a minute had passed, and then two, and then five and everything was still bathed in darkness and quiet until a crack of thunder hit again.

"Here, Cat," she whispered, her voice cracking, the hair on the back of her neck standing up.

From somewhere above she heard the soft thud of footsteps, and her heart stopped.

56

The damn rain started again as he pulled back into traffic on Washington Street. But it didn't really matter. He'd been waiting for her to pull out and he stayed close. He followed as she took a right onto Massachusetts Avenue and later a left onto Albany Street, pulling into an empty space in front of the morgue. The traffic came to a halt at a red light just ahead, and he watched as she ran into the morgue, sliding her ID on the entry. She worked here, too?

He had a clear view of the ER entrance to his left and the two police cruisers parked there. He cursed under his breath. But the morgue was a place he knew, the nooks and crannies all too familiar to him. The building seemed mostly to be in darkness as he pulled behind it and into the small parking lot there, but he could see small bits of light leaking out through the drawn shades and the frosted glass windows. He knew the morgue was a place where the aim was to keep prying eyes out.

Thunder and lightning lit up the sky once again and in the sudden flash of light, he saw the bulky generator half hidden behind the chain-link fence that surrounded it. He hadn't formulated a plan yet for what he was going to do, but it was always good to have a backup plan. He pulled out his little flashlight and squeezed through a large gap in the chain-link fence, a gap that was probably on some bureaucrat's long-forgotten list of things to fix. These idiots *made it so easy for him. He stepped to the generator and had a look, and there it was—the switch to disable and disconnect the generator from the main electrical supply. He pulled the necessary switches and smiled. It was good to be prepared for anything, he thought, as he wriggled back out through the gap.*

It was then that he saw two medical examiner vans backed up to a closed door, and as he watched, the back door opened and a man in a bright orange slicker appeared. He saw his chance and ran up the steps. "Hey, Sean, right? How are you?"

"Hey, Al. How are you? You coming back to work here? Tony said you might be."

"Maybe, but tonight I'm just here to pick up paperwork," he said, reaching for the door before it slammed shut.

Sean grunted. "Jessie's the only one in there."

"Tony said he was going to leave some paperwork for me. I'm working for a funeral home, I'm here for a death certificate. I know where to look. Thanks so much."

"Ahh, okay," Sean said, bounding down the steps.

Al nodded and waved as he slipped inside, letting the door close softly behind him. It was so easy to get into places. Thank God for stupid people.

He looked around to get his bearings. It had been a couple of years since he'd worked here. He was on the first, maybe the second floor. An elevator was right in front of him, a flight of stairs to the side. He'd need to have a look around, but first he'd have to get used to the harsh scent of old blood and formaldehyde again. He held his breath and walked along the corridor and pushed open the first door. The reek was even stronger here, and he remembered that this was where they did autopsies. Gleaming stainless-steel gurneys, scales, and glass cabinets filled the large space. He'd learned everything he'd needed to know about murder here: how to assess a body for evidence, and how to make sure no evidence was left behind. He let the door close softly and began to walk away. And that was when he heard it.

"Here, kitty, kitty," a female voice said, filtering up from some-

where below him. He angled his head, and there it was again. "Here, kitty, here, kitty. Where are you?" she called.

And he smiled. He'd used a puppy ploy himself just a few days ago. It had to be Jessie Novak looking for a cat. Just then something brushed against his legs and he jumped. He began to swear, but he caught himself. He had to be quiet if he wanted to keep the upper hand. He lifted the cat into his arms, wondering quickly if he should keep the cat with him or shut her in somewhere. A purring cat would probably be a nuisance or give him away. He padded softly along the corridor. "Sorry, kitty," he said, running his fingers through her fur as he opened the next door and threw the cat in. He could hear the cat mewing a loud protest. "Damn it," he muttered, hoping that the door and the distance would muffle the cat's complaints.

His day was getting better by the minute. He headed back to the stairwell and tiptoed down the steps just as a crack of lightning burst outside. He wondered for only an instant if it had hit the generator. It sounded that close.

But as he paused in the stairwell, the lights flickered and died, throwing the whole building into darkness. The only sound was the whoosh of his heartbeat in his ears. And then he heard it again, a whisper really.

"Here, Cat," the voice called. This time, the voice cracked.

She was afraid. He had her just where he wanted her. She was all his.

57

Jessie held her breath and listened. There it was again: the soft, barely-there footfalls from above. Someone else was here—but who? Maybe it had turned out to be a false alarm, and maybe the footsteps were Sean's or one of the other technicians. And then the footsteps just stopped, or maybe they'd never been real at all. She just needed to relax, find Cat and get out of here.

"Here, Cat," she called, almost too softly for a cat to hear. Silence filled the narrow hallway, and Jessie felt herself relax. It was only her damn imagination. But in that heavy silence, she suddenly had that eerie feeling that someone was right behind her. She held her breath and then a hand gripped her shoulder. Her heart stopped.

"Looking for a cat?" an unfamiliar voice asked. "I've found him."

Jessie froze, a hard knot forming in the pit of her stomach. She turned and the beam of a flashlight was all she could see. She blinked, raising her hand to her eyes. "Can you turn that away?" she asked.

"Sure," he answered, holding the too-bright light under his chin, creating an eerie shadow of his face. "Do you remember me?"

"No," she said. "Should I?" Her fear was fading. He seemed not to be a threat at all. Just another morgue worker she hadn't met.

"Al," he said. "I used to work here with Tony."

And the last of her adrenalin-laced response flittered away. "Tony. That's right, he mentioned you. Are you back to work here?"

"No, Dr. Dawson never liked me. The bastard."

At that, a small, tight lump formed in Jessie's throat. Roger Dawson was one of the kindest people she knew. He didn't dislike anyone without good reason. "I don't understand. So, what are you doing here? Can I help you?"

He laughed, a thin, mean laugh baring his yellowed teeth. "You can't help me. I did ask you once, and you turned me away. Remember that?"

A line of worry creased Jessie's forehead. She needed to get away from him. "Look, I'm kind of busy, so if you don't mind..." She began to push past him.

"Oh, Jessie Novak, don't take me for a fool. You know exactly who I am." He took a step toward her, casting an icy stare her way. "Remember me now?" he asked, dangling a pair of zip ties in his hand.

58

A stream of sweat ran along Sam's forehead as he passed the photo to Ralph.

"Jesus. Who the hell is behind this? And how does he even know who Jessie is?" Ralph said as he handed the photo to the others.

"The day Jessie found the glove on the garage roof, someone was there, behind her. She never saw him, and he was too fast for her, but she chased him down the stairs. He got away, but he'd seen her." Sam pulled out his phone and began calling Jessie. "Answer!" he shouted.

"But how did he get a picture of her?"

"Look closely. That's the scene at the dorm earlier this week. He probably took it with his cell phone and then printed it out somewhere." Sam hit *call* again and again, but his calls went right to voicemail, and this was not a message he wanted to simply leave. He left quick, curt messages. *"This is an emergency. Call me!"* He prayed she'd get the messages.

"Well, with any luck," Ralph said, "we've scared him off and he's long gone."

"I don't think murderers scare that easy," Sam said, his voice cracking. "Does anyone know where she went? Did she tell you where she was going?" he asked Ralph.

"No, she just said she had things to do. I'll call headquarters, see if she's there."

"I'll call the hospital, ask the units there to page her overhead," another said.

Sam nodded and called Jessie once again, but she wasn't answering. *"Jessie, call me! Let me know where you are!"* He slammed his finger into *end call*. He needed to text her, but what could he write? He hesitated but finally his fingers hit the screen once again.

Please call me or let me know where you are. IT'S IMPORTANT!

He hit *send* and watched the little delivered message flash on the screen and then he waited for the tiny dancing bubbles that would let him know she was responding, but there was nothing. No response at all. Maybe she'd gone home, or maybe she was out for a run; she didn't always bring her phone. Rufus! He'd know if she was home.

He scrolled through his contacts blessing Rufus for insisting once that he take his number. His fingers shook as he hit *call*. "Hey, Rufus," he said, trying to sound calm. "It's Sam. Is Jessie at home, by any chance?"

There was a pause as if Rufus was scratching his head. "Well, no. She's supposed to be with you. Is there a problem?"

"No, not at all. We probably just missed each other. But if you see her..."

"I... Oh, I'm sorry," Rufus said. "Don't know how I could forget, but she's probably getting my new cat."

A swell of relief surged through Sam's veins. "So, she's at a pet store, then?"

Rufus chuckled. "No, the cat was at a doctor's office. That's probably where she is."

He couldn't have heard that right. "A doctor's office?"

"No, not exactly, I guess. She's at the morgue. The cat's in an office there." And as quickly as he'd felt that surge of relief, a knot of tension formed in his chest.

"The morgue? You're sure?"

"Well, that's what she said."

"Alright, thanks, Rufus."

"When she gets home, I'll ask her to call you."

"Thanks again," Sam said as he ended the call. He turned to the others. "She's at the morgue, if Rufus is right. Picking up some damn cat."

"Ahh," Ralph said. "She said she'd be picking up a cat from someone at the morgue."

Sam shook his head. "Let's just get going. Call for backup there, just in case. Tell them no sirens."

The officer radioed headquarters with the information as they raced to their cars and turned back onto Massachusetts Avenue heading to the morgue, their windshield wipers working at double speed to keep up with the rain.

As they pulled onto Albany Street by the hospital, a jagged streak of lightning lit up the sky. Streetlights and traffic lights flickered and died. The hospital's generator had likely kicked in as the building stayed well lit, the red *Emergency* sign glowing brightly.

The morgue, however, directly across the street, was in total darkness. But Sam could still make out Jessie's car parked right in front. "Damn it," he muttered.

"Hey," Ralph said. "This place always looks dark. Between the frosted windows, the blinds and the shades, there's hardly ever light visible."

Sam swung his car into the parking lot behind the morgue with the second car pulling in right behind him. They parked and exited their cars. Sam tried texting Jessie once more. "Is it possible there's no cell coverage in there?" he asked, knowing full well that he was grasping at straws.

Ralph shook his head. "Even in a storm, I've been able to text or call using my phone from inside there."

"Looks like this whole place is locked up pretty tight," one of the detectives from the second car added. "But let me try that door by the ME van." He climbed the stairs and pulled hard, but the door wouldn't budge. He knocked once, twice and then a third time but the sound was muffled by the storm. He rejoined the others and shook his head. "Maybe we can get in through the front door," he said as they headed toward the main entrance on Albany Street, the stone lions standing on either side like sentries.

Sam tried to push open the door, but it was locked and immovable. An ID swiper, likely useless without electricity, was next to the door. Sam pulled out his ID and swiped it across the reader, but nothing happened, no green light, no buzzing, nothing. He turned his gaze back across the street to the hospital, still lit up. "The emergency room," he said.

"She's not there," Ralph said. "We checked."

"I know that," Sam said irritably, bounding back down the steps. "But this place is a maze of tunnels that run underground and connect the buildings. There's a tunnel that runs from the hospital, underneath Albany Street, to the morgue's lower level. That entrance is always open so the attendants can bring those who've died right to the morgue. Follow me," he said as he raced across the street to the ER entrance. Once inside, he flashed his badge. "Boston Police," he said, turning to the two detectives who'd been with him. "Stay here," he said to one of them, "and wait for backup. They should be here soon. Security can guide you to the tunnels."

He nodded as Sam led the way to the elevators, his thumb banging at the *down* arrow until the door opened and the trio stepped inside. At the lower level, the elevator ground to a halt with a thud, the doors squeaking open on to a series of seemingly endless tunnels, a maze of pipes hanging from the ceilings, painted the same dingy yellow as the walls. Bare overhead light bulbs illuminated their way. "This way," Sam said as they made their way under Albany Street to the morgue's lower level, their heavy footfalls echoing as they went.

Once they reached the morgue's entrance, Sam stopped and

turned. "I don't think our guy's in there—at least I hope he isn't—but we're still going to proceed quietly and just listen before we even call her name. Understood?"

They nodded in unison as Sam opened the door, the light behind them spilling on to a pitch-black room, their eyes blinking furiously to adjust to the dark.

59

He could never have guessed how easy this would be. But here she was. Jessie Novak, as beautiful and as snotty as he knew she would be. Just like the rest of them.

They all thought they were too good for him, that he was a nobody. She was trying to look away, pretend she didn't recognize him from the night he came to the ER asking about Rosa Suarez. He moved closer, so close he could feel the fear seeping from her skin. He reached out to touch her and she flinched and turned away. He wanted to grab her by the hair then, to drag her up to the roof. But there was time enough for that, he reminded himself.

"Have you figured things out, Jessie Novak?" he asked, pulling on a blue surgical glove. "You think you're pretty smart, don't you?" She didn't say a word, just stood there with her back against the wall, her lips parted as if she was getting ready to scream. But there was no one to hear her, and she must have known that. "Nothing to say?"

She remained silent. The bitch. He'd show her who was in charge. "Turn around and face the wall," he commanded her.

"Why?" she asked, her voice a whisper.

"Just turn around." And she did. "Put your hands back so I can see them." And she moved her hands, trembling though they were, behind her. He grabbed them then and quickly cuffed her with a zip tie. He smiled as he saw the red welts begin to rise under the ties, his signature. The police had never figured it out. This power, this control he had was almost the best part—but no, there was more to come.

"You can turn back to me now, Jessie." She turned slowly. "Looks like we have all night to talk, don't you agree? Your friends are looking for Jack Feeney. He's dead, by the way, in case you were wondering. And though I was reported to have died in a car accident, as you can see, the reports of my demise were premature." The fear made her eyes a beautiful shade of green. He moved closer.

And then he heard it: whispery sounds behind him, moving closer through the dark. He spun around but there was nothing to see. He swung his flashlight back and forth along the hallway, but there was nothing else, no shadows, no sound. Nothing. It was being here in a damn morgue. Ghosts.

That's all it was. He just wanted to get this done and get the hell out.

"Let's move back down there," he said, pushing her ahead of him along the blacked-out corridor.

60

She flattened her back against the wall, adrenalin surging through her veins once again. "Who are you?" she asked.

"I'm your worst fucking nightmare, that's who I am. I'm the loser you and the other girls ignored, tormented, laughed at." His lips were drawn tight over his yellow teeth in an evil half-smile. "Who's laughing now?"

He shoved her along and she stumbled, lurching forward but catching herself before she fell to the floor. He grabbed her left arm, yanking it with such force that she was certain her shoulder was dislocated. She ignored the pain. She had to figure out what to do—how to get away, and though he had the flashlight, she'd just searched through this whole building for a cat. She now knew every inch of the place. He was pushing her roughly toward the refrigerated body storage room. There was nothing there that she could use as a weapon unless she could come up with an idea. She had to get him to talk. She stopped and asked again. "Who are you? You know who I am, but who are *you*?"

He laughed again and spun her around to face him, the flashlight trained on her face once more. "You still haven't figured it out?"

Sweat beading her forehead, her heart racing, her breath shallow, she shook her head.

"My name is Allen Smith, Al to my friends, and I suppose you want to know everything. Dr. Dawson fired me because I was too smart for this place."

"I don't understand."

"Think about it. I'm a nice-looking guy and I'm pretty smart, but every single bitch of a woman I've ever met thinks I'm a joke. That includes my mother, and then a string of lazy foster mothers. I'd found a niche working here, but Dr. Dawson thought I was too rough with the female corpses and he let me go." He laughed again. "I went back to Worcester and got a security job rotating through the colleges out there. Great gig, right? Meet college girls, get laid, life will be great. But it wasn't."

Even in the dark, Jessie could see his eyes narrow, a snarl on his lips.

"They treated me like shit. Reported me to the company, who finally let me resign. Big favor, right? So, what's a man supposed to do? Get even, that's what real men do."

And Jessie understood that he was probably crazy. Her muscles tightened up. "So, you killed all these girls and a housekeeper, and Arnie Boone? Why?"

"Come on, figure it out. The girls deserved it. Arnie and what's her name, Rosa? They knew things. Arnie suspected all along. He and Jack Feeney and I were roommates. We worked together and lived together, and they figured things out, but couldn't prove it. They left the security agency before I did. When I was forced out, I guess I followed them. I didn't have a place to go and I liked them. I really did. But things didn't work out for me. Jack let me sleep in his shitty little room until I got back on my feet. I even went back to school. I didn't enroll, I just wandered around. It was a place to go while I figured things out, but the pretty girls still treated me as though I didn't exist, as though they were too good for me. Just like you, Jessie Novak. And just like Jack Feeney. He knew what I was up to. And he was about to turn me in. I had to kill him to shut him up. Just like you." He pushed her again. "Keep going."

She tried to grasp any thread of a plan from her brain, but her synapses wouldn't connect. Her mouth dry as cotton, her pulse racing, sweat pooled along the small of her back as she tried desperately to think, but nothing cohesive would come. She walked slowly, one shuffling footstep at a time.

"Speed it up," he snarled.

"I can't see where I'm going. I don't want to fall," she said. He shoved her again, and she realized that if she slowed down once more and he knocked into her, she could trip and cause him to stumble and fall. And with any luck, he'd lose his flashlight and she could use that as a weapon against him. Pathetic to count on luck at a time like this, but that was all she had. And she wondered if Rosa Suarez and the others had wished for luck as well. Somehow, thinking of them gave her courage. She'd do it for all of them.

Her hands were zip tied behind her back, and she wriggled them back and forth trying to break free. She had no idea how she'd get hold of his flashlight, but right now that was her only chance. In the silence that followed, as she slowed her steps, she was almost certain that she heard muffled voices behind them. But she knew it was likely an illusion, her brain grasping for help when none was coming. She took a deep breath, steeled herself for the fight of her life, and felt the heat of his hand as he shoved her again. She pushed back and let herself fall into him.

"You miserable bitch," he hissed as he lost his own balance, the flashlight still gripped tightly in his hand.

As Jessie had tumbled, she'd twisted onto her left shoulder, the pain shooting into her side. She winced against the agony and rolled to her right side. Smith reached out and pulled her roughly back up as he scrambled to his feet.

"Move," he said as he pulled her along, and Jessie wondered if he was somehow going to try to get her up to the roof. The morgue had five stories; she wondered if she could survive a fall from that height. She just might, unless... and an icy finger ran long her spine. He planned to kill her first just as he had Rosa. She wriggled her hands again and again against the zip ties, but they held fast.

They had just reached the body storage room, when a sudden

and unmistakable clamor of footsteps in the hallway stopped them. Smith pushed open the door and shoved her inside pulling the door softly behind him.

He laughed then, a sinister sneer to the curl of his mouth. "Well, isn't this just perfect?" he said. "I'm not sure who's outside but at least we're in here until I can figure out what to do next."

Despite the chill in the room, a line of sweat trickled down Jessie's face as Smith yanked open the first doors and began pulling out trays. The first three trays held bodies wrapped in white plastic shrouds. "Damn it," he muttered pulling open a fourth door, this one empty. "This," he said, turning to Jessie, "is where you're going to wait for me."

He lifted her, the bulk of him holding her tight as she struggled to free herself, kicking out with her feet and twisting her upper torso. But he was considerably bigger than her and stronger, and he grabbed her legs with one beefy hand and dumped her onto the tray, his other arm balancing her neck, his hand clamped over her mouth. She resisted then, but there was little room to fight back as he began to slide the tray into the wall.

"I'll come back for you, Jessie. You know I will." He leaned down, removed his hand from her mouth and kissed her. Revulsion surged through her and she reeled her head back and spat in his face. He laughed. "Save your strength," he said as he pushed the tray all the way.

She took one last gulp of air as he slammed the door shut, and deep blackness enveloped her. She knew there was no way to get out. Her hands were still restrained behind her back, and there was no release mechanism on this side of the door. And why would there be? This was a receptacle for bodies, not living people. It was refrigerated and airtight. Until he came for her, there was no escape. A white-hot bubble of fear burned into her brain and she opened her mouth to scream, but just like those nightmares where she couldn't call for help, no sound came. She tried to calm herself. Shouting, after all, would eat up the little oxygen left inside her tomb-like box. If the cold didn't kill her first, the lack of oxygen would. She twisted onto her side and jammed her feet into the ceiling of the unit, but there was only a soft thud when her feet made contact and nothing else. And then, in the quiet, she felt her cell phone vibrate. Someone was looking for her.

She needed to be quiet until that someone came for her.

If that someone came for her at all.

61

His hand on the door handle, he hesitated. It might just be Sean and the other workers out there, he reminded himself. He knew he could convince them he was from the funeral home, here to collect the paperwork. He took a deep breath, pulled the door open and stepped cautiously into the hallway, which luckily was still dark. His eyes had adjusted to the shadowy hall and he slipped the flashlight into his back pocket as he headed toward the stairwell. He turned left and moved slowly along the hallway, stopping short when he heard voices and an arc of light hit him in the face.

"Boston Police," a man shouted as he appeared like a mirage out of the darkness. "Who are you?"

He smiled and shrugged. "Al Smith. I work here. Death certificates."

"Where's Jessie Novak?"

"I don't know who you're talking about."

The man with the silvery eyes stepped forward, his fist raised. One of the men with him grabbed hold of his arm. "No," he said softly. "Not yet."

"Jesus," another man said suddenly. "Al Smith! The security guard from Tempus who was supposed to have died in a car accident."

And he realized he might not be able to talk his way out of this one.

"Hands up and turn around," the smartly dressed black man said, grabbing his hands roughly and slipping cold metal handcuffs around his wrists. He patted him down and emptied his pockets, the zip ties and gold chain and cross making a clicking noise as they were pulled from his pocket.

He heard a sharp collective intake of breath. "You motherfu—" someone shouted, pushing him roughly against the wall.

"Where is she?" someone else said, an anxious edge to his voice.

"You can see for yourselves. Or maybe you can't really see in the dark, but believe me, she's not here."

And suddenly, the lights buzzed and flickered and glowed once again, the power surge making the light bulbs burn more brightly; the motors that operated the equipment thrummed loudly and he blinked at the brightness.

"Where the hell is she?" the man shouted as a swarm of blue-uniformed men surrounded him.

He cursed silently. He was just as trapped as she was, but he had the upper hand. He still might be able to negotiate his way out of this. Jessie's air would run out soon, and without her testimony, they'd have nothing but a little DNA on a glove. He could still walk away a free man. "I don't have a clue," he said, his eyes cold as ice.

62

Sam pushed Al Smith roughly against the wall and moved in so close he could feel the killer's breath on his face. Sam swallowed hard, beads of sweat breaking out on his forehead, his fist poised to strike, when Ralph pulled him back and stepped between them.

"Hey, take it easy," he said. "We'll find her." He turned back to the group of policemen crowded into the narrow hallway. "Search this whole building. Jessie Novak is in here somewhere." He pointed to the senior officer. "Please get Dr. Dawson and Tony Jones, the senior tech here, ASAP. They know this building." The group dispersed and began their search.

"What about me?" Smith asked.

Sam took a deep breath and looked him square in the eye. "Allen Smith," he began, "you are under arrest for multiple counts of murder and attempted murder. Things might go easier for you if you help us out. If not, you bastard, I will personally come after you with everything I have."

"I have rights," Smith said.

"And here they are," Ralph interjected. "You have the right to remain silent and refuse to answer questions. Anything you say may be used against you in a court of law. You have the right to consult an attorney before speaking to the police and to have an attorney present during questioning now or in the future. Do you understand your rights as I have stated them?"

Smith bit the edge of his lip. "What if I help you?" he asked, stalling for time.

"Tell us where Jessie is," Sam said, "and only then will we talk."

Smith's face grew pale as ash. A line of sweat trickled along his hairline. "I want to see a lawyer," he said. "Until then, I got nothing to say."

The stale air grew thick with Sam's angry glare. Every cell in his body was tensed, ready to fight this worm. He took a step closer.

Ralph stepped between Sam and Smith. "I'll just take him outside, Sam. We're wasting time. He can sit in a cruiser with some policemen while we search."

Sam stood, his back rigid, his fists clenched at his side, his jaw tight. He nodded and tried calling Jessie once again. But it went right to voicemail. "Her phone! That's it," he said to no one in particular as he raced up the stairs. "I'm going to keep calling Jessie. We're bound to hear her phone. I'm willing to bet that wherever she is, she has it with her. Just listen. Even if she's turned off the sound, just listen for the vibration. Did someone check the roof?"

"Empty. No one's been up there."

Sam nodded and began to open doors on the first floor until a cat came scrambling out. He grabbed it. "This is the cat she came for," he shouted. "She's here somewhere." He passed the cat to a uniformed officer. "Put it in my car, will you?" The officer nodded and took off, cradling the cat in his arms.

Just then, more officers, uniformed and plainclothes, burst through the main entrance. Sam pointed them toward the sergeant in charge. "He can fill you in," he said. "Every inch of this place needs to be searched. The basement is some kind of storage area, this is the reception and family area, second floor holds the autopsy suites and lockers, third floor are offices and I have no idea what else is in here." He swiped a line of sweat from his forehead. "I'm going to go back downstairs and just start where we found Smith. You," he said, pointing to a group of patrolmen, "come with me."

Sam made his way back to the basement, the policemen on his heels. "I'll start down there," he said. "You start at the other end and check every nook and cranny. Understand?"

Sam started looking through the areas along the hallway, checking under empty metal gurneys and peering into boxes. He spun around, trying to decide exactly where they'd run into Smith, his eyes searching—and then he saw it. A discarded zip tie. He picked it up and called Jessie's name once again. Still no answer, but across from where the zip tie lay was a heavy steel door. He pushed it open, the sudden chill sending a shiver up his spine, and then his gaze fell to the bank of body storage lockers in front of him.

"Jessie!" he screamed. "Can you hear me?" He began to pull open the locker doors and drag out the trays, unzipping the top of each body bag quickly before shoving the bodies back in and moving to the next locker. It seemed an eternity before he pulled out a locker and found Jessie, her skin dusky and cool. He felt for a pulse, his fingers moving along her neck and then her chest, but there was nothing. He felt a panic he hadn't known before, a heavy suffocating weight in his chest, the pain of it almost unbearable. But he pushed it away. He wouldn't lose her now. He took a deep breath and tried again, his fingers gently probing her neck until, at last, he felt it—a weak, barely-there pulse. He pulled her limp body into his arms, raced back up the stairs and called for help.

"I'll call for the EMTs," somebody shouted.

"There's no time. I'm gonna run across the street with her. Just go ahead of me, stop the traffic." A bevy of officers streamed out and stood in the street, hands held up, while others turned sirens on. Traffic came to a sudden halt as Sam dashed across the street and into the ER.

"Help!" he shouted. "Help me." Suddenly, he was surrounded

by doctors and nurses who took Jessie from him and placed her onto a stretcher.

"What happened?" somebody asked.

"I'm not sure. She was in one of those cold storage lockers in the morgue."

"She's not breathing," one of the doctors yelled. "How long was she in there?"

"I don't know," Sam said. "Please, please—just save her." They pulled the stretcher into one of the trauma rooms and he tried to follow, but a nurse held him back.

"Wait outside, please," she said. "This is our Jessie Novak, too."

Sam nodded and slumped against the wall, sliding down, his head falling forward onto his knees as tears streamed from his eyes. He could only watch helplessly. "Don't let me lose her," he whispered as a sob racked his shoulders.

Staff hurried into the room and then out—doctors, nurses, an x-ray tech, a respiratory tech—and Sam stood and tried to get a glimpse as the door opened again and again, but all he could see was a wash of blue scrubs surrounding the stretcher that held Jessie. Orders were shouted, meds were passed, a ventilator and another imposing machine were wheeled in and then Sam saw them—the tiny blips on the monitor above the stretcher. She was alive. And that was something.

He pulled away when a social worker tried to get him to move to the family room. He stood stiffly as another detective and a member of the Forensics team rushed by him and into the trauma room, emerging shortly with her clothes and the zip ties that had circled her wrists. "Hey," he called, "did you see her?"

The detective shook his head and held up the evidence bags. "They just passed these to us. She's in good hands, Sam." He patted his shoulder. "Need anything?"

"No, just get that bastard for me."

He nodded. "We will."

And then he was gone. Sam was alone again. He began to pace up and down the trauma hallway, trying to figure out how this had happened, how everything had gone so wrong. But his brain wouldn't let go of Jessie; there was no room in his thoughts for anything or anyone else.

"Jesus Christ," a familiar voice called. "I just heard. What happened?"

Sam turned to see Tim Merrick, a trauma surgeon and Jessie's friend. Sam tried to explain, but the words wouldn't come. "I'm afraid she's dying," he said through tears. "Please, can you find out how she is?"

Tim pushed open the trauma room door and slipped inside, leaving Sam alone once again. He leaned back against the wall, loosened his tie and closed his eyes.

"Hey, Sam," Donna, the ER's nurse manager, laid a hand on his shoulder. Her face was drawn. "Let's go to the family room."

A knot of fear took hold in his chest. He backed away. "No," he said. "Don't tell me. Please..."

"It's not over, but it's serious. We need to talk. Tim Merrick is going to join us."

The hallway spun, the lights were blinding, the air heavy. Sam swayed as Tim Merrick appeared and placed a steadying hand on his back. "Easy, Sam. Let's go. We have some decisions to make."

But Sam, his brow furrowed, stood perfectly still. He wasn't going anywhere.

"Sam, Jessie has no next of kin in her records. There's no one. Right now, you're all we have. All she has," Donna said gravely.

"I... I'm not leaving. Just tell me."

"You saw her for yourself when you brought her in," Tim said. "She suffered from hypoxia, which means that her body, her vital organs—her heart, her brain, her kidneys—were deprived of oxygen, which can be fatal. But the saving grace for Jessie is that the cooling of her body in that locker allowed her body to protect itself, to decrease the need for oxygen. Her heart is beating on its own but she is intubated, on a warming blanket, and we're trying to get her blood pressure up and improve her cardiac output and perfusion, her circulation. Does that make sense?"

Sam nodded, his eyes suddenly bright. "It means there is hope, right?"

"There's always hope," Tim said. "She has no kidney or heart damage that we can see yet. But this is still going to be very touch and go, Sam. We're going to move her to the ICU where the critical care team will look after her. She'll be surrounded by monitors and machines to help her to recover."

"Can I see her?" Sam asked.

"She's heavily sedated, she has an arterial line in, IVs, a breathing tube connected to a ventilator, a warming blanket, medication pumps. You won't really be able to get close to her. I think you should go home and get some sleep."

"I'm not going anywhere. I'm staying put. Can't I just see her before she goes up to the ICU?"

"Yes, of course you can," Donna said. "Is there anyone else you want to call for her? She doesn't have a next of kin listed, at least not that I can find."

"I suppose I should call Rufus," he said, and then he remembered Angela Novak. "Or her mother."

"Her mother? She's never talked about her," Donna said. "You'll call her?"

He nodded. "Can we just go in?"

Tim and Donna led him into the trauma room, which grew suddenly silent. The staff who'd been scurrying to their tasks, setting up portable monitors, moving pumps and the machinery required to keep Jessie alive, stopped and moved away, allowing Sam to move to her side. He took her hand, the sight of the red marks on her wrists threatening his thin veil of composure. He held his breath, leaned down and kissed Jessie's still cool cheek. "Please," he whispered, "I love you. Just wake up. Just be okay." Suddenly, a hand pulled him away. "Sorry, sir, we really need to get her up to the ICU. You can see her later."

Sam backed away reluctantly, tears spilling from his eyes. He'd never felt so alone in his life.

63

TUESDAY, DAY 10

The overhead fluorescent lights in the ICU were almost blinding, and combined with the whir of medication pumps, the whoosh of ventilators, and the constant beep of monitors, there was precious little room for any other sound. But Sam, slumped over Jessie's bed, his hand holding hers, was keenly aware of the minutes ticking by on the wall-mounted clock and the soft footsteps moving along the corridor.

"Morning, Sam," a soft voice said. "The team will be in to see her soon."

His suit coat on the back of a chair, his tie askew, his sleeves rolled up, fresh stubble on his face, Sam looked up to see one of the nurses who'd been caring for Jessie.

"Do you mind waiting outside?" she asked.

He stood reluctantly, kissed Jessie's cheek and started out. "You'll come and get me?" he asked.

"I will," she said, watching as he slipped through the automatic doors to the waiting area.

Sam poured himself a cup of cold, stale coffee from the carafe on a table and sat heavily, his mind numb, his body screaming for sleep. He was just taking a sip of coffee when Ralph appeared at the doorway.

"Morning, Sam. Any news?"

"Not yet. What about you? Anything from Smith?"

Ralph nodded and sat next to Sam. "He told us everything, the miserable little fuck."

"So, how? Why?"

"Suffice it to say, he's a classic narcissist anti-social prick." And Ralph shared what he knew. "His mother died when he was about twelve and after that, he was a lonely foster kid, kicked around from one house of horrors to the next." He sighed. "He's admitted to all of it, including Boone and Feeney. He was convinced that they knew everything, same as Rosa Suarez. He called them 'loose ends.' Poor Tony's beside himself. He always thought Smith had resigned from the ME's office, said he even tried to fix him up with Jessie."

Sam dropped his head into his hands and sighed. "What about the fingernails?"

"Souvenirs, he said. We found them in little plastic lunch bags in his pocket. And the chain with the cross that was in Alison McCray's hand? It belonged to him. He stole it from his mother when he was a kid, said it had protected him ever since, and he needed it back. Said that Alison had pulled it from his neck when she struggled. That's why he took Sarah Gorman's cross, to replace his. But said he'd like his own back and asked if we had it." Ralph shook his head. "You just can't make this stuff up."

"What about the car accident death?"

"He said that was easy enough to fake. Just write a short obituary, send it to a newspaper, and send the printout to Tempus. After that, he was able to vanish into thin air."

"But why kill them in the first place?"

"He said those girls treated him like he was nothing. Hadn't realized until after the first one what a thrill it was—watching them die. And he learned from working with the ME how to make a death seem like a suicide, and it worked. Said to tell Dr. Dawson he's a good teacher."

"But why did he escalate so much in the last week?"

"He felt as if it was all collapsing down around him, he needed to get his confidence back. To get the thrill back."

"Why Jessie? She doesn't fit."

"Ahhh," Ralph said. "He spoke to Jessie the night that Rosa Suarez fell. He's the one who went into the ER and tried to get information. He was afraid that she'd survived, but said Jessie wouldn't help him; she told him to call the police. He had no idea what her name was or anything about her until he saw her pick up his glove on the garage roof and then again at the next two scenes, and he put it all together. She was his last loose end. He planned to leave Massachusetts once she was dead. Said he got lucky finding her at the morgue."

"Jesus," Sam said, rubbing his eyes, trying desperately to erase the image of Jessie in that cooler. "So, we've got him."

Ralph nodded. "And now, we need to get you home for some sleep."

He shook his head.

"I knew you'd say that. Go home for a shower, at least. I'll stay. Go home. Looks like you haven't slept in a week."

Sam ran his hand through his hair, his eyes the flat gray of a sidewalk in winter. "Maybe I should at least wash up and change. You'll stay? I won't be long."

"I'll be right here," Ralph said, sinking into the orange vinyl of the couch.

Sam started for the door and turned. "Jessie's mother is coming up from Texas. I don't think she'll get in until late tonight or tomorrow, but just so you know."

Ralph's brow wrinkled, a puzzled look on his face. "I thought her mother was dead?"

"Long story," Sam said. "For another time."

It wasn't much more than an hour later when Sam returned, freshly showered and shaved, and two Dunkin' coffees in hand. He passed one to Ralph. "Anything?"

Ralph shook his head. "Dr. Merrick told me they're keeping

her sedated, a 'medically induced coma,' he called it, for at least another day. He said to call him." He passed a slip of paper to Sam.

Sam nodded and sat heavily. "I don't know..."

"Don't say it. She'll be okay. Hang onto that. And call Dr. Merrick."

"I have to call Rufus. That cat..."

"I got the cat to him, told him the barest minimum, thought you should be the one to update him."

"Should I pick Rufus up? Bring him in to see her?" Sam asked.

"No," Ralph said, almost too quickly. "It can wait another day. He's an old man, and she's like his kid, right?"

Ralph sat by Sam into the early afternoon when the nurses finally returned and said Sam could come back. "Sorry for the wait, but all of the specialists had to see her, then she had to go for a CT scan and a cardiac echo. And we wanted to get her cleaned up. But you can come in now."

"And the results?"

"Looks good," she said.

And Sam smiled, his first since he'd found Jessie's lifeless body. He and Ralph stood at the same time, the vinyl couch squeaking as they did.

Ralph headed out. "Call me if you need anything," he said as Sam stepped back into the ICU.

Though the breathing tube was still in her mouth, and she was surrounded by mechanical devices designed to keep her alive, she somehow looked a little better. Her skin was pinker, her hair had been pulled back, and she looked more like his Jessie. He went around to the side of her bed, kissed her forehead and sank into the chair. "I'm back, Jessie," he said, gripping her hand. "Squeeze my hand if you can hear me."

And there it was, just the slightest fluttering of her fingers. Sam's heart raced as he stood and shouted for the nurse. "Squeeze my hand again, Jessie."

And she did. He was certain of it.

The nurse and the ICU team rushed back in, and Sam explained what had happened. "She's waking," he whispered. "I know she is. Watch." And he squeezed her hand again and asked her to squeeze back, and her hand curled the slightest bit around his to a collective gasp in the room.

"We've lightened her sedation," said a doctor whose name he couldn't remember. "But I didn't expect this response so early. This is good, very good." He turned to Sam. "We'll try to wean her from the vent tonight. You should go home. Let us get back to Jessie. Come back tomorrow morning."

It sounded more like an order than a request to Sam. He nodded. "You'll call me?"

One of the nurses led him back to the hallway. "We will. I promise."

64

WEDNESDAY, DAY 11

It was just after midnight when Sam stepped back into the hospital. He'd hardly slept before he'd said the hell with it and called Tim Merrick, who told him to come back in, that Jessie would be off the vent and breathing on her own in a few hours. "Come in. You can stay with her. Things look very good. I'll meet you in the ICU."

Sam rushed to shower and get dressed, and by the time he made it to the ICU his heart was racing, his breath coming in short spurts. When he stepped from the elevator on the fifth floor, Tim Merrick was waiting for him. He followed him to Jessie's room, the overhead lights so bright it might have been noon.

"She's sleeping, but likely a real sleep since her sedation has been weaned down. Go on in," Tim said. "She still has the tube in, but they'll take that out in a few more hours."

"Her mother's arriving this morning. Will you make sure they know to let her in?" Tim nodded as Sam slipped soundlessly to Jessie's side and gripped her hand in his own. "I'm here, Jessie," he whispered. "I'll be right here when you wake up."

The hours passed slowly, the time interrupted only by the stream of nurses and doctors who came in and out, hung new IV medicines, adjusted pumps and settings and disconnected the ventilator a few times so she could breathe on her own, and each time her breathing seemed to improve, at least to Sam. It was almost six a.m. when a small group of weary-looking young doctors surrounded Jessie, asking Sam to step back a little. "We'd like to take out her tube, but we want to make sure she's fully awake first."

Sam melted into the background, determined not to leave, and held his own breath.

"Jessie," one of them said, "can you wake up for us?" He squeezed her hand.

Jessie's eyes flickered and then opened wide, her terror still raw. She struggled, her back arched as she reached to pull out the breathing tube. "Jessie, it's us," a nurse said. "We're trying to help you." Jessie seemed not to have heard.

"Ativan IV," someone shouted.

"Wait," Sam said, pushing his way to Jessie's side, his gaze holding hers. "Jessie, you're safe. You're in the ICU. I won't let anyone hurt you. I promise. Just let them take that damn tube out so I can kiss you."

The nurse plunged the needle into Jessie's IV but not before Jessie looked right at him, or maybe through him. She didn't seem to recognize him. He gripped her hand.

A nurse used a small syringe to deflate the little balloon that held her breathing tube in place in her trachea. "Take a deep breath," someone said, and when she did, the nurse pulled the tube out. Coughing, Jessie wrenched herself forward, gasping for breath. A nurse clamped an oxygen mask onto her face. "Just breathe," she said, checking the monitor.

Jessie fell back onto the pillow, her eyes closed.

"Are you awake?" Sam asked, running his hand through her hair.

But she was asleep, the soft rhythm of her breathing the only sound as the team left the room.

Jessie's mother arrived later, and she introduced herself, but Sam would have known her anywhere. She and Jessie shared the same dark hair, the same hazel eyes, pert nose and porcelain skin. "I'm Angela," she said softly, "and you're Sam?"

He nodded and hugged her briefly as she began to cry, tears that slipped soundlessly along her face. She swiped them away. "I'm sorry," she said, leaning over Jessie. "Mom's here," she whispered. "I'll never leave you again, honey. I love you. Just wake up. Please." She swayed a little, her shoulders heaving with quiet sobs.

Jessie's fingers seemed to flutter once again at the sound of her mother's voice. "See that," Sam said, guiding her to a chair by Jessie's bed. "She heard you."

Angela Novak closed her eyes and sighed.

Sam brought her up to date on Jessie's condition and she'd gripped his hand tightly while he spoke. "Thank you for saving my girl." She sat quietly by Sam, dabbing at her eyes.

"It's all good," Tim Merrick announced when he stopped by. "Sleep will help her to heal and to remember when the time comes."

Jessie's mother sighed and stood. "I'm going to the chapel," she said. "I need to do something."

It was late morning when Ralph appeared. "How is she?" he asked.

"Off the vent, breathing on her own and resting," Sam said. "So, I'd say she's good, but I don't want to get ahead of myself. She didn't seem to know me when she opened her eyes, but I guess... I guess we just have to wait."

"If it's okay, I brought someone in who really needed to see her."

"Who?" Sam asked, his brow furrowed.

Just then Rufus appeared in the doorway, his skin pale, his hands trembling, looking older than his seventy years. Sam went to him and embraced him. "Come on, have a seat," he said, leading him to the chair by Jessie's bed. "She's going to be okay," he reassured the old man.

A tear streamed down Rufus's face as he took Jessie's hand in his. "She's got to be. She's all I've got in the world."

"Hey," Sam said. "How's the cat?"

Suddenly the years melted away and Rufus smiled, the wrinkles in his face fading. "Your friend Ralph here and that young man, Tony, brought her to me yesterday. Cat is settling in nicely."

"What are you going to name her?" Sam asked.

"Well, I guess Jessie didn't get a chance to tell you, but her name is Cat. I like it, keeps it nice and simple."

"I like that, too," Sam said.

"Is her mother here?" Ralph asked.

"In the chapel."

"Well, we don't want to be in the way," Ralph said, guiding Rufus from the room. "We'll come back later."

"Please tell her I was here," Rufus said, his eyes clouded over with tears. Sam stood and hugged him.

"I will, Rufus. I will."

65

Jessie's eyes burst open, the bright light almost too much to bear after the all-enveloping blackness of the cold locker into which she'd been forced. She moved her hands and wriggled her feet and looked around. She was in a bed in the ICU, oxygen flowed into her lungs through a nasal cannula, an IV dripped fluid into her arms, and an overhead monitor beeped out her heart rate. Her throat burned, her wrists throbbed, but she was alive. Someone had come for her after all. It was then she saw Sam, his mouth open, his eyes closed, his body slumped in a chair. A soft snore interrupted the gentle rhythm of his breaths.

"Sam," she started to say, but she could almost feel the worry, the fear peeling off of him in layers even in sleep. And she noticed the hard angle of his jaw, and the softness of his lips set against the fuzzy growth of new beard. She wanted to reach out and run her fingers through the stubble and she pulled herself up a little, rattling the bedrail as she did.

And Sam stirred, a smile breaking out on his face, his eyes flecked with that familiar silver shimmer, as he stood and leaned into her, pulling her gently into a long embrace. "Oh, Jessie," he whispered. "Thank God you're okay. Your mother's here, and Rufus will be back, and they wanted you to know they love you, and I'm..." And he blinked away a sudden moistness in his eyes. "I love you, too."

She ran her fingers along the curve of his chin, feeling the rough edge of his beard as she took his face into her hands and kissed him with a longing she hadn't even known she'd felt. But there it was—as simple and as complex as anything that really matters.

He loved her. And she loved him right back.

A LETTER FROM ROBERTA

Dear reader,

I want to say a huge thank you for choosing to read *Her Mother's Cry*. If you did enjoy it, and want to keep up to date with all my latest releases, just sign up at the following link. Your email address will never be shared and you can unsubscribe at any time.

www.bookouture.com/roberta-gately

As an ER nurse, I've always been interested in forensics and crime investigation, and I've thoroughly enjoyed researching and writing every aspect of this story. I hope you loved reading *Her Mother's Cry* as much as I enjoyed writing it. And if you did, I would be so grateful if you could spare the time to write a review. It makes such a difference helping new readers to discover one of my books for the first time.

I'd also love to hear your thoughts about Jessie Novak, so please get in touch on my Facebook page or on Twitter, or through my website.

Thank you for your support!

Roberta Gately

www.robertagately.com

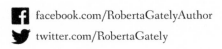

facebook.com/RobertaGatelyAuthor

twitter.com/RobertaGately

ACKNOWLEDGMENTS

I am enormously grateful to Cynthia Manson and Judy Hanson, my incredible agents and even better friends, for their extraordinary guidance, their cherished friendship and their unshakable faith in my ability to craft a story. I am more grateful than a simple thank you can ever convey.

To Therese Keating and Maisie Lawrence, my brilliant editors —your guidance, your edits and your encouragement have inspired me every step of the way, and have helped this story to come alive. To the wonderful team at Bookouture, including Noelle Holten, Kim Nash, Sarah Hardy, and so many others who have helped bring Jessie Novak to readers, thank you. I am forever grateful to be a part of the extraordinary Bookouture family.

Thank you to my good friend Kate Conway, who continues to provide me with the insider's view of South Boston, helping to carve out the perfect niche for Jessie Novak. And many thanks to Detective Sergeant James P. Wyse (BPD Ret.), for his technical guidance and tips into homicide investigation, and for his lifetime of service at the Boston Police Department. And to Christian Kiriakos, Director of the Office of Decedent Affairs in the Office of the Chief Medical Examiner in the state of Massachusetts, thank you for your advice into the protocols and policy of that office. To my cherished Gately and Quinn families, my dearest friends, and my nursing colleagues—with love and gratitude for your endless encouragement on this writing journey. ♥

Made in United States
North Haven, CT
31 October 2021

10682598R20177